SCENT OF MAGNOLIA

A NOVEL

ASHLEY FARLEY

Also by Ashley Farley

Life on Loan

Only One Life

Home for Wounded Hearts

Nell and Lady

Sweet Tea Tuesdays

Saving Ben

Sweeney Sisters Series

Saturdays at Sweeney's

Tangle of Strings

Boots and Bedlam

Lowcountry Stranger

Her Sister's Shoes

Magnolia Series

Beyond the Garden

Magnolia Nights

Scottie's Adventures

Breaking the Story

Merry Mary

Chapter 1

Scout

Scout adds her unmarked car to the cluster of Seattle's first responder vehicles parked haphazardly at the crime scene. Turning off the engine, she grips the steering wheel, bows her head, and squeezes her eyes tight. *Please, God, don't let it be Sally Strickland.*

She stuffs her stubby ponytail into a black baseball cap and grabs her trench coat from the trunk. Blue and red flashing lights are dim in the early morning fog as she hurries up the dank alley to the back door of a pool hall where the victim is lying facedown in the mud. Scout's heart skips a beat when she notices the young woman's blonde hair, the same white-blonde shade as Sally.

"Talk to me," Scout says to her friend and coworker, homicide detective Sandra Reyes.

"Looks like a drug overdose. Fentanyl would be my guess."

The smell of frying bacon from a nearby diner mixes with the stench of death. Locals are starting their day off with a hearty meal while, less than fifty feet away, a young woman is dead from drugs that either some jackass hoping for sex forced on her or that she willingly took to satisfy an addiction. Some days this job really gets to Scout.

Crouching down next to the body, Scout turns the girl's right hand over to inspect the inside of her wrist. Instead of the heart tattoo Sally's mother has described in detail, she discovers an angry red scar from an apparent suicide attempt.

"Can I see her face, please?" Scout says to a crime scene investigator.

The investigator rotates the victim's head so the right side of her face is visible. The girl's young age is apparent despite the caked mud covering her cheeks and forehead. She can't be over fourteen years old. And she's definitely not Sally Strickland.

"Do you have any idea who she is?" Sandra asks.

"Nope." Scout gets to her feet. "I've never seen her before in my life."

She walks over to a group of young people standing behind the yellow crime scene tape at the opposite end of the short alley. "Morning."

The kids respond in unison, "Morning."

"She a friend of yours?" Scout asks, tossing a thumb over her shoulder toward the dead girl's body.

A dozen sets of eyes dart about, avoiding Scout's gaze.

"I've memorized the faces of every reported runaway in this country, and she's not one of them. Which means I have no way of getting in touch with her family. What if that were one of you lying dead in a dirty alley? Wouldn't you want your family to know your fate? Wouldn't you want them to bring you home and bury you in the family plot where you belong? Wouldn't you want to end their constant worry so they could try to put the pieces of their lives back together?"

Her lecture is met with stony silence.

"Call your parents! If nothing else, let them know you're

alive." From an inside coat pocket, Scout removes a stack of McDonald's gift cards and hands them out to the runaways. "Get yourself some food. And try to stay out of trouble. You know where to find me if you learn anything about our Jane Doe."

Mumbling their gratitude for the gift cards, the group, with chins tucked and eyes glued to the ground, disperses into different directions. One runaway remains at the yellow tape—a tiny girl with pale hair and skin and electric blue eyes. The others call her Tinker Bell because she's light on her feet and walks on her toes. Scout wonders if she was a ballerina in a previous life.

Tinker Bell bites down on a quivering lip. "Her name is Chloe Thompson. She's from Spokane and has only been on the run for a few days, which is probably why you don't know about her. I tried to help her, but she was a real mess." Tinker Bell taps her forehead. "She has some serious emotional problems. She left home on a whim, and she desperately wanted to go back, but she was afraid to contact her parents."

Scout takes out her phone and types the victim's name and hometown in her Notes app. "Was she into drugs?"

"I don't think so. She's been hooking up with some guy, though. I know nothing about him."

Scout pockets her phone and gives Tinker Bell's shoulder a gentle squeeze. "You did the right thing in telling me." She presses a business card into the girl's palm. "Call me if you think of anything else."

After spending a heart-wrenching afternoon with Chloe Thompson's parents, Scout enters the Bail Out a few minutes after five and orders a tequila on the rocks from the bartender.

Drink in hand, she bypasses several tables of coworkers and chooses an empty booth on the far wall.

She's nursing her tequila, replaying the day's events over in her mind, when Barrett sits down in the booth across from her. Setting down his whiskey shot, he sheds his leather jacket, draping it over the back of the bench seat. Her heart flutters at the sight of his black T-shirt stretched tight over his muscular chest. With his scruffy beard and dark locks curling at the nape of his neck, her father would label him a thug, but beneath his rugged exterior lies a gentle giant. "I heard what happened. How're you holding up?"

"It's been a long day. I'm relieved it wasn't Sally Strickland, but I'm devastated for the Thompson family." Scout tugs her wheat-colored hair free of the elastic, letting it fall to her shoulders. "Every time I lose a runaway, I travel back in time seventeen years. Why can't I move on from my brother's disappearance?"

Barrett cocks his head as if to say *really*. "You know why. Because you need closure."

"Right. If only I knew how to get it." Scout drains the last of the tequila and sets the glass on the table with a clunk. "Ford would never intentionally leave me hanging like this. I have a strong social media presence. There must be a legitimate reason he hasn't contacted me."

"Because he doesn't want to be found." Barrett kicks back the shot of whiskey. "Your parents still live in the same house. Ford knows the way home."

Scout refuses to accept the possibility her brother is avoiding her on purpose. "I can think of other legitimate reasons that would prevent him from going home." Scout ticks them off on her fingers. "He's incapacitated and can't travel. He's in jail. God forbid he might be dead."

"When we idolize someone, Scout, we have a tendency to overlook their flaws."

Scout glares at Barrett. "You're always so hard on him when you've never even met him."

"I'm a homicide detective, trained to deal with the facts. Your brother disappeared during the early hours of the morning three days after Christmas seventeen years ago. The police ruled out the possibility of abduction. Which means he ran away. While visions of sugarplums danced in your head, he climbed out of his bedroom window with his guitar slung over his back. He may very well be unable to travel, but he still has access to a phone. He called your mother for crying out loud."

Scout's pointer finger shoots up. "Once. Five years after he left. It was late at night and the line was static. Mom could barely hear what he was saying. What if Ford escaped from his kidnappers and made it to a phone to call Mom, but the kidnappers caught him and killed him?"

Barrett snorts. "You're letting your imagination get the best of you again."

Scout laughs at herself. "Okay, so maybe that is far-fetched. But I can't rule out the possibility something happened to him. He could have amnesia."

"If he has amnesia now, he didn't have it when he left home or when he called your mom five years later. Running away is a coward's way of solving one's problems."

"Says the man from the happy family with loving parents and close-knit siblings." Scout's phone vibrates the table, and she glances down at the screen. "Why are Mom and Mary Beth calling me at the same time? This can't be good."

Barrett grabs their empty glasses. "I'll get us some refills while you talk to them."

Scout picks up the phone but hesitates as she decides whose

call to accept. Finally, she clicks on Mary Beth's number. "You and Mom are calling me at the same time. What's wrong?"

"Alice committed suicide this morning," Mary Beth blurts.

While she's relieved it's not bad news about Ford, Scout feels guilty she hasn't thought about her childhood friend Alice in years. "That's too bad. How'd she do it?"

"Scout! That's awful. Only you would ask such a thing."

"I'm a detective, Mary Beth. It goes with the territory."

"If you say so. Anyway, the funeral's on Friday. You need to be here."

"Since when did you get so bossy?"

"Since I became the mother of a toddler. Besides, if I'm not firm with you, you'll try to weasel your way out of coming. And there's no excuse for missing Alice's funeral, Scout."

One legitimate reason pops into Scout's mind. "Did you call Kate?"

"I left several messages with her assistant. I'm waiting to hear from her now. You can no longer hide behind your animosity toward Kate. We're all adults now, Scout. The time has come for you to put this petty vendetta behind you."

Scout sighs. "I don't expect you to understand my feelings for Kate. But you're right. I should be there for Alice's family. Can I stay with you?"

"As much as I would love that, your mom would be heart-broken if you don't stay at home."

Scout notices Barrett heading back toward the table with another tequila for her and a Miller Lite for himself. "I've gotta run, Mary Beth. I'll text you my flight information."

Barrett slides her drink across the table. "Why the long face?"

Scout stares at the clear liquid in her glass. "An old friend committed suicide."

"Gosh. That's awful, Scout. I'm so sorry."

"Thanks. Alice lived across the street from me growing up, but we haven't been close since we were kids. Life has not been good to her. She has a drug addiction, suffered from bipolar disorder, and self-medicated a lot with illegal drugs. She's been in and out of rehab most of her adult life."

"That must have been tough on her family."

Scout looks past him to the back room. "The pool table is open. Let's grab it." She crawls out of the booth and makes a beeline for the poolroom at the back of the pub.

Barrett racks the balls and Scout breaks, sending the solid blue number two ball to the far corner right pocket. She sinks three more solids in two turns before missing.

"How long will you stay in Alabama?" Barrett asks as he lines up his shot.

Scout props herself against her cue stick. "As short amount of time as possible. The funeral is Friday. I imagine I'll head back to Seattle on Saturday."

Barrett makes his shot and scrutinizes the table for another opportunity. "You have years' worth of vacation time built up. Why not stay for a while?"

"Why would I do that? There is literally nothing to do in Langford, Alabama. And two days is as long as I can stand to be in the dictator's presence."

Instead of laughing at her father's nickname, he scolds her with his dark eyes. "Give your parents a chance, Scout."

"People don't change, Barrett."

"Maybe people don't, but circumstances do." He takes an angle shot and misses. "You're an adult now. You might find you have more in common with your parents than you think."

She considers the possibility. "I haven't thought about it like that, but maybe you're right. After all this time, we're virtually strangers to one another. Maybe we can start over on a level playing field."

"You never know. At least stay through the weekend. Besides spending some much overdue time with your parents, you could search for clues about your missing brother."

"That investigation is dead," Scout says, leaning over the table as she lines up her next shot.

"Says who? Your eighteen-year-old self? You're an accomplished detective now, Scout. With your keen senses and seasoned eyes, you're bound to come up with something. The answers are there. You just need to find them."

"Maybe." She cleans the table and returns her cue stick to the wall rack. "That's a wrap. I'm outta here."

"Hey! What about dinner?" They have a standing deal that the loser pays for dinner.

"I wish I could. But I need to make travel arrangements."

Barrett tugs on his jacket. "I might as well go home too. I've been procrastinating on some paperwork."

They exit the Bail Out together, pausing in front of Barrett's motorcycle parked on the curb. "Good luck in Alabama, kiddo. If you need me. I'm only a phone call away."

When he kisses her cheek, she imagines what his lips might feel like on hers. But she's not his type. He prefers beautiful women with sexy bodies. He would never look twice at a girl with a lopsided smile and boyish figure.

Scout experiences a sick feeling in her gut as she watches him speed away on his bike. And she can't shake the feeling of impending doom during the drive home. Her life is about to change, and there's nothing she can do to stop it.

She's lived in the same dingy apartment building in a seedy part of downtown since first arriving in Seattle fifteen years ago. Many of her friends have upgraded to swanky buildings with open floor plans and rooftop pools. Scout doesn't see the point in paying premium rent for a place to lay her head. She no longer believes in the concept of home. Over the years, she's witnessed too much heartache born out of dysfunctional families and broken homes. Creating a happy home is a pie-in-the-sky dream only a blessed few ever achieve.

Barrett's words come back to her as she books her airline ticket. She's a confident young woman now, no longer the confused teenager who left home for college and never looked back. Maybe a fresh perspective will lead her to a new discovery about Ford's disappearance.

Scout folds an assortment of black tops and blue jeans into her small rolling suitcase. There was a time when she enjoyed wearing fun clothing in festive colors. But Ford drained all the life out of her world when he abandoned her.

Chapter 2

Kate

Kate studies the eager faces gathered around her conference table. She's toying with her staff, making them wait for her reaction. She plants her hands on the table, as though bracing herself to deliver bad news, and says, "I absolutely love it!"

The men and women exhale a collective sigh of relief.

"This is our most spectacular line of handbags we've launched to date. Our clients will be thrilled come spring. You've clearly put forth your best efforts. You can all look for fat bonuses in your next paychecks."

Cheers and applause fill the conference room.

She closes her laptop. "Take the rest of the day off. Grab an early dinner. Celebrate. You deserve it."

"How generous of you," says Anya, her head designer. "It's already five thirty."

"Is it really?" Kate checks her Apple Watch. "I didn't know it was so late. In that case, enjoy your evening. First thing tomorrow morning, we'll start executing the new designs."

As the designers and marketers exit en mass from the

conference room, her administrative assistant brushes past them on her way in. Vivian waves a stack of pink while-you-were-out messages at her. "Some woman named Mary Beth has been trying to reach you. She's called three times in the past hour. She claims it's urgent. She says she knows you from Alabama." Vivian peers at Kate over the top of her tortoiseshell glasses. "When did you attend Alabama? I thought you graduated from NYU."

"The state, Vivian. Not the university. I grew up in Alabama." Kate takes the messages from her assistant and walks down the hall to her office. Seated at her desk, she stares down at her phone screen. She hasn't spoken to anyone from Langford since she moved with her father to New York seventeen years ago. Something tragic must have happened if Mary Beth went to the trouble of tracking her down. *Please don't let it be June.*

Kate inhales an unsteady breath before punching in the number.

Mary Beth answers on the first ring, and the old friends exchange a moment of awkward pleasantries. "I'm afraid I have some bad news," Mary Beth says finally. "Alice committed suicide last night."

Kate relaxes back in her chair, relieved the news isn't about June. "I'm sorry to hear that. Her family must be devastated."

"Alice hasn't been well for a long time. Naturally, they're upset, but this wasn't her first attempt, and no one was surprised. Anyway, I thought you'd want to know. We were so close as children."

Memories rush back to Kate of swimming parties and summer nights playing kick the can in the neighborhood. But those happy times quickly slide away, and visions from her miserable high school days flash before her.

"The funeral is Friday. I hope you can make it. It would

mean a lot to Alice's family, and I'd love to see you again. We have much to catch up on."

As Mary Beth rattles on, Kate opens her top drawer and removes a tattered photograph taken in the Montgomery's backyard at one of their many talent shows. Ford's fan club—Kate, Mary Beth, Alice, and Scout—surround him while his guitar dangles from his neck. "I assume Scout will be there."

"She's flying in from Seattle tomorrow."

Since when does Scout live in Seattle? Kate wonders. She really is out of touch. She opens her mouth to tell Mary Beth she can't make the trip. Instead, she asks for a hotel recommendation.

"Try the Meeting Inn. I've heard amazing reviews about their recent renovations. I hope you'll come for a casual dinner tomorrow night. I'll text you the address."

"I'd like that, Mary Beth. I look forward to seeing you then."

Dropping her phone on the desk, Kate spins around in her chair and stares down seven flights at Madison Avenue. *What just happened?* She vowed never to return to Langford. Yet she gave Mary Beth zero pushback about attending the funeral. Kate rarely makes impulse decisions. She attributes her success as a top fashion designer to her cautious nature and sound business acumen.

Dad is going to freak when I tell him. And speaking of Phillip. She glances at her watch. His reception starts in a few minutes.

In the adjoining bathroom, Kate freshens her makeup and ties her mahogany hair back in a tight knot. Grabbing her tote bag, she takes the elevator down to the lobby and summons a taxi. The trip to Washington Heights takes longer than usual in rush hour traffic, and she arrives as a hospital's senior vice president is announcing her father's appointment to head of pediatrics.

Kate stands on her tiptoes to glimpse her father as he takes the podium. He looks sharp in a navy suit with red-and-white stripe tie. She snickers when he struggles to adjust the microphone to accommodate his tall frame.

Bart appears beside her with two glasses of red wine. "Kate! You're looking as lovely as ever," he says, offering her a glass.

"Thanks." She accepts the glass and turns her attention back to her father.

Bart leans in close. "Can we talk afterward?" he whispers near her ear.

"Shh!" She presses a finger to her lips as her father begins his speech.

Phillip expresses his gratitude for his appointment before attributing his success to his humble beginnings as the only pediatrician in a small Alabama town. "I treated patients with everything from strep throat to leukemia. I learned many valuable lessons from my time in Langford, from those courageous patients and their loving parents. But I gained the most wisdom from being a single parent for my daughter from the time she was a year old."

Her father talks on about how parents are the real heroes and the hardships families face when coping with critically sick children. He's wrapping up his comments when Bart tugs on her coat sleeve and leads her outside to a small courtyard.

"I miss you, Kate. Won't you please give our relationship another chance?"

Kate is tempted to say yes. She misses having a date for certain functions. And she misses having someone to spend Friday nights with when she's not in the mood to go out. But she doesn't miss Bart. "There's no point, Bart. You know how I feel."

"Come on, Kate. True love is overrated. Compatibility is what matters. We belong to the same social circles, and we share the same political views. We both like to sail and snow ski and go for long walks in the park on Saturday afternoons."

"Those are things friends do together. But when it comes to marriage, I'm holding out for more." She kisses his cheek. "It was good to see you, but if you'll excuse me, I need to congratulate Dad."

Returning to the reception, Kate makes her way around the room, speaking to her father's many colleagues. The crowd is thinning by the time she locates Phillip near the door. She hugs his waist. "You did great, Dad! Congratulations. I'm really proud of you."

"Thanks, sweetheart." He kisses the top of her head.

She pulls away from him. "Are you almost finished here? I need to talk to you about something important."

"Sure thing." He gestures at the door. "My driver's waiting out front. Can I give you a ride home?"

"That would be great."

They exit the hospital and climb into the black sedan waiting at the curb. Phillip pats his longtime driver on the shoulder. "Good evening, Charles. Please drop us at Duke Ellington Circle. We'll walk the rest of the way."

Charles finger salutes him. "Yes, sir, Dr. Baldwin."

Her father settles back in his seat. "Is this about Bart? I saw you two talking. He's a fine young man and a good friend. Is there any chance you're getting back together?"

"None." Kate offers him a sympathetic smile. "I'm sorry to upset you, Dad. I know you hoped Bart would be your son-in-law. He *is* a fine young man and a good friend, but he's not the one for me."

Phillip gives her a solemn nod. "I understand. I just want to see you settled and happy."

When they reach their destination, they get out of the car and head south on Fifth Avenue. The leaves haven't begun to change, but the air has the crispness of fall as they walk along Central Park.

Kate takes hold of her father's elbow. "You surprised me when you mentioned Langford in your comments earlier. Why don't you ever talk about the past?"

"I thought it best, since your childhood was so unhappy."

"My childhood was happy. It's my high school years I'd like to forget." Kate stares down at the sidewalk. "Mary Beth called me today. Alice Johnson committed suicide."

"I'm sorry to hear that," her father says with a sympathetic cluck of his tongue. "I remember Alice well. She was my patient."

"As was every other child in town."

Phillip chuckles. "True. But poor Alice struggled with anxiety from early on. She was in high school when I sent her to Atlanta for treatment. They diagnosed her with bipolar disorder."

Kate shakes her head in disbelief. "I knew she had problems, but I didn't realize they were that bad." She inhales a deep breath. "I told Mary Beth I'd come for the funeral."

Phillip stops walking and turns to face her. "Why? You haven't been friends with Alice since you were children."

"I can't explain it. I feel a powerful pull, like a magnetic attraction, to Langford. Maybe it was hearing Mary Beth's voice. Or maybe I'm intrigued by the prospect of seeing June again."

"June isn't your mother, Kate," he says, and they start walking again.

"Maybe not, but she played a major role in my upbringing. Is it wrong of me to want to see her again?"

"Under the circumstances, it's dangerous for you to revisit the past. After your mother left, I should've married the first woman who came along. Any mother would've been better than no mother."

"That's not true, Dad. You were an amazing single parent." Kate increases her pace to keep up with her father as they cross Fifth avenue. "For your sake, I wish you had remarried. I hate that you've been alone all these years."

Phillip smiles over at her. "I'm not alone. I have you."

"It's not the same, and you know it." She loops her arm through his, and they continue the rest of the way to her apartment building in silence.

Phillip pulls Kate out of the way of residents entering and exiting her building. "I'm warning you, Kate. Once you open this can, you won't be able to put the worms back in."

"I have unfinished business in Langford that has hung over my head long enough."

"Then I'll come with you. We'll make a mini vacation out of it and drive down to the coast. We'll book a guide and try to catch a tarpon on the fly."

"I appreciate your concern, but this is something I need to do alone." His disappointed face is a stab of guilt in her heart. "But a fishing trip sounds nice. Can I take a rain check?"

"Of course." Phillip squeezes her arm. "If things don't go your way in Alabama, I'll be on the next plane headed south."

She stands on her tiptoes to kiss his cheek. "Don't worry, Dad. Everything will be fine."

"I hope you're right, sweetheart."

Kate watches her father disappear into a throng of commuters before entering her building. In her apartment, she books her travel reservations, packs a suitcase, and makes a salad with leftover rotisserie chicken for dinner. After storing her plate in the dishwasher, she brews a cup of lavender tea and takes it out to her garden terrace.

Her mind drifts as she thinks back to one of the most defining moments of her life. During her first months of kindergarten, she came home from school one day in tears. Mrs. Rice, their sour-faced housekeeper and nanny, could do little to console her. She was still upset when her dad arrived home from work that evening. After much coaxing, she showed him her masterpiece—a drawing of him and Mrs. Rice.

She explained, "The teacher told us to draw a picture of our families. She asked if Mrs. Rice was my mama. I told her I don't have a mama. Why don't I have one, Daddy? All the other kids do."

Her father lifted Kate onto his lap. "You have a mama, sweetheart. She just chooses not to live with us."

Kate's golden-brown eyes widened. "Where does she live?"

"I don't know, honey. I wish I did."

She pouted her lower lip. "Make her come home."

He chuckled, fingering her lip. "How can I do that when I don't know where she is?"

"What's my mama's name?"

"Her name is Honey."

Kate repeated the name, relishing the way it felt on her lips. "I like that name. Why don't we have any pictures of her?"

"I have one." Her father leaned forward as he freed his wallet from his back pocket. He handed her the worn photograph of the prettiest woman Kate had ever seen, with flowing golden hair and a spattering of freckles across her nose.

"She's really pretty."

"Yes, she is, sweetheart."

"I'm sad, Daddy." Kate buried her face in his chest. "Can Miss June be my mama?" she asked, her words muffled by his shirt.

"You know Miss June is Ford and Scout's mother. But she loves you as though you were her own daughter."

"I don't like Mrs. Rice. She's mean."

"She's not mean, Kate. But I agree, she's a better housekeeper than nanny."

Kate looked up at her father with fresh tears in her eyes. "Can you get me a new mama?"

He tightened his arms around her. "I can't do that, sweetheart. But I *can* see what I can do about getting you a nicer nanny."

Chapter 3

June

June puts the finishing touches on the porch table—pink gingham linen napkins, magnolia scented candles, and a bouquet of assorted roses from her garden. Her husband's favorite dinner is almost ready—crab casserole in the oven, homemade cornbread in the warming drawer, and arugula salad in the fridge awaiting lemon vinaigrette dressing. She nurses a glass of crisp rosé while she awaits her husband's arrival home from work. At six thirty sharp, Buford walks through the door, and she hands him a whiskey sour.

"What's the occasion?" he asks when he notices the decorative table.

"I have exciting news," June says, even though she's sure he'll find her news anything but exciting.

"Really? So do I." He opens the glass-paned door leading to the porch. "Why don't we take our cocktails outside? It's a shame to waste this pleasant weather."

As they cross the back porch, June fills her lungs with the cool air. "Smells like autumn."

"Mm-hmm. Won't be long until the leaves change." They

stroll past her rose garden. "You need to do something about these roses, June. They're taking over the backyard."

June lets out a breath of indignation. "I'll have you know, *Southern Living* recently contacted me about doing an article on this overgrown rose garden."

Buford appears surprised. "That's wonderful, June. Congratulations. I know how hard you work in the yard. What do I know about roses anyway?"

Warmth fills her chest at the rare compliment.

They move past the rose garden to the glaring space in the back corner of the yard where her beloved magnolia tree once stood. "Even after two years, I still miss that magnolia. What do you think about putting a hammock in this space?"

"A hammock? Don't you need trees from which to hang it?" asks Buford.

"I was thinking we could get one of those metal stands."

"Those contraptions are eyesores. I thought the idea was to hang a hammock in the shade. And in order to have shade, you need trees. So why not plant two maple saplings? In a few years, you'll have big enough trees from which to hang your hammock."

June considers his suggestion. "There's not enough room for two maples. Maybe I'll just replace the magnolia. It's not summer in the South without the magnolia bloom's citrusy scent."

They continue around the side of the house to the live oak in the front yard. June lowers herself to a sprawling branch and tilts her chin up, letting the late-day sun's dappled rays warm her face.

"Tell me your news," Buford says.

"You go first," she says with eyes closed.

Buford clears his throat. "I'm thinking of running for governor."

Her pale blue eyes open wide. "But you've been out of politics for more than ten years."

"Correction. I haven't held an office in ten years. But I've been doing important work for the party behind the scenes." He smooths back the graying hair at his right temple. "I'm disappointed, June. I thought you'd be more supportive."

"You know you can count on me for support." She stands up and turns to face him. "I'm just surprised. I thought you were finished with politics."

"I've been holding out for the right opportunity."

June imagines her husband through voter's eyes. He's handsome and physically fit, and his strong personality commands attention. The intense scowl he wore in younger days has developed into permanent grooves in his forehead. She imagines his handlers will insist he have Botox to soften those lines. "Governor? Wow! That's a big deal."

"And you'll make a wonderful first lady. Coincidentally, we're hosting a dinner party here on Sunday night. Bring in your caterer and hire a bartender. I can't have you running around in your apron when you should entertain our guests."

"I'm insulted, Buford. When have I ever worn my apron while entertaining guests?" Turning her back on him, she starts toward the driveway.

Buford hurries to catch up with her. "Don't be so sensitive, June. You know what I meant. This event is important. I can't afford any screwups."

June shakes off her irritation as she continues around the side of the house to the mudroom. "I assume we're talking about a seated dinner. For how many people?"

"Ten or twelve at the most. This is a meeting. We'll eat at the table in the dining room, where we can have an open discussion."

June pauses before opening the back door. "And who's on

the guest list?"

Buford names several people she knows. The last one steals her breath. Raquel Ramsey is back in their lives. Or perhaps she never left.

"I see." June pours the rest of her rosé into a boxwood bush and goes inside.

Buford follows her into the kitchen. "Tell me your news."

"I have both bad and good news. I assume you heard about Alice Johnson."

"Of course. Everyone was talking about her at the firm today. She was a creepy little girl. Obviously, she never got her act together."

"Don't be cruel, Buford. She was a troubled child who grew into a troubled adult." June makes a big show of putting on her apron and tying it around her waist. "The good news is, Scout is coming home for the funeral."

Buford grunts. "I hardly consider that good news."

"Buford! That's awful. You haven't seen your daughter in years. Show some excitement."

He dumps his ice in the sink. "That's like asking me to show excitement about a tornado threat."

June plants her hands on her hips. "How can you say that about your own daughter?"

"Because she's a black cloud of anger and frustration," he says, pouring a splash of bourbon into his glass.

"Wonder where she gets that from," June mumbles under her breath.

Anger flashes in his hazel eyes. "What did you say?"

June stares him down. "You heard me." She takes the crab casserole out of the oven and places it onto a trivet on the counter. "Scout is no longer the volatile teenager we remember. She's highly successful at her job."

"Some job, chasing vagabonds."

"Runaways," she says, correcting him.

"Same difference." He downs his bourbon. "At least I can count on her visit being brief. With luck, she'll be gone before the dinner on Sunday."

"You're incorrigible," she says, removing the salad from the refrigerator and drizzling on the dressing.

"Why? Because I don't want my apple cart upset. I'm content with our lives. We've lived in peace these past . . ."—he waves a hand around as though swatting at a fly--"however many years it's been since she left."

"Sixteen years, six weeks, and four days. And peace is over-rated, Buford."

"After the hell those kids put us through, I'll take the way things are now over the way things were then any day."

"No one ever said parenting would be easy." She serves their plates and pushes past him on the way to the porch.

She lights the candle and sits down at her place. When he joins her, they say the blessing together and eat in silence, as they so often do.

While she'll never admit it to her husband, June agrees their apple cart is way more peaceful now than during the children's teenage years. Things couldn't be better. She has a beautiful home and leads an active social life. She's grateful her foster daughter is in her life, but Mary Beth can't replace her children. Scout lives across the country, though, and only the Lord and Ford know where he is. The estrangement eats at her every single day.

In all the years Scout's been gone, Buford has never once reached out to his daughter. He knows that June talks to Scout every few months on the phone, but he never asks about her wellbeing. He was desperate for children when they were first married. Was it because he wanted to be a father? Or because he needed props for his first election campaign for senator?

Chapter 4

June

March 1986

Buford had never mentioned the cocktail party he and June were attending in Mobile was actually a thousand-dollar-a-head political rally. When he abandoned her within five minutes of arriving, she found herself surrounded by a group of young women who fawned over her as though she were a celebrity. They complimented her attire and appearance. One pretty redhead even told her she was the luckiest girl in Alabama. "I'd give anything to be in your shoes."

June pasted on a smile and said thank you, even though she had no clue why they were being so nice. Southerners were known to be welcoming, but their praise was excessive. She felt like she was back in college at Chapel Hill, being rushed for a sorority.

Their odd behavior made sense when the governor took the podium after dinner and announced Buford's candidacy for senate. She graciously accepted congratulations from the women and men seated at their table, but inside, she was seething. How could her husband make such an important decision without consulting her first?

Toward the end of the evening, a sophisticated woman with

silky black hair and almond-shaped brown eyes approached June in the bathroom. "You're June Montgomery. I've heard so much about you."

June, having never seen the woman before, was taken aback. "Oh? From whom?"

The woman coughed up a condescending laugh. "Aren't you just darling? From Buford, of course." She thrust a hand at June. "I'm Raquel Ramsey, his campaign manager."

June glanced down at her hand without shaking it. "Funny, he's never mentioned you to me," she said, digging in her clutch for her lipstick.

Raquel retracted her hand. "You and I will be working a lot together in the coming months. Buford asked me to help improve your image. Aside from being a homemaker, do you have anything of interest on your resume?"

June swiped the lipstick across her lips and dropped the tube back into her clutch. "I don't have a resume. I belong to the Junior League, and I volunteer every week on the children's ward at the hospital. I love to garden, and our home will be featured in the October addition of *Southern Living*."

"How wonderful. Just in time for the election." Raquel admired her reflection in the mirror. "Buford warned me you're the quintessential Southern belle."

June glared at Raquel's reflection in the mirror. "Why would he *warn* you about something like that? Since when is it bad to be southern?"

Raquel powdered her nose and snapped her compact shut. "The older generation of Alabama women will think you're a sweetheart. But most of them are already loyal to the party. It's the younger ones, the feminists, we want to target with this campaign. We were hoping for a more progressive first lady, but we'll figure out a way to improve your image."

"My image doesn't need improving. Now, if you'll excuse

me, my husband is waiting for me," June said, and exited the restroom.

June looked everywhere for her husband, finally catching up with him in the valet line. She waited until they were in the car heading back to Langford before blurting, "You could've told me."

"The powers that be asked me to keep the lid on it until tonight."

"I can't believe they wouldn't let you tell your wife. This affects my life too, you know."

"I wanted to surprise you, June. I thought you'd be happy for me."

"You surprised me all right," she mumbled.

A self-satisfied smirk appeared on his lips. "Isn't it fabulous? Imagine me, James Buford Montgomery in the United States Senate."

"Since when do you have political aspirations?"

Buford puffed out his chest. "I have a calling. My country needs me."

"Making a healthy donation to the armed forces would be a lot easier than becoming a senator," she said, looking away from him and staring out the window.

"The senate is merely a steppingstone to the White House. I will one day run for president of the United States." He stroked her thigh through the black crepe fabric of her cocktail dress. "I can't do this without your support, honey. I need my beautiful wife and children by my side."

The mention of children brought silence to the car. Her inability to conceive was a sore subject.

Truth be told, June was more upset that he had kept her in the dark about the campaign than she was about him running for the senate. She relished the idea of traveling around the state with her husband, of being on his arm at political rallies and for television appearances. She'd buy a whole new wardrobe. She would charm the press, and they would love her. She'd be the modern day Jackie Kennedy.

Much to her dismay, Buford never invited her to accompany him on the campaign trail. Raquel Ramsey was the woman by his side in all the television appearances.

Buford was gone most weeks during the months that followed, and when he was home on the weekends, his primary focus was getting June pregnant. In late May, after yet another negative pregnancy test, she asked, "Why the rush, Buford? We're only twenty-six years old. We've got plenty of time to start our family."

"I'm ready to be a father now," he snapped, but June suspected he was more interested in having a pregnant wife to flaunt at campaign events.

June soon grew lonely, and with so many empty hours to fill, she decided to plant a rose garden. One Sunday in late June, she was planting two new varieties of David Austin roses when she noticed a moving truck, hauling a yellow Volkswagen Bug with California license plates, pull into the driveway at the house next door. A young woman with yellow-blonde hair got out of the passenger side, slammed the door, and vanished inside the house. The long limbs of the man June assumed was her husband appeared from behind the wheel. He paused for a minute, staring up at his new house with a satisfied smile, before following his wife inside.

June kept a close eye on the Cape Cod next door during the days that followed. She spotted the man often—drinking coffee on his back porch in the mornings, dragging stacks of folded boxes to the curb for garbage pickup, and inspecting the trees and shrubs in his yard. But June didn't see his wife again until she ventured over with a welcome casserole on Friday afternoon.

As she was approaching the porch, the back door swung open, and the young woman floated across the porch, her long sundress billowing around her sandaled feet.

Noticing June, she asked, "Who are you?"

June was awestruck by her ethereal beauty, her sun-kissed skin and angelic face. "I'm June Montgomery, your next-door neighbor." She held up the dish in her oven-mitted hands. "I brought you a casserole, to welcome you to the neighborhood."

The woman, her lip curled in distaste, looked down at the casserole and back up at June. "They warned me about this."

June shook her head in confusion. "I'm sorry. Who warned you about what?"

"My friends in California told me to be aware of Southern hospitality, that you people will use it to get into my personal business." She flapped her hand at the back door. "Just put it in the kitchen. I've gotta run. I'm meeting friends."

As she watched the woman speed off in the yellow Bug, June wondered who she was meeting and if they had friends in common.

June continued to the kitchen, where dishes and cookware covered every inch of counter space. For lack of a better place to put it, she slid the casserole into the oven. As she was turning to leave, she glimpsed a blank canvas on an artist's easel in the adjacent room. She glanced around to make certain no one was watching before venturing inside the room. Natural light streamed in from a large picture window onto beautiful land-scapes of rocky beaches decorating the back wall.

"Hello there," said a deep voice behind her.

June's face warmed as she turned to face the new home-owner, his large frame taking up much of the doorway. "I'm sorry. I'm being nosy. Are you an artist?" Her hand shot up. "Sorry. Nosy again. None of my business."

He chuckled. "I don't mind. I'm actually a pediatrician. My wife's the artist."

Once again, June's eyes travel to the paintings. "She's quite talented."

"She claims I squashed her creativity by making her leave California. Hence the blank canvas." He inclined his head at the easel. "She made her choice. She was aware of my dream of becoming a small-town pediatrician when she married me."

June considered this information too personal to share with a stranger. With an outstretched hand, she closed the distance between them. "I'm June Montgomery from next door. I brought you a casserole. Chicken tetrazzini. I put it in the oven. It's still warm, but you can freeze it if you already have dinner plans."

"That's very kind of you. Thanks. And I'm Phillip Baldwin."

June tugged her hand free of his soft grip. "I should go. If you need anything, you know where to find me."

Phillip followed her outside to the porch. "Actually, there is one thing you might help me with. I've noticed you working in your yard. Mine, as you can see, is a jungle," he said, sweeping an arm at his backyard.

June studied the overgrown shrubs. "You definitely have your work cut out for you. The previous neighbor was an elderly woman, and she let things get run down. Does your wife enjoy yard work?"

"Honey isn't the domesticated type. She's a bit of a free spirit. A bit of a handful too."

June coughed up a nervous laugh. "Being a homemaker isn't for everyone."

"You seem to find it enjoyable," he said with a warm smile.

"I do. I've never been particularly ambitious. Some would

consider that a character flaw." June shrugged. "I'm just following in my mama's footsteps."

"Nothing wrong with that." He returned his attention to the yard. "Anyway, I plan to organize the kitchen in the morning and spend the rest of the weekend cleaning up this mess. Maybe you can tell me what's worth keeping and what I should clear out."

"Sure. If you'd like, I can spare a few minutes now before my husband gets home."

"That'd be great. What does your husband do?" Phillip asked as they moved toward the yard.

"He's an attorney, but he's also running for US Senate. He's on the campaign trail more than he's at home right now."

Phillip appeared impressed. "A senator? That's impressive. I admit I'm not much of a politician."

"Neither was he until a few months ago."

Phillip gave her a curious look but refrained from commenting. "What is this leggy plant?" he asked, pointing to a row of top-heavy shrubs bordering the back porch.

"Nandina." June picked off one of the plant's small leaves. "I'm not a fan of Nandina, although the berries are nice to use for decorating at Christmas. These are way overgrown. They're blocking the view from your porch. You can find something more suitable for this space."

"Such as . . ."

"I can think of several smaller shrubs. You should visit a nursery. Sun and Shade Garden Center on Old Mobile Highway is my favorite."

June lost track of time as they wandered around the yard. Phillip already knew a fair amount about plants and trees. Most of the ones he couldn't identify were indigenous to the South. When she glanced at her watch, she was surprised to see an hour had passed since she left home. "I should go.

Buford will be home any minute, and I need to get dinner ready."

"Don't let me keep you. Thank you again for the casserole and the gardening advice."

June felt his eyes on her as she hurried down the driveway to the back door. The phone was ringing when she entered the house. "June! Where have you been? I've been trying to reach you for an hour."

"I took a casserole to our new neighbors. What's up? I thought you'd be home by now."

"About that . . . Raquel booked a last-minute segment on the six o'clock news at the local ABC affiliate in Huntsville. Since we're already in the northern part of the state, we've decided to campaign through the weekend."

June gripped the phone's receiver. "You mean you're not coming home?"

"Not until Sunday. But I can stay for a few days next week. I need to catch up on some work at the office. . . . I realize the situation is difficult for you, June. Being away from you is hard on me too. But the election is only a few months away."

"Why—"

"Listen, honey. I've gotta run. They're calling for me. Talk to you soon."

When the line went dead, June hung up the phone receiver and rested her forehead against the wall. If he realized the situation was difficult for her, why didn't he ask her to join him on the campaign trail?

Angry and frustrated, June dumped her chicken tetrazzini down the disposal and went to bed hungry.

She worked in the yard most of the morning on Saturday. After taking a quick break for lunch, she returned to raking dead leaves from the bed beside the garage. She was emptying the contents of her wheelbarrow into the compost pile when she spotted Phillip attacking his Nandina. The yellow Bug wasn't in the driveway, so she grabbed her shears and made her way over to his yard.

"Need some help?" she called over his waist-high picket fence.

He straightened, wiping sweat from his forehead with the back of his gloved hand. "Please! I have no idea if I'm doing this right."

June smiled. "There's not an exact science to butchering Nandina."

For the next two hours, they hacked Nandina stalks down to stubs and then dug their roots out of the ground. Once they'd emptied the flower bed, they stood back to admire their handiwork.

"I can't leave it barren," Phillip said, his brown eyes golden in the sun. "Care to accompany a novice to the garden center?"

"I don't consider you a novice, but I'm happy to go along for the ride. Shall I drive?" She gestured at the empty driveway. "Since you obviously don't have a car."

Phillip laughed. "We could only bring one car from California. And Honey refused to leave her Volkswagen behind. Buying a car is on my list for next week."

"We'll need my Wagoneer, anyway, to bring your plants home. Let me run get my keys."

On the way to the garden center, Phillip said, "Tell me about your husband. Have you two been together long?"

"Yes! Buford and I were childhood sweethearts. He's my one and only."

Phillip's brown eyes grew wide. "You mean you haven't . . . not even in college?"

She shook her head. "Nope. At least I didn't. We broke up our sophomore and junior years. I'm sure Buford fooled around some. But I never met anyone else I wanted to date. I hope you'll get to meet him soon. I think you two will really hit it off."

"I hope so too. He sounds like a super nice guy."

A dreamy expression fell over her face. "Buford's the best. He's intelligent and fun to be with, and he knows so much about so many things."

"He's a lucky guy. Your face says it all. I wish my wife looked like that when she talked about me."

Phillip's sad tone surprised June. A hopeless romantic, she assumed all marriages were as blissfully happy as her own.

Chapter 5

Scout

Scout is stunned by the transformation in her hometown's downtown area. Upscale boutiques now occupy storefronts where the five and dime as well as the greasy spoon diner used to be. New awnings adorn buildings, and the courthouse sports a fresh coat of white paint. On the corner in the center of town, a coffee shop has replaced the shoe repairman and offers outdoor seating at umbrella'd tables on the sidewalk.

The founding fathers named the town's primary thoroughfare Meeting Avenue to encourage locals to gather in the public square for community building. Downtown had been a ghost town when she was growing up. But today, the streets are crowded with pedestrians flocking to various eateries for happy hour and early dinners.

A catchy song comes on the country music station, and Scout turns up the volume. According to the radio display, the popular country music artist Rex Bell is singing "Sunshine." She listens closely to the lyrics which speak of a brother's love for his younger sister.

As she leaves the business district, she admires stately

homes with immaculate lawns. She passes the elementary school on the right, and a block later, her family's early twentieth-century house comes into view—white siding, square fluted columns, oversized windows with black shutters, and a Carolina blue front door—the signature color her mom adopted during her college years as a Tar Heel.

Scout experiences a pang of disappointment at the sight of the empty driveway. She thought her mom would be here to greet her. Did she remember to text her mom her ETA?

As she parks her rental car in front of the detached garage, memories from the last time she was home rush back to her. All her valuable possessions were packed in her silver 4Runner, and her parents were seeing her off to college. They'd wanted to accompany her to Auburn, and help set up her dorm room and meet her new roommate. But she'd insisted she could handle the move-in day alone.

Her father had actually smiled at her that day. "Do us proud, Scout. We're all counting on you."

Scout was never a great student to begin with, and her grades had taken a nosedive after Ford went missing. Her father pulled major strings to get her into Auburn, and he was livid when she disgraced him by failing to show up for her freshman year.

She'd waved goodbye to them. "I'll call you tonight," she'd yelled out the window as she backed down the driveway. But when she reached the interstate, instead of heading northeast to Auburn, she'd gone west in search of her missing brother.

Scout spent all her savings over the next six months looking for Ford on the street corners of every major city between Langford and Seattle. She showed his picture to every homeless young person she encountered. While she never found a trace of him, she discovered a career helping runaways.

She removes her suitcase from the trunk and wheels it to the house. The door is locked but she locates the hidden key where it's always been—under the pot of colorful flowers on the back stoop. The fresh lemony scent of Magnolia greets her as she passes through the mudroom into the kitchen. She stops dead in her tracks when she sees the handsome navy cabinets, marble countertops, and sunny nook with windows overlooking the backyard. The pine farm table, also a new addition, is set for dinner for three. Oops. She neglected to tell her mom she's going to Mary Beth's for dinner.

She peeks in the family room and her father's study as she continues down the center hallway to the front of the house. The antiques are all the same, but the upholstery fabrics, draperies, and wallpaper are all different. When she was growing up, her mom had changed wall colors as often as she did hairstyles. While her white-blonde hair is permanently fashioned in a shoulder-length bob, June's home's interior remains a work in progress.

Lifting her suitcase, Scout darts up the circular staircase to her bedroom, where she receives yet another shock. Her purple walls are now pale gray, and an upholstered headboard has replaced her four-poster bed. She quickly inspects the drawers and closet and finds not a trace of the girl who once lived here.

Across the hall in Ford's room, however, nothing has changed. His swimming ribbons and football trophies remain on display. His Crimson Tide blanket is folded at the foot of his bed, and the glass paperweight he made in kindergarten is on their grandfather's desk, a mahogany secretary with small drawers and cubbyholes.

Beside the paperweight is Ford's brown leather wallet, the contents removed except for his driver's license and student ID. One thing has nagged at Scout all these years. Why would Ford leave behind his wallet but take his tattered backpack, worn hooded sweatshirt, and acoustic guitar? Not his new electric guitar their parents had given him for his birthday in July of that year but the first guitar he'd owned as a child. Was Ford sending them a message? Was he telling them the three cherished items he took with him were more important to him than his identity?

Her mom calls up from downstairs. "Scout! I'm home!"

Scout hollers back. "Be down in a second."

Suddenly eager to see her mama, she quickly changes into a black, short-sleeved turtleneck and dark-washed jeans with the legs tucked into her scuffed-up, square-toed cowboy boots.

Hurrying down the stairs, she stands in the kitchen doorway and observes June stir something in a pot on the stove. How is it possible her mama looks so young and fit and hardly has any wrinkles. Has she had a facelift?

June brings the wooden spoon to her mouth, sampling the creamy liquid in the pot. Their eyes meet, and June returns the spoon to the pot. She moves toward Scout with arms extended. "Welcome home, darling girl."

Scout falls against her mama. She never expected this overwhelming wave of emotions.

"Let me look at you," June says, holding her at arm's length.

Scout's lip quivers and tears well in her eyes

"Oh, honey." June takes her face in her hands, thumbing away her tears. "You're beautiful. You're all grown up."

Scout laughs through her tears. "Not entirely. My breasts still think I'm twelve."

June spins her around. "What're you talking about? You have an adorable figure."

Tell that to Barrett, Scout thinks, but says, "I wouldn't go that far."

June turns back to the stove. "You must be starving. Dinner will be ready soon. I'm trying out a new shrimp recipe."

"I'm sorry, Mom. I forgot to tell you. Mary Beth invited Kate and me over for dinner."

A flash of disappointment is quickly replaced by a sincere smile. "I understand. You girls haven't seen each other in ages. You'll have a big time catching up. I hope you'll carve out some time for me while you're here. How long can you stay?"

A pang of guilt rips through Scout. After her long absence, she can't very well tell her mom she's leaving on Saturday. "I'm not sure yet. I may stay through the weekend."

"That would be wonderful. Your dad will be thrilled. Do you have time for a glass of wine?"

Scout looks to the stove clock for the time. "Sure!" she says, although she'd prefer a glass of tequila. "Does Dad still come home at six thirty? I was hoping to see him." *Hoping* is a stretch. She's anxious to get the awkward reunion over with.

"Every single night of the week." June rummages in a drawer for a corkscrew. "I'm sorry I wasn't here when you arrived. I've been home all day, but I ran to Langford Market when I realized we were low on wine."

"No worries. I was checking things out. The house looks great." Scout spreads her arms wide. "And the new kitchen is amazing."

June smiles as she unscrews the cork. "I'm pleased with the way it turned out. Next spring, we'll be on the front page of *Better Homes and Gardens* in their kitchen edition."

"That's incredible, Mom. How many magazine features is that now?"

June's cheeks pinken. "This will make eleven."

"Are you still working with the same decorator? I've forgotten her name."

"No, Janice retired." June pours pink wine into two glasses. "I'm working with Mary Beth now. I'm surprised she hasn't mentioned it to you. She has impeccable taste."

"Of course she does. She learned from the best."

Her mom waves away the compliment, even though Scout

can tell she's flattered. "She may have learned a thing or two from me, but Mary Beth has the keen eye of a genuine artist," June says, offering her a glass.

Scout, eyeing the pink wine, accepts the glass and they toast. "Cheers."

They go outside to the rockers on the screened porch. Scout studies the yard, noticing not only how much her mom's rose garden has grown but also the gaping hole in the back corner where the magnolia tree once stood. "What happened to the magnolia tree?"

"It died, sadly. I'm thinking of planting a new one. You know how much I love a magnolia bloom's scent."

"You don't say?" Her mom has been making her own magnolia-scented candles for as long as Scout can remember.

"Oh, hush." June playfully smacks Scout's arm and sits back in the rocker. "So, what's new in your world? Any updates on the Sally Strickland case?"

Scout smiles. Even though they talk on the phone only every three or four months, her mom always keeps abreast of her most important cases. "Still no sign of her. Sally's parents flew out again about a month ago."

"Hmm." June sips her wine. "What makes her mom so sure Sally will turn up in Seattle?"

"When Sally was a little girl, their family took a trip to Seattle. Sally fell in love with the city and often talked about living there after college."

"Sounds like Sally has a loving family. Why do they suspect she ran away?"

"Sally was seeing a boy they disapproved of. Her parents had reason to believe he was abusing her."

June grimaces. "How awful. Poor girl. I hope she's somewhere safe."

Scout thinks back to the days following Ford's disappearance. Her mom had been frantic and insisted they contact the police. But her father, a senator at the time, feared the story of his son's disappearance would be leaked to the press. Her mom won the argument in the end. Because Ford *was* a senator's son, the police came right away, but found no evidence of abduction.

"What's new with you, Mom?"

"Well . . . let's see . . . Your father is thinking of running for governor."

Scout furrows her brow. "Isn't he too old to be governor?"

"Apparently not. Lots of governors are over sixty."

"How exciting. You'll get to redecorate the governor's mansion. Will you sell this house when you move to Montgomery?"

June's expression pinches with concern. "I haven't gotten that far. But I refuse to sell my home. I assume we would come back to Langford after his term ends." She sits up straighter in her chair. "There's no point getting the cart before the horse. I can't see him winning the election. He's been out of the public eye far too long."

"I wouldn't be so sure. I learned a long time ago not to underestimate Dad's influence." Scout sips her wine. "So that's what Dad's been up to. I asked what was going on with you."

"I'm president of my garden club, which keeps me busier than you might expect. And I've been keeping Billy for Mary Beth in the afternoons. Her nanny quit and she's looking to hire someone new." June repositions her body toward her. "Wait until you meet him, Scout. He's a rounder, but when he wears himself out, he crawls into my arms, and I read to him until he falls asleep."

Her mom's blue eyes are bright as she babbles on about Billy. A stranger might mistakenly think she's talking about her own grandson. Who knows? Mary Beth's children may be the closest thing June ever gets to having grandchildren.

"Sounds like you spend a lot of time with Mary Beth."

"Of course. She's my foster child, after all. Besides taking care of Billy, your father and I have dinner with Mary Beth and Jeff once or twice a month. They come here or we go there. Your father and Jeff have become golfing partners."

"Really? I can't see Dad having much in common with a builder." Scout checks her phone for the time. "Speaking of Dad, he's twenty minutes late. So much for his punctuality." She gets up from her chair. "I should be going."

June follows her into the kitchen. "I can drive you over to Mary Beth's if you'd like," she says in a hopeful tone.

Scout places her glass in the sink. "I'll just walk. It can't be far." She clicks on Mary Beth's address and her Maps app opens. "Yep. Only a five-minute walk."

"Have a wonderful time," June says, kissing her cheek. "Give the girls a hug. I'm looking forward to seeing Kate tomorrow."

Scout exits the house and hurries down the driveway. Emotions overwhelm her as she heads toward town. While she's happy to see her mom again, she feels guiltier than ever for having stayed away so long. In her absence, life in Langford has gone on without her.

Her phone vibrates, and she's grateful to see Barrett's face on her screen. "How're things in Alabama?" he asks.

"Confusing. I expected an awkward reunion with Mom. Instead, I feel so . . ." She collapses onto a nearby park bench. "I don't know what I feel, honestly. I was so happy to see her, I cried. I've been angry at her for so long. Now I'm not even sure why."

Barrett pauses a beat. "Sorting through your emotions won't be easy, Scout. But you're there and that's a start. Don't expect these issues with your parents to be resolved overnight."

Scout sinks down lower on the park bench beneath the

weight of her burden. She wishes she was back in Seattle, sitting across the table from Barrett at the Bail Out. She works too hard and rarely socializes, but it's a life she understands.

"What's the point, Barrett? Things are fine with twenty-six hundred miles separating us. I told Mom I'd stay through the weekend, but I'm not sure I can. This family stuff is so messy. Who needs this heartache?"

"You do, Scout. It hurts because it matters. You can no longer hide. Fixing the problems with your parents is part of moving on with your life."

Scout exhales a reluctant sigh. "All right. I guess I should stay the weekend."

"Thatta girl. Your mission in Alabama is important. Your wounds have been festering for a very long time. And they may get worse before they get better. Stay the course. You're tough. You'll survive."

Scout swipes at her wet eyes. "Thank you for being honest with me. I needed a swift kick in the rear."

He chuckles. "Any time."

Scout remains seated on the bench after they hang up. While she's not yet ready to face Mary Beth and Kate, she doesn't want to return home either. Jealousy cuts like a knife as she thinks back to the conversation on the porch, the way June was going on about Mary Beth. Her best friend has taken Scout's place in her mom's life, and Scout has no one to blame but herself.

Chapter 6

Scout

September 1993

S cout tuned out her mama's voice, calling her to come
back to the house. She'd discovered a litter of kittens
behind the woodpile on the side of the garage. And with
the mama cat nowhere in sight, she couldn't just leave them
unattended. The fluffy balls of white fur needed her to keep
them safe.

Mama hollered again. "Mary Scout Montgomery! Come
here this instant!"

Scout's head shot up. Mama sounded furious, and since she
rarely lost her temper, Scout decided she'd better go see what
she wanted.

"I'll be back in a flash, little kittens." She dashed across the
lawn to the back porch where Mama stood with hands planted
on hips, her pretty face twisted in anger. "I'm sorry, Mama. But
I found some kittens. Six of them." She took hold of Mama's
hand. "Come quick. You've gotta see them. They're so cute."

"We don't have time for stray animals now," Mama
protested, even though she allowed herself to be dragged toward
the garage. "Kate is waiting for us. You'll be late for your first
day of school."

"But I can't find the mama cat. I looked everywhere. If we don't save the kittens, a vicious wild animal might kill them."

Peeking behind the woodpile, they saw the mama cat had returned in Scout's absence and was currently nursing her kittens.

"See! All is well. The mama has come back. Now we need to get you ready for school."

When Mama tugged on Scout's hand, she jerked it away. "No! We can't leave them out in the wilderness. They might die."

"Our yard is hardly the wilderness, Scout." Mama leaned over so she was face-to-face with Scout. "But I tell you what, after school we can make some flyers and post them around the neighborhood. I'm sure we can find the owner."

"Okay. Fine. Can I keep one?" Scout asked, as she skipped alongside Mama back through the yard.

"You already have a bunny and a turtle."

"But I don't have a kitty. Please, Mama."

Mama smiled down at her. "We'll see. Let's find the owner first. The kittens may all be spoken for."

Scout noticed Kate heading over from next door. "Why does she have to come with us on the first day of school?"

"Because her father has to work." Mama gave Scout a push toward the house. "Now run inside and grab your things. And tell your brother to hurry."

Scout trailed behind the others on her way to school, thinking up names for her kitty should she be allowed to keep one. When they arrived at the classroom, she was relieved to see the teacher had assigned seats, and hers was on the opposite side of the room from Kate. While she was glad to be separated from Kate, she was a tiny bit jealous that Kate got to sit by the window.

While she waited for class to begin, Scout studied the other kids in the room, many of whom she recognized from preschool and the country club pool. All the other little girls were into sissy stuff. Scout preferred to be outdoors.

Scout perked up when a skinny girl with yellow braids and a soiled dress sat down in front of her. She wondered why this girl didn't have a backpack like all the other children. She tapped the girl on the shoulder. "Hi! My name is Scout. What's yours?"

"Mary Beth. I'm new here."

Scout giggled. "We all are, silly. Today's the first day of kindergarten."

Mary Beth's cheeks turned a pretty shade of pink. "Oh. Right."

At recess, Scout jumped rope and played hopscotch with the other kids. But at lunchtime, when she noticed Mary Beth eating alone, Scout broke off from the crowd and sat down at her table. She opened the Jurassic Park lunchbox she'd insisted on buying, even though Mama refused to let her see the movie. "Where's your lunch?" Scout asked when she noticed Mary Beth didn't have any food.

"No one told me to bring lunch."

"In that case, I'll share mine," Scout said, giving Mary Beth half of her PB&J.

Mary Beth grinned. "Thanks. School isn't like I expected. My brothers told me the kids would be mean to me because I'm poor. But you're really nice."

Scout frowned. "What's *poor* mean?"

"Means we don't have any money."

"Doesn't your daddy work?" Scout asked, as she bit into her sandwich.

"I don't have one of them either."

Scout offered Mary Beth an apple slice from a Tupperware container. "Do you have a mama?"

Mary Beth's big blue eyes fell to the table. "Might as well not. She isn't ever home."

"Who takes care of you?"

"My brothers are supposed to. Mostly, I take care of myself."

Sadness filled Scout's heart for this little girl. "I found a litter of kittens this morning behind our garage. Wanna come see them after school?"

Mary Beth's fanny came out of her chair. "Sure! That'd be great."

When the bell rang that afternoon at three o'clock, Scout and Mary Beth exited the building hand in hand. Betty, the Montgomery's longtime housekeeper, was waiting out in front of the school.

Mary Beth whispered to Scout, "Is that your mama?"

"No. She's our housekeeper."

Mary Beth cast a suspicious glance at Betty. "What's a housekeeper?"

"She keeps our house clean. She dusts furniture and vacuums floors and makes the best ever chocolate chip cookies." Scout turned to Betty. "Where's Mama? Why didn't she come for us?"

"She's playing tennis. She sent me to walk you home. Who's your friend?"

"This is Mary Beth. She's coming home with me to see the kittens."

Betty scowled. "Miss June didn't say anything about you having a friend over." She turned to Mary Beth. "Did you get permission from your mama?"

Mary Beth stared down at her big toe peeking through the end of her sneaker. "She won't mind. She's at work."

Betty's bushy eyebrows became one. "Who was supposed to pick you up from school?"

"Nobody. I'm supposed to walk home. I know the way."

Ford, with Kate on his heels, ran up to them. He flashed a hand at Mary Beth. "Hi. I'm Ford, Scout's brother. Who are you?"

"Mary Beth," she mumbled, and inched closer to Scout until she was hiding behind Scout's back.

Out of the corner of her mouth, Scout said to Mary Beth, "What're you doing?"

"I'm afraid of brothers. They're mean," Mary Beth whispered.

"Not mine. Ford's the nicest boy I know."

"Come here, child. Let me get a good look at you." Betty took hold of Mary Beth's hands and inspected her arms. "Good, Lord. You're covered in bruises. Did your brothers do this to you?"

Mary Beth nodded, her front teeth clamped down on a trembling lower lip.

Betty stroked the top of the little girl's head. "Don't cry, sweetheart. Everything will be fine."

Mary Beth and Scout skipped the whole way home. They were devouring slices of Betty's strawberry cake at the kitchen counter when Mama returned from playing tennis, her tanned legs showing from beneath her short white skirt. Before Scout had a chance to introduce Mary Beth, Betty whisked Mama away for a private conversation in the family room across the hall.

When Mama returned to the kitchen, she wore concern on her face. She sat down next to her new friend. "Hello, Mary Beth. I'm Scout's mama. You can call me Miss June. I'm worried your mama doesn't know where you are. What time does she get home from work?"

Mary Beth appeared afraid. "I'm not sure. I'm usually asleep."

The lines on Mama's forehead deepened. "Do your brothers feed you dinner?"

"No, ma'am. I usually eat a can of Vienna sausages."

"Oh. I see. In that case, you'll have dinner with us tonight, and I'll drive you home afterward." Mama turned to Scout. "I have good news about the kittens. They belong to my friend Judy. She lives behind us on the next street over. She would like you to have one as a reward for finding them. We can go there now if you'd like to pick out a kitten."

Scout shot out of her chair. "Yippee! Let's go."

Mama drove Scout and Mary Beth to Miss Judy's, where they spent the afternoon playing with the kittens. Scout finally settled on a girl kitten she named Coconut, Coco for short. By the time they walked home, dinner was ready.

Mama said to Mary Beth, "I hope you like fried chicken and macaroni and cheese."

Mary Beth's face lit up. "Yes, ma'am!"

They'd no sooner sat down to eat than her daddy arrived home.

"Who are you?" he asked Mary Beth in his lawyer tone of voice.

"This is Scout's friend from school," Mama said. "Her name is Mary Beth."

"I see." He joined them at the table and ate his dinner in silence. Scout had learned it was best not to bother him when he was in a mood.

The kids were finishing dessert when Scout overheard her parents talking in the kitchen. "I need you to drive Mary Beth home," Mama said. "And be careful. She lives in an unsafe part of town."

Her father didn't argue. He was gone a long time, and when he got back, his face was grim. When he summoned Mama to his study, Scout pressed a juice glass against the closed door, but she couldn't make out what her parents were saying.

The next morning, Scout asked if Mary Beth could come home with her again from school, and Mama readily agreed. When they arrived home that afternoon, clothes Scout had outgrown covered her bed. Mama stripped Mary Beth naked and put her in the bathtub, scrubbing her skin and washing her hair three times. She dressed Mary Beth in shorts and a white knit shirt and folded the rest of the clothes into paper bags. Mary Beth ate dinner with them again that night, and afterward, Scout's daddy drove her home. And from that day forward, Mary Beth was as much a part of the family as Coconut.

Chapter 7

Kate

Kate enters the handsomely appointed lobby of the new Meeting Inn and wheels her suitcase to the reception desk. She's digging her wallet out of her purse when a voice says, "Kate? Is that you?"

She glances up at the attractive man behind the desk and then does a double take. "Lance?"

"It's been a long time," he says, his smile meeting the piercing blue eyes that once left her weak-kneed.

She bobs her head. "A really long time." Her old boyfriend has aged well. He'd been a lanky kid in high school, and the weight he's gained since has softened his facial features.

"It's good to see you," he says, those eyes now twinkling.

Kate, curious about his position at the hotel, checks his coat for a name tag. But there is none. She remembers her old high school boyfriend as being highly motivated. Surely, he's not a desk clerk. "I gather you work here. Are you the manager?"

"I'm the new owner. We're short-staffed tonight, so I'm pitching in."

Kate scans the lobby. "You did a remarkable job on the renovations. If I didn't know better, I'd mistakenly think I was back in New York."

"That's right. I heard you were a big-time fashion designer." His fingers dance across the keyboard. "I assume you're in town for Alice's funeral."

"I am." Kate slides her credit card across the counter. "I'm so sorry for all her family has been through."

Lance gives his head a solemn shake. "Such a sad situation. Whenever I saw Alice around town, I tried talking to her, but she always wore a blank look. She's been in and out of rehab for years."

"That's a shame."

Lance hands her a packet of room keycards. "Maybe we can have a drink while you're in town." When her eyes travel to his left ring finger, he chuckles. "I'm not married."

A flush creeps up Kate's neck. "A girl can't be too careful these days." Grabbing her suitcase handle, she starts off toward the elevators. She punches the up button and turns around to face him. "About that drink . . . I'd love to catch up. As of now, I'm planning to stay until Monday."

"All right, then. We'll figure out a time," he says, his grin reminding her of the boy he once was.

She thinks about Lance on her way up in the elevator. She'd broken off her relationship with him when she moved to New York with her father during the winter break of her senior year in high school. She'd cared about him more than any boy she'd dated, and she's often wondered about him over the years.

The elevator deposits her on the fifth floor and she lets herself into the corner suite, which offers a sitting area, plush marble bath, and view of downtown. As she stares out the window, she's surprised to see the charming boutiques and eateries lining both sides of Meeting Avenue.

Kate unpacks her suitcase, putting her hanging garments in the closet and placing her folded clothes in drawers. She brushes her hair, freshens her makeup, and changes into a gray shirtdress before heading out. The brisk evening air feels refreshing on her face after an exhausting day of travel. She longs to walk past her old house, but the detour would make her late for dinner. She'll wait until after the funeral tomorrow, when she has more time to reminisce.

Mary Beth lives on a charming street in a gray craftsman-style house with black shutters. Kate smiles when she sees the hot-pink front door. Her old friend was a big fan of anything pink.

Mary Beth welcomes her with a warm hug. "Look at you, an elegant and sophisticated fashion designer. I admire your work. I have several handbags and too many pairs of Honey B. shoes to count."

Kate smiles. "And you haven't changed a bit. Still as pretty as ever." With deep blue eyes and golden hair, Mary Beth was the one the boys chased in high school. "Do you have a career? I'm embarrassed to say, I don't know."

"I own an interior design firm."

"That explains why your house is fabulous. I love the pink door."

"Come on in," Mary Beth says and closes the door behind them. "I'll give you the nickel tour while we wait for Scout."

Kate admires the decor as she follows Mary Beth through the various rooms. Everything is done in grays and whites, with accents of different shades of pink. "How long have you lived here?"

"We moved in two years ago, right before my son, Billy, was born. My husband is a contractor. The house was built in the early 1920s. It needed a ton of work. We took it down to the studs."

In the kitchen doorway, Kate stops in her tracks when she

sees the dark gray cabinets and Carrera marble countertops. "Now, this is a dream kitchen."

"Thank you. We worked hard on it." Mary Beth removes a bottle of expensive champagne from the refrigerator. "Our reunion calls for a celebration. Not to belittle the sad occasion that has brought us back together."

"Sounds like Alice led a tormented life. We'll honor her by remembering our carefree childhood years."

Mary Beth pops the cork and fills two stemless flutes with the golden bubbly, handing one to Kate.

Scout appears in the kitchen doorway, the same scrawny girl with lopsided smile Kate grew up with. "I knocked. But I heard your voices and let myself in. I hope you don't mind."

Mary Beth lets out a squeal and throws her arms around Scout. "You're here! Finally."

Scout gives Kate a curt nod over Mary Beth's shoulder. "Kate."

Kate nods in return. "Scout. It's nice to see you. It's been a long time."

Mary Beth fills another glass of champagne and holds it out to Scout.

"I'd rather have tequila," Scout says, dismissively.

If Scout's rudeness irritates Mary Beth, she doesn't let it show. "Of course. How would you like it served?"

"On the rocks, please."

Mary Beth opens a cabinet, pulls out a bottle of Casamigos, and pours two fingers over ice. The years fall away as Kate watches the scene unfold. The threesome is back in middle school again. Scout is in a mood, and Mary Beth is placating her while Kate watches from afar.

"Do you two see each other often?" Kate asks.

"I've been out to Seattle twice," Mary Beth says.

"But I haven't been home since I left for college," Scout admits, sipping the tequila.

This surprises Kate and suddenly she wants to know more. "Where did you go to school? If I remember correctly, you were hell-bent on attending Auburn. Did you become a veterinarian?"

"I didn't go to college. And I'm not a veterinarian."

"But—"

A little boy in footed pajamas comes barreling around the corner from the hallway. He throws himself at Mary Beth's legs. "Mama! Can I stay up longer?"

Mary Beth scoops him up and kisses the top of his damp blonde head. "Long enough to meet my friends. This is Miss Kate and Miss Scout. Ladies, this is Billy."

Suddenly shy, Billy buries his face in his mama's neck.

A male version of Mary Beth enters the kitchen. His hair is golden like hers, but his eyes are a lighter shade of blue than his wife's. With a warm smile, he introduces himself as Jeff. "I've heard so much about both of you."

Kate shakes his hand, and Scout gives him a hug. "Same. I'm glad to finally meet you."

Jeff lifts his son out of his mama's arms. "Come on, Tiger. It's time for bed. We need to let the ladies do their thing."

Kate waits for father and son to leave. "I'm confused, Scout. How is it you've never met Mary Beth's husband? Did you not come home for their wedding?"

"I just told you. I haven't been back since I left for college," Scout snaps.

An awkward silence fills the room. "I'm sorry," Kate says. "I didn't mean to pry."

"We had a small destination wedding at Jeff's parents' mountain house in Cashiers, North Carolina," Mary Beth explains, which tells Kate nothing.

Kate suspects there's more to the story. Mary Beth and Scout obviously had some sort of falling out. But she doesn't press for details.

Mary Beth removes a hummus platter from the refrigerator. "Why don't we sit on the patio for a while before we eat dinner?"

"That sounds perfect." Kate grabs the bottle of champagne and Scout the tequila, and they follow Mary Beth out a pair of french doors to a blue slate terrace that offers comfortable seating around a stone fire pit.

Kate inhales the intoxicating smell of roses. "The scent reminds me of my childhood days playing in Scout's backyard. I tried growing roses in my balcony garden, but I don't have much of a green thumb."

Mary Beth smiles. "Me either. June wanted me to start a rose garden in the back corner of the yard. But planting a few bushes around the patio seemed more manageable."

Scout plops down in a chair and digs into the hummus. "What *is* for dinner? I'm starving."

"I'm glad to see your appetite hasn't changed," Kate says. "It's a shame you can't market your metabolism."

"My metabolism is a curse. If I could give it to you, I would. It's like owning a car with a hole in its gas tank."

Kate laughs. "I could see where that might be a nuisance. And expensive."

Mary Beth refills their glasses with champagne. "To answer your question, Scout, we're having a Mexican smorgasbord. I thought it appropriate for our reunion."

Kate settles back in her chair as a long-forgotten memory resurfaces. "That's right. Miss June used to take us to the Taco Palace nearly every Friday night. Is it still open?"

"Yes," Mary Beth says. "But it's under new ownership, and the food's not as good."

"Was the food ever any good? Or were our tastebuds unso-phisticated?" Kate drags a celery stick through the hummus. "We used to think McDonald's was gourmet."

Scout sits up straight. "Hey! What's wrong with McDon-ald's? It's my go-to place for comfort food."

Mary Beth giggles. "I'm not surprised."

"Speaking of food," Kate says. "I've eaten in Michelin Star restaurants, but I've never tasted anything better than Betty's grilled pimento cheese, bacon, and tomato sandwiches."

"Amazing!" Scout says. "Maybe she'll make them for us while we're here."

Kate, reminded of the purpose of their visit, says, "I admit I remember little about Alice. Did she hang out with us a lot?"

"I invited her over all the time, but she never stayed long. She always invented some excuse to go home," Scout says.

Mary Beth gives Scout a reproachful look. "Because you tormented the poor girl."

"That's right!" Kate says. "I remember you once made her kiss a frog, Scout. You pinned her to the ground and pressed the slimy creature to her face. Alice ran home, screaming and crying."

Mary Beth giggles, her hand pressed to her lips. "You blamed me for that escapade, Scout. Fortunately, June realized you were the guilty one. But the 9-1-1 call was a different story. I took the fall for that prank."

Scout slumps down in her chair. "Because Mom would've beaten my behind. You only got a scolding."

Mary Beth gawks at Scout. "You deserved a beating for telling the operator your house was on fire."

A light bulb switches on inside Kate's head. "The passage of time has allowed me to see things more clearly. You let Mary Beth take the blame for all the bad things *you* did because you knew she would get a lighter sentence. You were the instigator, and she was your scapegoat."

Scout pops a cherry tomato into her mouth. "And you were the Goody Two-shoes who stood by and watched."

Kate lowers her gaze to the fire pit. "My father faced his share of challenges as a single parent. He had a demanding career and dedicated what little free time he could manage to me. I didn't want to make things harder on him by getting into trouble."

Scout pours herself more tequila. "I never thought much about you not having a mother, Kate. We were just all June's children."

Kate runs her thumb around the lip of her champagne glass. "It might have seemed that way, and I'm grateful for all June did for me, but I never felt like one of her children."

Sorrow fills Scout's face. "I realize I was a brat. And I feel awful about the way I treated Alice. I honestly never meant her any harm. She was just an easy target. If I only had the chance, that is one of many things I'd take back. Or at least ask forgiveness for."

Scout has always rubbed Kate the wrong way. Their personalities are so very different. But comments like these reveal a snippet of the genuine soul beneath her gruff exterior.

"Why didn't you go to college, Scout?" Kate asks in a soft and sincere voice.

Scout looks away, staring out into the dark night. "I went to look for Ford. My search landed me in Seattle, where I joined the police force and eventually became a detective specializing in runaways."

Her answer leaves Kate speechless. Now, more than ever, she's convinced she made the right decision in coming home.

Chapter 8

Scout

July 2002

Scout's parents hosted an adults-only party on the Saturday night of July Fourth weekend. Mama relegated the adolescents to the yard with a package of hot dogs, several bags of chips, and a six-pack of Coca Cola. After feasting on grilled hotdogs, they stretched out on blankets to wait for the final round of neighborhood fireworks.

"I have an idea." Ford sat bolt upright. "Let's play a game. How about flag football? Girls against boys."

Scout crossed her arms over her chest. "Football is boring. Let's play truth or dare."

"I'm out." Alice scrambled to her feet. "I gotta go home. I hear my mom calling me. See y'all tomorrow."

Four sets of eyes watched her disappear down the driveway. "I didn't hear her mom calling, did y'all?" Ford asked.

"Nope. She's afraid to play truth or dare with us." Scout broke off a stick from a nearby azalea bush, pointing it at Ford. "I'm the moderator, and you're going first. Truth or dare?"

Ford stared up at the starry sky. "I'll take a dare."

"Hmm. Let's see." Scout's eyes traveled the backyard,

landing on his guitar. "Go inside and play a song for the grown-ups."

Ford, who loved performing for audiences of any kind, jumped to his feet. "I'll take that dare any day."

As he started off toward the house with guitar in hand, Scout called after him, "Play that Beatles song I love. 'Here Comes the Sun.'"

Ford stopped walking and turned to face them. "Seriously, Scout? I hate that song."

"But you play it so well. The grown-ups will love your version. It's so sweet."

"*Sweet* is not the image I'm hoping for. But whatever." He spun back around and continued inside.

Scout and the others ran to the porch and watched through the open window as Ford made his way to the center of the family room. The crowd grew silent as he strummed his guitar. His performance was flawless, and when he finished, everyone clapped loudly.

When Ford emerged from the house, the others followed him out into the yard, but Scout lingered behind to eavesdrop on the grown-ups. Cigarette smoke wafted out of the window, and she pinched her nose to keep from gagging.

Her parents were near enough to the window for Scout to hear her father's friend say, "Buford, you old dog. Looks like you've got the next Paul McCartney on your hands."

Dad beamed with pride. "As long as he doesn't make a career out of his talent."

The friend chuckled. "Right. He's going to follow in his daddy's footsteps and become an attorney. Maybe even a senator."

"Or president," Dad grumbled.

Next to Dad stood Mama and her tennis partner, Miss Barbara. "I can't believe how much Ford has grown since I last saw him," Barbara said. "You and Buford aren't especially tall. Where did he get the height?"

Mama held her hands out as if to say *who knows?* "Both my brothers are over six feet. I guess he inherited it from me."

Scout thought, *Meanwhile, I got the shrimp gene.*

Ford called her from the yard. "Come on, Scout. We're waiting for you."

Scout left the window and returned to the group.

Ford, who had picked up her stick in her absence, waved it at her. "It's your turn. Truth or dare?"

Scout rolled her eyes. "Dare. Duh."

"Go make that dog shut up." Ford pointed the stick in the direction of the house behind them, whose vicious German shepherd barked incessantly.

"Piece of cake," Scout said, already on her feet and running.

Ford shouted, "Don't, Scout! I'm just kidding. Bruno will bite you."

She darted across the lawn and scrambled over the brick wall into the neighbor's backyard. Scout was on the ground playfully wrestling with the German shepherd when three sets of wide eyes peered over the wall at her.

"Whoa. How'd you make Bruno like you?" Ford asked, seemingly amazed.

"He loves these expensive caramels Mama keeps in the glass bowl beside the front door." Holding out her arm, Scout revealed a handful of individually wrapped caramels.

Scout climbed back over the wall, and the foursome returned to their spot to continue their game.

Scout, once again in control of the stick, said, "Kate, it's your turn."

Kate tapped her chin. "Hmm . . . I pick truth."

Scout's blue eyes flashed with mischief. "Have you kissed a boy yet?"

Kate glared at her. "Um . . . No."

"I don't believe you," Scout said.

Kate's brown eyes were like peppermint patties. "Why would I lie about something like that? I would have told you anyway."

"I'm just surprised. All the boys have crushes on you." Scout jabbed the stick at Mary Beth. "Your turn."

"I pick truth," Mary Beth said without hesitation.

Scout couldn't think of a good question, so she opted for one of their tried-and-true commands. "Tell us your deepest, darkest secret."

Mary Beth lowered her gaze. "My mama has a new boyfriend. Lamar is a real jerk. He got into a fight with my oldest brother last night. Johnny pulled a switchblade on him, and Lamar kicked him out of the house. Lamar told him not to come back, even though it's not his house. My other brothers are saying they're leaving too, and they're not even eighteen yet. If they do, I'll be left alone with Lamar while Mama's at work."

Mary Beth sniffled, and even though Scout couldn't see her face, she assumed she was crying.

Ford moved closer to Mary Beth. "Has Lamar hurt you?"

"No. But he creeps me out the way he looks at me. Like he might try to do something . . . you know . . . inappropriate."

"You need to tell my parents," Scout said.

Mary Beth gave her head a vehement shake. "I can't bother them with this. They've done so much for me already."

Kate chimed in, "Then tell my dad. He's a pediatrician. He'll know how to help you."

"He'll help me right into a foster home," Mary Beth said, using her shirttail to dry her tears.

Kate considered this. "That's probably true. By law, he would be obligated to call social services."

"Mama will be spitting mad when she finds out Johnny is

gone. With any luck, she'll break up with Lamar." Mary Beth straightened her spine. "I'm sorry for the outburst. Who's next?"

"It's Ford's turn again," Scout said.

Her brother chose truth this time, giving Scout the chance to ask him what she'd been dying to know all summer. "Why have you been hanging out with us lately instead of your friends?"

A flushed creeped up Ford's neck. "My friends have been smoking cigs and getting drunk off liquor they steal from their parents. I can't pollute my body. I have to stay in shape for football. Coach says I have a good chance of playing varsity this year."

"Wow! Congratulations." Kate offered him a high five. "Playing varsity as a freshman is a big deal."

With a thin smile, Ford said, "I'm pumped. It just sucks not having any friends."

Scout placed a reassuring hand on her brother's shoulder. "Don't worry about your friends. They'll come around."

Ford hung his head. "I'm not so sure about that."

Kate volunteered, "Then make new friends with the guys on the football team. Aren't you already spending a lot of time with them in the weight room?"

Ford perked up. "That's true. I like some of those guys a lot. I could ask them to grab food after a workout or something."

Scout's heart sank. How was it Kate always knew just what to say to comfort her brother?

Chapter 9

June

Buford never comes home late from work without calling to let June know. When she hasn't heard from him by eight o'clock, she fixes her plate and takes it outside to the rocker on the porch. At nine o'clock, with still no word from Buford, she leaves his dinner in the warming drawer and stores the leftovers in the refrigerator.

She's changed into her nightgown and is smearing cream on her face when she hears Buford banging around in the kitchen downstairs. A loud clattering sound startles her, and she slams down the jar of cream.

June grabs her robe and heads for the stairs, calling out to him on the way down. "Buford! What did you break? It better not have been my good dinner plate."

She finds her husband on his hands and knees with a wad of paper towels, wiping up spilled shrimp casserole off the floor. He looks up at her with bloodshot eyes. "I'm sorry, honey. The plate slipped out of my hands."

"Give me that." She takes the paper towels from him. "You're replacing this dinner plate."

He sits back on his haunches. "I'll buy you a whole damn set."

"Juliska doesn't come in sets." June mops the food into a pile and deposits the soiled paper towels into the trash can. "Where have you been anyway?"

"Having dinner with important donors at the club." Clambering to his feet, he fills a highball glass with ice and splashes bourbon on top.

"You could've texted me. I've been waiting for you all night. Who were these important donors? Was Raquel there?" June cringes at the jealous tone in her voice. She tells herself she has no reason to worry. Her relationship with Buford is solid.

"No one you know. And yes, Raquel was there. She's my campaign manager." He studies the bourbon before taking a gulp.

"You've had enough of this." She takes the glass from him. "Did your drunkenness impress your dinner guests into contributing large donations?"

"I wasn't drunk during dinner," Buford says, his eyes swimming in his head. "Raquel and I stayed afterward. We had some business to discuss."

June raises an eyebrow. "Mm-hmm. I bet. If you already ate, why bother with the food I left you?"

"I didn't eat much at the club. I was busy explaining my campaign strategy."

June removes the container of leftover casserole from the refrigerator and spoons a heaping serving onto a plate. "You missed Scout. Mary Beth invited her to dinner. She waited for you as long as she could."

He plops down in a chair at the counter. "Scout is the main reason I ate at the club."

"You'll have to face her at some point, Buford." June places the plate in the microwave to reheat. "Are you going to the funeral tomorrow?"

"I hadn't planned on it. I hardly knew the kid."

"But you knew her parents. Bud and Judy were our neighbors for years," June says as she sets a place for him on the counter with placemat, napkin, and flatware.

"I have an important meeting with a client in the morning anyway."

When the microwave dings, June removes the plate and places it in front of him. "The reception is family only, and the girls will need to eat, so I figured I'd have Betty throw together a brunch. You can swing by during your lunch hour. I'm sure you want to see Kate."

"Kate who?" he asks as he inspects the contents of his plate.

"Kate Baldwin. Phillip's daughter."

Buford grunts. "Right. Phillip, your old boyfriend. Is he coming to lunch too?"

June ignores his comment. "I doubt Phillip will come. Although it would be nice to see him again." She intends her comment to irritate Buford, but with a jolt, she realizes how much she means it. Even after all these years, she still misses her long talks with Phillip. No one has ever understood her like he did.

June glances over to find her husband glaring at her. "Why are you looking at me like that? Is something wrong?"

"I'm wondering what you're scheming in that pretty little head of yours."

"Nothing. I was just thinking about old times," June says, and shakes her head to clear her thoughts of Phillip.

Buford shovels in a forkful of shrimp casserole. "This is a bad time for Scout to come back into our lives. I need the support of certain key figures in order to be included on the primary ticket next spring. A scandal could ruin that for me."

June laughs out loud. "That's absurd, Buford. No one is going to cause a scandal."

He jabs his fork at her. "Watch yourself. If you step out of line, you could cost me the election."

June drops her smile as cold dread descends upon her. "Like you cost yourself the election the first time you ran for senate?"

Buford's face beams red. "Why you little . . ." When he lurches toward her, he tumbles off the stool and grips the counter to prevent himself from falling to the floor.

June darts out of the kitchen and up the stairs to Ford's room, where she sleeps occasionally when she wants to feel close to her son. Buford rarely drinks too much, but when he does, it's never pretty. She knows better than to antagonize him, but sometimes she can't help herself.

Locking the door, she slips beneath the covers and listens for Buford's footfalls on the stairs. When she's certain he's gone to bed, she closes her eyes and allows herself to think about Phillip.

June had been so angry the last time she saw Phillip, three days after Christmas seventeen years ago. The conversation had taken place in his driveway, like so many of their important talks. Kate had gone to say goodbye to a friend, and the movers were packing the last of the boxes in the moving truck. Phillip and Kate were to spend their last night at home, sleeping on air mattresses in front of the fireplace while reliving old memories, before leaving for New York in his SUV at the crack of dawn the following morning.

June wraps her cashmere sweater tighter around her. "My offer still stands. We would love to have Kate live with us. It breaks my heart to think of her missing out on her senior year."

"Kate and I have discussed your offer at length, and we appreciate your generosity, but moving to New York with me is what she truly wants. She might as well get to know the city before she starts at NYC next fall."

Phillip had been the first person June had called when they discovered Ford missing the following morning.

"I haven't seen him since last night when he came over to say goodbye," Phillip had said. "Don't worry, June. He'll show up. He's in college now. He probably spent the night at a friend's house and forgot to let you know."

"I'm sure you're right," June had said, even though her mother's intuition warned her there was something seriously wrong.

"I'll have Kate call around to some of their friends. We'll let you know if we hear anything."

June and Phillip had stayed in contact during the days following Ford's disappearance. But after a week, those calls and texts had dwindled and then stopped completely. Phillip had been her best friend for nearly twenty years, and her heart ached for him every bit as much as it ached for her missing son.

June dozes off to sleep and awakens sometime later to find Scout sitting on the edge of her bed.

"Hey, honey." June rolls onto her back, stretching an arm over her head. "What time is it?"

"Around midnight. Why did you redecorate my room?"

June eases into a sitting position. "Having two guest rooms comes in handy when we have more than one couple in from out of town for member-guest tennis and golf tournaments at the club."

"But why my room? Why not Ford's?" Scout asks, her blue eyes darting around the room.

"Because Ford left all his stuff here. You took all yours with you."

"Not all of it," Scout says in a defiant tone.

"I donated your American girl dolls to a local charity. They were practically brand new. I stored everything else in two boxes in the attic."

Scout lets out a heavy sigh. "Dad kept giving me those dolls for Christmas every year, even though I never played with them. He never understood me."

"Your father doesn't understand anyone. Not even himself."

Scout furrows her brow. "Do you think Dad had something to do with Ford's disappearance?"

"Not intentionally. Although your father was awfully hard on him."

"Ha. That's an understatement."

June draws her knees up to her chest. "Your brother wasn't himself that Christmas. His grades were awful and football wasn't going well."

"You never told me that," Scout says in an accusatory tone.

"It was obvious the way he was moping around."

Scout picks at a loose thread on the wool blanket. "I was too wrapped up in my own life to notice," she admits.

June rests her chin on her knees. "Ford was an intelligent young man. He needed to get out from under your father's thumb and find himself."

"If you believed that, why did you insist Dad report his disappearance to the police?"

"Because Ford was a senator's son. I had to rule out the possibility of abduction."

Scout digs her thumb into her chest. "I was a senator's *daughter*. Were you worried someone had kidnapped me when I ran away?"

"God help the abductors." June intends her comment to be funny, but Scout doesn't laugh. She reaches out to Scout, her fingers grazing her arm. "You left your phone behind. That's a pretty good sign you didn't want to be found. I was terrified for your safety, sweetheart. I didn't sleep for six months after you left. But, like your brother, I knew you needed the space to chart your own course."

Scout shoots her a sharp look. "But we were your children. We needed you and you abandoned us."

"*You* abandoned *us*, Scout. You packed your car for college and never came back." June sighs. "I couldn't have stopped you. You were a passionate young girl, determined to find the brother she adored."

"That's fair. Do you think he's still alive? He's only called that one time, fifteen years ago. Anything could've happened since then."

June places her hand on her chest. "I believe in my heart he's alive. I keep hoping he'll show up at the front door one day."

Scout slides off the bed to her feet. "I'm determined to find Ford if it's the last thing I do."

"I hope you do, sweetheart. It's way past time for him to come home."

Chapter 10

June

October 1986

June and Phillip grew closer as their spouses became increasingly absent in their lives. She encouraged his developing enthusiasm for gardening, and he taught her about California wines and New Orleans jazz. He invited her over for cocktails, and she served him simple suppers on her screened porch. He was easy to talk to, more so than any of her girlfriends, and she found herself confiding her innermost thoughts, hopes, and dreams for the future. Because they were both devoted to their marriages, it never occurred to June to feel guilty about spending time with a member of the opposite sex. After all, men and women, like Buford and Raquel, have platonic friendships all the time.

One Saturday morning in late September, they were standing in the driveway drinking coffee when Phillip confessed, "I'm at my wits in with Honey. I worked with drug-addicted teens during my residency, and I know the signs. She's smoking a lot of marijuana. Her clothes reek of it every time she walks through the door at night. But I think she might be popping pills and using cocaine as well."

June kept a straight face despite her surprise. She had

plenty of friends who experimented with drugs in college, but those people were now too busy having babies and furthering their careers for such reckless behavior. "Is this something new? Or was she using drugs back in California?"

"It's a possibility. I was working all the time. It would've been easy for her to hide it."

"It's not my place to say this, Phillip, but I think she's being unfair to you. You're working hard all day, and she's partying all night. Does she ever even cook dinner for you?"

He gave his head a grave shake. "Not one time since we moved here."

"Have you tried putting your foot down?"

"I've discussed it with her so many times, I'm all talked out. She's furious at me for making her leave California. She says I ruined her life."

"Seems to me like her life is just fine with all the new friends she's made."

"One would think so. I'm beginning to worry there's no making her happy." Bewilderment crossed his face. "I'm ready to start a family, and she's partying like a college girl."

June offered him a smile of encouragement. "She'll come around. She just needs a little more time to adjust to her new life."

"She could learn so much from you. Who knows? If you two had children the same age, you might become friends."

June smiled. "I can see it now, two little girls or boys playing in the backyard while Honey and I sip margaritas on the porch." As much as she relished the idea, deep down June knew she and Honey would never be friends.

Two weeks later, June was poaching an egg for her breakfast when the mention of her husband's name on the local TV news got her attention. Spooning the egg onto a slice of buttered toast,

June turned off the stove and upped the volume on the television.

The news anchor, Amelia Lake, was reporting about an accident that happened around two o'clock that morning. "The senate candidate was driving home from a fundraiser at a historic mansion in Natchez, Mississippi, when his car careened off the highway and struck a tree. No injuries were reported. The police are investigating the possibility that alcohol was involved. Montgomery's campaign manager, Raquel Ramsey, is rumored to have been traveling with the candidate at the time."

June's stomach soured, and she scraped her breakfast down the disposal. Changing into yard clothes, she left the back door open in case the phone rang and spent the morning taking her frustration out on the weeds in her garden. When noon rolled around, she was hot and thirsty and ready for a break. Pouring herself a glass of sweet tea, she turned on the television, hoping for an update about the accident. Her husband's face filled the screen. Raquel, wearing a stylish gray dress and dark sunglasses, stood next to him.

June chomped down on an apple as she watched her husband place a possessive hand on the small of his campaign manager's back. "For those at home who haven't met her, I'd like to introduce my campaign manager, Raquel Ramsey. I couldn't have come this far without her organizational skills and firm hand in keeping me in line."

Murmured laughter spread throughout the journalists gathered for the press conference.

"As you are probably aware by now, Raquel and I were in a car accident last evening on the way home from a fundraiser. When I swerved to miss a deer, my car skidded off the road and ran into a tree. We are both grateful to be alive."

When Buford opened the floor for questions, one journalist

asked, "Why were you in Mississippi when you're running for office in Alabama?"

"That's what I wanna know," June said to the television.

"We were invited to an event in Natchez to support fellow party candidates from Alabama," Buford explained.

The newscaster transitioned from Buford to a press conference being held by the Mississippi State Police. "A blood test shows Mr. Montgomery's blood alcohol level was way over the limit. We expect to file charges for driving under the influence by the end of the day."

"Good," June said, dropping her apple core into the trash and returning to her yard work.

Around two o'clock, she looked up from tending her summer perennials to see Phillip in his driveway. He appeared frazzled, with hair in disarray and a five o'clock shadow on his face. She set down her clippers, peeled off her gloves, and walked over to him. As she drew closer, she could see angry red marks on both sides of his neck.

"Have you seen Honey?" he asked.

"Not today." June noticed the yellow Volkswagen in the driveway. "Her car is here. Are you sure she's not at home? Maybe she went out for a walk."

"She rarely drives when she goes out. One of her friends usually picks her up." Phillip raked his fingers through his unruly hair. "She was a mess when she came home last night around one o'clock." He lifted his fingers to his neck. "She physically attacked me and tore the house apart. When she finally calmed down, she admitted she'd taken LSD. She was having a bad trip."

June's heart went out to him. "That's awful. I can't imagine how disturbing it must have been for you to see your wife like that."

Phillip grimaced. "It wasn't a pretty sight. When she finally crashed on the sofa around daybreak, I curled up on the floor beside her and zonked out. I woke up a few minutes ago to find her gone. I have no clue how she got past me without me hearing her."

"Do you think she left town?"

Phillip shook his head. "None of her clothes or precious art supplies are missing. She knows I'm upset with her. She'll probably hide out somewhere for a few days until things settle down."

"I'll ride with you if you want to try to find her."

He considered her suggestion before answering. "I've wasted enough of my day already. After I change, I'm going to head over to the garden center to pick out some new azaleas. I could use some company."

"And I could use the distraction." When he gave her a quizzical look, she added, "I'll explain in the car."

"I'll be right back," he said, disappearing inside. He emerged ten minutes later in fresh clothes with hair combed and the last of a banana sticking out of his mouth.

On the way to the garden center, June told him about Buford's accident and the likelihood the police would charge him with driving under the influence. "He was with that Raquel woman again. I have a sick feeling Buford is sleeping with her. Whenever I see them on television, she's always at his side. And every time I invite myself on one of his trips, he insists I'm better off at home."

"Don't let him take advantage of you, June. If he is having an affair, you need to call him out on it."

June shivered despite the sweltering afternoon. "Let's talk about something more pleasant than our spouses."

Phillip nodded. "Amen to that."

All thoughts of Buford and Honey were forgotten as they

selected a dozen new azaleas and planted them along the border of his back flower bed.

As they were putting away their yard tools, Phillip said, "Care to have dinner with me? My treat. I have a hankering for one of Luigi's veggie pizzas."

"Pizza sounds wonderful." Tonight, of all nights, June dreaded being alone.

~

June had just come down from showering when Phillip arrived with a large pizza. She placed the pizza in the oven to keep warm while they enjoyed vodka tonics in the rockers on the back porch.

"Any sign of Honey?" June asked, sipping her cocktail.

"Nope," Phillip said with a grim face.

"I'm sorry. I know you're worried."

Phillip shrugged. "She'll eventually show up, and when she does, I'm going to give her an ultimatum. Either she gets her act together or I'm sending her back to California."

June's head swiveled toward him. "That's drastic, Phillip. Are you ready to take that step?"

"I'm hoping I won't have to. But Honey is on a collision course with disaster. I have to get her attention." Phillip shifts in his seat, setting his golden-brown eyes on her. "What about you? Have you heard any more about Buford's accident?"

"The story is all over the news. But there are no new updates. And Buford has yet to call me."

"Sounds to me like you need to take drastic measures as well."

June and Phillip discussed their marriage over another vodka tonic and a bottle of red wine while they ate their pizza at the table on the porch.

A tipsy June confessed, "I love him so much. I don't know what I'll do if I find out he's cheating on me."

Phillip stares at her, his eyes wide in astonishment. "What do you mean? Won't you divorce him?"

June has asked herself this question countless times. She's happy with her life. She doesn't want a divorce. "I can't say for sure. If he's truly sorry, I might forgive him."

"You don't strike me as the type who would condone an open marriage."

"I'm not at all." His statement shocked her. But later, as she stood at the sink doing dishes, she sensed Phillip's presence behind her and turned to face him, wrapping her arms around his neck and pressing her lips to his.

Phillip pulled away. "I thought you weren't into open marriages."

"I'm not," she says in a breathy whisper. "But I'm angry and confused. I feel so lost . . . I just . . . I need comforting. Is there anything wrong with that?"

"We both know it's wrong. And we'll regret it in the morning. But we're friends who can give each other the comfort we need." Phillip swept her off her feet and carried her upstairs to the master bedroom.

The sex was tender, as one might expect between two friends, and June cherished the moment, knowing it could never happen again. They'd made a grave mistake by letting their spouses get the best of them. Going forward, June and Phillip would have to be stronger in order to save their marriages.

They dozed off, and sometime around eleven, Phillip got up to go to the bathroom. On his way back to bed, he stopped to look out the window. "What in the world?" he said out loud, as though talking to himself.

June sat up immediately, drawing the blanket to her chest. "What's wrong?"

"I'm not sure. There's something in my front yard. I can't tell what it is. Some sort of mound." He squinted as he moved closer to the window. "Dear, Lord. I think it's a body. I recognize the fabric on the dress. It's Honey." Spinning away from the window, he quickly gathered up his clothes and got dressed.

June went to the bathroom for her robe. "Should I call an ambulance?" she asked, trailing him down the stairs and out the front door.

"Not yet. Let me check her condition first."

June waited in her front yard, watching as he rushed to Honey's aid. He kneeled beside her, feeling for her pulse and lowering his ear near her mouth. He then scooped Honey up, much like he'd done with June earlier when he'd taken her to bed and carried her over to the driveway.

He called out to June on his way to his car. "She's in bad shape. I can't wait for an ambulance. I'll drive her to the hospital myself."

"Let me know what I can do to help," June said, as if she hadn't already done enough. She'd been having sex with Phillip while his wife lay passed out in their front yard, presumably overdosing on drugs. June's stomach knotted, and she feared she might vomit. If Honey died, it would be all her fault.

After watching Phillip speed away, June retraced her steps to her bedroom, where she stripped off the soiled linens and remade the bed with fresh sheets. Downstairs in the kitchen, she started a load of laundry and brewed a cup of chamomile tea. During the gloomy hours that followed, she paced from window to window, watching for headlights in the driveway next door.

She was standing at the front storm door when Phillip finally returned around seven thirty in the morning. When he saw her, he waved and walked toward her. She met him on the dew-covered front lawn. "How is she?"

"She's alive. She overdosed on cocaine and pills and who knows what else. I came home to pack a suitcase for her. She's agreed to go to rehab, to try to save our marriage."

Relief overcame June. "I've been so worried. This is all my fault. If I hadn't seduced you—"

"Don't go there, June. I was an eager participant." He cupped her cheek. "I don't regret what happened. We both were in a bad way last night and needed comforting. But it can never happen again."

Her chin quivered. "I agree. Our friendship is important to me. I'd hate to do anything to jeopardize that."

"So we'll never speak of this again?"

"Never." June held out her hand, and they shook on it.

Phillip kissed her cheek. "You're an amazing woman, June. Never settle for less than you deserve."

She turned away from him and hurried inside, crumpling in a heap on the living room sofa and crying herself to sleep. A loud clap of thunder woke her around two o'clock. To distract her mind from her problems, she spent the dreary afternoon cleaning out closets.

She was reading a novel on the back porch, listening to the rain fall softly on the copper roof, when Buford arrived home around six o'clock.

"What's for dinner?" he asked, sitting down in the rocker beside her.

Without looking up from her novel, June said, "I wasn't expecting you. I'm having a salad. You'll have to figure out something for yourself."

"I'm sorry, honey. I don't blame you for being upset."

She slammed the book shut. "I'm not upset, Buford. I'm furious."

"In case you're interested, the party leaders got the charges dropped."

June glared at him. "That's too bad. You deserved a DUI."

Buford winces. "You realize I could've been killed in that accident last night?"

June ignores his question. "Tell me the truth, Buford. Are you having an affair with Raquel?"

He recoiled, as though she'd hit him. "Hell no! What makes you ask that?"

Relief washed over her. She'd known Buford since he was a boy, and she didn't think he was lying. He seemed genuinely sincere. "Because you spend every waking hour with her. Every time I see you on television, you're standing close to her with your hand on the small of her back. You're never home anymore. You've completely shut me out of your life these past few months. I haven't attended a single campaign event with you."

"Because I was worried the pace of our schedule would be too much for you. I'm beginning to see that leaving you out was a mistake. The next two weeks are critical, especially in light of the accident. Raquel is organizing one last tour of the state with stops in all the major cities. I want you to come with me. We'll live it up, stay in nice hotels and eat in fine restaurants. What do you say, June? It'll be like a second honeymoon."

June accepted without hesitation. So what if he was using her to salvage his election? She was thrilled to finally be invited into his world. By charming potential voters, she would prove to Raquel Ramsey what an asset she was to her husband's campaign.

Chapter 11

Kate

K ate is helping herself to the complimentary coffee bar in the hotel lobby when a voice from behind says, "I hope you're finding the accommodations suitable."

She turns to find Lance's intense blue eyes staring down at her. "Better than suitable. Everything is over the top. I slept like a baby."

"Glad to hear it," he says, gathering up trash from the coffee bar. "Can I offer you a ride to the funeral?"

Kate snaps a plastic lid on her cup. "Thanks, but I'll walk. I need the fresh air."

Lance eyes her black heels. "In those shoes?"

"No. In these." She opens her tote bag, revealing black walking shoes.

"Right. I forgot. You're a New Yorker." Lance deposits the handful of trash in a nearby waste bin. "I hate going to these things alone. Can I twist your arm into riding with me? You'll get plenty of fresh air at the cemetery." When she hesitates, he adds, "You could always ride to the service with me and walk back."

Kate glances at her watch. She doesn't have time to walk by her old house on the way to the cemetery anyway. She'll have to wait until later today. "Sure. Why not? Truth be told, I don't like going to these events alone either."

He gestures at the gray Tahoe waiting in the valet circle. "My car's out front whenever you're ready."

"I'm ready," Kate says, and goes ahead of him out the revolving door.

The inside of Lance's car smells like new leather and his intoxicating cologne. As he merges onto Meeting Avenue, she admires the way his muscular body fills out his dark gray suit.

Kate searches her bag for her sunglasses and slides them onto her face. "Have you always been in hotel management?"

"I'm actually a real estate developer. I work with a group that develops upscale shopping complexes all over the state. The hotel was a fun side project for me." He chuckles. "I didn't expect to ever be working the desk, but I'll eventually get the right management in place."

"Do you travel a lot to check on your other projects?"

"A few days a month. I'm rarely gone overnight. My dad says I'll never find a wife if I keep working so hard. But I don't consider my career work. It's like playing a real-life game of Monopoly."

Kate smiles. "I can relate. Some days I feel like I'm accessorizing my Barbie with handbags and shoes. My dad says the same about me working so hard. I've dated plenty of men. But I've never found one whose company I enjoyed as much as my work."

"Have you ever been serious with any of these men?"

Kate nods. "The most recent one, the guy my dad hand-picked for me. Dad was heartbroken when Bart and I broke up. But I wasn't feeling it. I'm holding out for the real deal."

"As you should," Lance says as they pull into the cemetery and join the long line of cars parking along the road.

Kate shakes her head in disbelief. "I don't get it. You live in a small town where everything is within walking distance. So why does everyone drive everywhere?"

"Good question. I've never really thought about it. That's just the way we do things. But I can see how it might seem strange to a city girl."

By the time they walk to the gravesite, the service is already in progress. Kate spots June Montgomery right away, her shock of white-blonde hair standing out in the sea of black. Even from the distance, Kate can tell June has changed little in all these years.

Kate's attention is drawn to another striking woman standing behind June. She appears to be older than June, with skin freckled from the sun and her gray hair in a low knot. When the woman's eyes meet Kate's, an eerie feeling crawls up her spine. Does she know this woman? Is she someone from her past?

Kate turns her attention to the minister as he delivers the eulogy. When she looks for the woman again, she's nowhere in sight.

At the end of the brief service, the minister says, "Thank you all for coming. If you would like to speak with the family, they will greet guests for a few minutes under the tent."

"That was fast," Kate whispers to Lance. "I'm surprised they're not having a reception."

"I agree. It seems strange. That was hardly worth your trip." Lance looks over at the line forming under the tent. "I may cut out if you're sure you don't need a ride. I spoke with Alice's parents when I stopped by their house last night on my way home from work."

Kate waves him on. "Go ahead. I'll be fine. Thanks again for the ride over."

He kisses her cheek. "I'll catch up with you over the weekend, and we'll have that drink."

"I'm looking forward to it," Kate says, already anticipating seeing him again.

She waits twenty minutes for a chance to express her sympathy to the Johnsons. Alice's mother sobs when she sees Kate. "Bless your heart for coming all this way. Alice was so proud of your success. She's smiling down on us from heaven right now. I'm sure you've heard what a tormented life she lived. Her best years were the ones she spent with you and Scout."

Kate hugs the woman. "I'm sorry for all your family has been through. I will keep you in my prayers."

She's stepping away from the family when Scout grabs her by the arm and drags her from beneath the tent. "I've been looking all over for you. Mom wants you to come to lunch. Do you need a ride?"

Scout's bossy attitude takes Kate back to their childhood. "Is that an invitation or a summons?"

"It's whatever you want it to be. Are you coming or not?" Scout asks in an impatient tone.

"I accept the lunch invitation. I was headed over to see your mom anyway. But the weather is so nice, I'm going to walk."

"Suit yourself," Scout says, and disappears into the crowd.

Kate heads off in the opposite direction to look for a bench to change her shoes. As she strolls the short distance to her old neighborhood, she observes the changes homeowners have made to the houses, some of them improvements but others she doesn't care for, as is the case in her old home. She barely recognizes the once charming Cape Cod, which is now a two-story square block with zero character.

In the front yard, the sight of a tire swing dangling from a sprawling live oak brings back more memories. Kate's father, true to his word, hired a nanny to replace Mrs. Rice. Izzy was an exotic creature with caramel skin and electric green eyes. Although she wasn't much of a housekeeper, she was an enthusiastic playmate for Kate. But Izzy had a brood of her own children and was often out for long periods of time on maternity leave. Her sister, Bertie, filled in for her during these absences. Bertie, neither housekeeper nor nanny, was a warm body who watched soap operas and chain-smoked cigarettes on the back deck.

Kate is so lost in the past she doesn't notice June coming toward her from next door until she's standing beside her. "The current owner enlarged the house to accommodate their five children."

"They ruined it," Kate says.

"True. But they got the space they needed." June holds Kate at arm's length. "Look at you. So lovely and all grown up."

"And you haven't changed a bit."

"I wish. But I appreciate the compliment just the same. Congratulations on your success. I'm one of your biggest fans."

Kate smiles. "I'm flattered. That means a lot coming from someone with your elegant style."

"I hope you're hungry. Betty has been cooking up a storm this morning." June hooks an arm around Kate's waist and walks her across the street. "How's your father?"

"He's doing well. Thank you for asking. He was just named head of pediatrics at the hospital."

"That's wonderful. Tell him congratulations for me. Did he ever remarry?"

"No, ma'am. He's married to—"

"His patients." June finishes her sentence with a knowing smile.

Kate enters the Montgomery's house, admiring priceless

antiques and impressive woodwork, all of which she'd been too young as a child to appreciate. As she passes through the center hallway, she notices the house is in pristine condition without a speck of dust on any surface and all the silver and brass polished to a shine.

In the kitchen, Betty engulfs her in a bear hug. She smells like cinnamon and vanilla, the scent reminding Kate of cold December days making sugar cookies and gingerbread men. The housekeeper is thicker around the middle and her dark hair is now streaked with gray, but her genuine smile and warm brown eyes haven't changed.

Mary Beth hands Kate a mimosa, and they migrate to the porch where a table is set with linens, June's sterling flatware, and a vase of roses from her garden. Betty serves plates of shrimp and grits, pickled cabbage slaw, and cornbread still warm from the oven. June offers the blessing, and they talk for a minute about the funeral service.

"I'm not sure about your travel plans," says Mary Beth. "But if y'all are staying in town for the weekend, I thought it might be fun to make a girl's trip to our lake house." She smiles at her husband. "Jeff has offered to keep the baby. We can leave early in the morning, spend the day on the water, and stay overnight."

Kate has nothing planned for the weekend, and the weather forecast is projected to be unseasonably warm. She looks across the table at Scout. Question is, Can she stand that much togetherness with her oldest friend? And what about her tentative date for drinks with Lance? "That sounds nice, but my flight leaves from Mobile at one o'clock on Sunday."

"You could drive separately in your rental car," Jeff suggests. "You'd be closer to the Mobile airport from the lake than here."

"I didn't realize that." Kate is tempted. A day on the water sounds heavenly. Maybe she can entice Lance into having drinks with her tonight. "Count me in. A trip to the lake sounds like fun."

Mary Beth's gaze shifts to Scout. "What about you, Scout? When are you leaving?"

"Sometime on Sunday. I haven't booked my flight yet. I was planning to spend some one-on-one time with Mom," she says, looking over at her mother.

June waves her hand in a dismissive gesture. "Go with the girls, honey. I don't want you to miss out on the fun."

Scout drags her fork through her grits. "I guess I could stay until Monday morning. That way, we'd have Sunday afternoon and evening together."

"We'll make that work," June says with a hesitancy that makes Kate wonder if she has other plans for Sunday.

Mary Beth claps her hands. "Then it's settled. We'll leave from my house around eight o'clock in the morning."

The rest of the meal is spent discussing plans for their trip. Afterward, when Jeff heads back to work, Mary Beth and Scout help Betty clean up while June takes Kate upstairs to her room. "I want to show you my collection."

Kate enters June's walk-in closet, taking in all the racks of garments tailored in sequins, silk, leather, and cashmere, as well as the wall of handbags, accessories, and shoes. Sweeping her arms wide, she says, "This is where my love of fashion began. I have often thought of the days we spent in here playing dress-up. Your taste is exquisite, June. You truly were an inspiration to me growing up."

June's face lights up. "I'm touched, sweetheart. That means more to me than you'll ever know. I have two shelves specifically designated for my Honey B. treasures. From my first pair of driving shoes to my most recent purchase." From the shelf, June removes a quilted brown leather boxy shoulder bag with a twisted rope chain and gold honeybee emblem that represents Kate's trademark. "I can hardly wait to carry it."

Kate spends a few minutes inspecting the items on the shelves. "I'm not surprised you've purchased many of my favorites."

When the women exit the closet, Kate walks over to the window and looks out at her old house. She never realized Scout's parents had such a bird's-eye view of her life. "How well did you know my mother?"

"I barely knew her at all. She had her own group of friends, most of whom were artists."

"Dad doesn't talk about her much. He told me she was a free spirt, but she was also troubled. He couldn't give her what she needed, so she left to find her happiness. Do you know how she was troubled?"

June pauses a moment before answering. "She had serious substance abuse issues."

"Whoa. My father kept everything about my mother from me. He thought he was protecting me, and I respect that. He always had my best interests at heart. But I never suspected drugs. Did she go to rehab?"

"Twice, that I'm aware of. She really pulled her life together after the first time. You came into her life, and she appeared genuinely happy. She adored you. That much was obvious. Then something caused her to fall off the wagon. Your father was concerned for your safety and sent her back to rehab. When she came home, she lasted about a month before she packed up her stuff and took off to God knows where."

"Dad is sure she went back to California."

June narrows her eyes. "That's the logical explanation. She never liked Alabama."

The uncertainty in June's expression hints at something more. "Is there another plausible explanation?"

"There's a woman in town who looks an awful lot like Honey. I've caught glimpses of her several times in recent years. I'm sure it's not her. They say everyone has a double. Why would she stay in Langford when she was so desperate to leave?"

"Unless she was desperate to leave my father, not the town." Kate angles her body away from the window. "Did you ever see any of Honey's work?"

"I saw some paintings she brought with her from California. She was extremely talented. As far as I know, she never painted while she lived in that house." She dips her head at the house next door. "She claimed the move to Alabama suppressed her creativity. The entire time she lived there, the same blank canvas stood on the easel in her studio. Have you ever tried to find her?"

"I've searched for her online and sent my DNA to one of those genetic testing websites. But I have had no luck. Since I'm a nationally known designer, I figured if she wanted to know me, she would've reached out to me. But I've been thinking a lot about her lately, and that's part of the reason I came back to Alabama."

"What's the other part, if you don't mind me asking?"

Kate's lips curve in a soft smile. "I wanted to see you again," she says, and leaves it at that. Because she's not yet ready to talk about her other unfinished business.

Chapter 12

Scout

Scout waits until the coast is clear—after their lunch guests have left and her mother has gone to the grocery store—before going through Ford's room with a fine-tooth comb. She finds nothing new of interest among his dusty old clothes, trophies, and sporting equipment.

She climbs the walk-up steps to the attic to continue her search. The attic runs the full width of the house with dormer windows on the front. The contents are meticulously organized. In a zippered wardrobe, hanging alongside her mom's outdated evening gowns, are the old Halloween costumes June's seamstress made for Scout and Ford when they were young children —Raggedy Ann and Andy, Winnie the Pooh and Piglet, Dr. Seuss's Thing One and Thing Two. There are tables with broken legs, lamps with missing shades, and boxes of books stacked high, old toys, and Christmas decorations.

Locating the boxes from her old bedroom, she drops to the floor and explores the contents. A scrapbook with ticket stubs and playbills from traveling Broadway shows. Her father's cigar box containing her marble collection. She was better at shooting marbles than any boy in the neighborhood. A bundle of love letters from a high school boyfriend. She shudders when she imagines her mom reading the letters from the boy who took her virginity. A small needlepoint pillow bearing their family's motto—*To whom much is given, much is expected.*

Leaning against an old chest of drawers, she flips through the pages of a photo album documenting Scout's childhood and adolescent years. Mary Beth is featured in most of the photographs, wearing the pretty dresses June had bought for Scout, but Scout refused to wear. There are pictures of Ford playing his guitar, their many talent show nights, and a whole page of Mary Beth playing dress-up in June's closet. It's a wonder they were such good friends when Mary Beth loved girly activities, while Scout preferred being outside inspecting ant farms with a magnifying glass.

At the bottom of the box, she finds an old shoebox that houses her most cherished possessions. Scrambling to her feet, she takes the shoebox to the dormer window where she finds her fort still intact—two flattened beanbags, a mountain of cast-off decorative pillows, and a host of old blankets. She drops to the beanbag and removes the lid. She's digging into the contents when Barrett calls.

"How was the funeral?" he asks, the tightness in his voice warning Scout something is wrong.

"Short. What's up? Did something happen?"

"This will probably be a nothing burger, but if I don't tell you and it turns out to be a whopper—"

Fear grips Scout's chest. "Tell me, Barrett."

"A badly decomposed body washed up near Elliott Bay Marina."

Scout's heart sinks. "And you think it might be Sally?"

"Based on the size of the body, it *could* be Sally. But it's a long shot, Scout. There are thousands of missing people who are approximately the same size."

Barrett wouldn't be calling if he honestly thought it was a long shot. "What're you not telling me?"

"I've told you everything you need to know for now. The coroner is performing an autopsy."

Scout puts the call on speaker as she searches the airline's website. "Shoot. The next flight back to Seattle isn't until tomorrow morning."

"Don't you dare cut your time with your family short. It could be days, maybe longer, before we identify the body."

"You're right." She takes the phone off speaker. "I'm looking for an excuse to get out of an overnight trip to Mary Beth's lake house."

"Why? Mary Beth is your best friend. You should have some fun for a change."

"I'm not looking to have fun. I'm looking for clues about my brother's disappearance. You were right. Things look clearer through adult eyes."

"Good luck. I hope you find something. Call me if you need a sounding board."

"I will. And let me know when you get the autopsy results," she says and ends the call.

Scout debates whether to put Sally Strickland's parents on alert but decides against it. There's no reason to upset them unnecessarily.

Returning her attention to the shoebox in her lap, she removes the items and places them on the floor beside her. A silver dollar in a plastic sleeve her father gave her one Christmas. A stack of foreign paper currency leftover from one of his many trips abroad when he was a senator. A blue satin ribbon, which must have belonged to Mary Beth, because Scout always wore her hair in a pixie cut. And three photographs from Christmas Eve, four nights before Ford disappeared.

She studies the images. In the first, Mary Beth is wedged

between her parents on the sofa, Buford with his arm around her waist and June looking lovingly at her. In the next picture, Ford is playing his guitar, Mary Beth is singing, and her parents are watching with rapt attention. She has an angelic voice. Scout wonders if she still sings in her church choir.

Ford is featured alone in the last photograph, his intense gaze on his fingers as they strum the guitar. Scout detects a sadness in his face she never noticed before. Her mother mentioned he was not himself that December, that his grades were bad, and he was unhappy with football. Was there something else going on with him? As kids, he'd shared all his secrets with Scout. When had he stopped confiding in her? She knows exactly when. Around the time their lives went to hell.

Sinking deeper into the beanbag, Scout closes her eyes as her mind travels back in time.

Chapter 13

Scout

August 2003

Scout's home life was peaceful when her dad was in Washington. Mama made simple dinners, and mealtime was more enjoyable without Dad constantly reminding Scout and Ford to mind their manners. Mama insisted they behave at the table too, but she was much nicer about it. Dad had changed in recent years. He'd always had high expectations of his children before, but he'd raised the bar to unobtainable levels. Nothing they did made him happy. Especially Ford. Scout felt sorry for her brother the way their father verbally abused him.

During the school year, the household ran like clockwork. Ford and Scout got themselves to school on time and did their homework and chores without being told. They were conscientious students and all-around good kids, staying out of trouble as much as possible to avoid the senator's wrath.

Scout dreaded August when the senate was out of session, and Dad came home for an entire month. Every year, their parents rented a house in Gulf Shores during the first week of August. Mary Beth had an open invitation for these trips, and

93

the two girls spent their time tanning on the beach and swimming in the Gulf.

The summer before Scout started high school, they'd just returned from their week at the beach when the Montgomery family dynamics experienced a drastic change. They were eating dinner at the kitchen table that Sunday night when Dad quoted his favorite Bible verse for the umpteenth time. "Remember, children, to whom much is given, much is expected."

Ford brought his elbow down on the table with a thud. "Geez, Dad! Get a new line already."

Dad's body went still, and he stopped chewing. "It's not a line, son. It's from the Bible, the Lord's will for our lives."

"Whatever. You say it so much, I hear it in my sleep." Ford repeated the verse in a high-pitched voice.

Scout slouched down in her chair, wishing she could crawl under the table. Her brother was asking for trouble by talking back to Dad, and she wanted no part of it.

Dad's face flushed red. "Don't you dare condescend to me, young man. I'm trying to raise children of character. But you two aren't making it easy."

Ford glared at their father. "How so? We make straight As and do everything you expect of us."

"It's true, Buford," Mama chimed in. "They're great kids, and you say that Bible verse a lot. Let's talk about something more pleasant." She turned her attention to Ford. "Are you excited about football practice starting tomorrow?"

Ford let out a breath as the tension left his body. "*Excited* isn't the right word. The practices will be brutal. But I'm pumped for the season. Coach thinks we're gonna have an awesome team this year."

"June!" Dad said in a warning tone. "Stop encouraging him to play football. He should join the debate team. He's wasting his time on a meaningless activity when he should be building his resume for law school."

"Who says I'm going to law school?" Ford stared at his father as he slurped up a forkful of spaghetti noodles.

Dad's upper lip curled as he watched Ford. "Polite young men don't suck their noodles. Either twirl them or cut them." He demonstrated how to properly twirl noodles on his fork.

"Like this?" Ford said and slurped up more noodles.

Dad shuddered and then appeared to shake off his disgust. "As you're aware, Ford, the last four generations of Montgomery men have been lawyers. I expect you to take over the firm when I retire."

Ford grunted. "Don't hold your breath."

Dad gulped down his brown liquor. "If you want me to pay for your college, you'd better get serious about your future. Football is a dangerous sport. You could encounter an injury that could cripple you for life."

"Or football could get me a full-ride scholarship." Ford jabbed his fork at Dad. "Which means you won't have to pay for it, and I get to choose my own career."

"That's enough." Dad's hand shot up with a finger pointed at the ceiling. "Go to your room right now."

"Fine." Ford pushed back from the table, toppling his chair over and bolting from the room without picking it up.

"Why are you so mean, Daddy?" Scout shouted.

"You haven't begun to see mean, little girl. Now get upstairs to your room. I've had enough from the both of you for one evening."

Scout deposited her plate in the kitchen before darting up the stairs. She tapped lightly on Ford's door. "Are you okay?" she whispered through the door.

Ford yelled back, "I'm fine! Now go away and leave me alone!"

Scout stomped down the hall to her room, where she dove onto the bed, burying her face in her pillow to stifle her cries of frustration. She was used to her father's bad moods. Everything was fine as long as she and Ford kept quiet and nodded politely when he lectured them. But Ford had intentionally antagonized him tonight. He'd crossed the line, and Scout had a sick feeling things were about to go from bad to worse.

When her fit subsided, she changed into her pajamas and brushed her teeth. She was reading *Lord of the Flies*, her summer reading assignment for school, when she heard the faint sound of Mary Beth's voice. She sneaked out of her room and tiptoed to the top of the stairs, where she could see her parents and Mary Beth in the hallway below. To Scout's horror, the front of Mary Beth's white nightgown was covered in blood.

Scout rushed down the stairs. "What happened, Mary Beth? Are you hurt?"

"Everything is fine. Nothing for you to worry about here." Dad placed a firm hand on Scout's shoulder and walked her over to the stairs. "Go back upstairs and tell your brother to come down here now."

Scout scurried back up the stairs and barged into Ford's room without knocking.

"Hey!" Ford looked up from his guitar with eyes red-rimmed and swollen. "What're you doing? Don't you know how to knock?"

"Have you been crying? What's wrong? Are you upset about what happened with Dad at dinner?"

Ford tossed his guitar onto the bed and jumped to his feet. "Mind your own business." Gripping her skull with his large hand, he walked her backward into the hall. "Now, for the last time, leave me alone."

"Ouch! You're hurting me." Scout dug her fingernails into his arm until he let go of her head. "Dad wants to see you.

Something bad happened to Mary Beth. She's downstairs, and her nightgown is covered in blood."

Frown lines appeared on Ford's forehead. "Is it her blood or someone else's?"

"I don't know. Go find out." Scout followed him down the hall, leaning against the railing as she watched her brother descend the stairs and join the others.

"What's going on?" Ford asked, his eyes on Mary Beth's bloody gown.

"There's been some trouble at Mary Beth's house. You need to come with me to help sort it out."

June gasped. "Buford, no! He's too young. It's too dangerous."

"Stop treating him like a little boy. He's a big, strong football player now. Southern men protect their families, and Mary Beth is our family." Dad turned to Ford. "Let's go."

Ford shuffled after their father as they left the house. Minutes later, the headlights on Dad's Mercedes sedan came into view through the storm door as he backed out of the driveway and drove off toward town.

Scout hurried down the stairs to Mary Beth. "Are you bleeding? Did you cut yourself with a knife or something?" She noticed her friend's bare feet. "How did you get here? Did you walk all the way without shoes?"

Mama placed an arm around her shivering friend. "Give Mary Beth some space, Scout. Let's go to your room and find her a clean nightgown."

Scout hurried up the stairs ahead of Mama and Mary Beth. She rummaged through her drawer for the lacy nightgown Mama had bought for her that she'd never worn.

Mama helped Mary Beth into the clean gown and balled up the soiled one. She cupped Mary Beth's cheek. "Don't worry, sweetheart. Buford will get to the bottom of it. Now, you girls try to get some sleep." She kissed both their foreheads before leaving the room, with the bloody gown tucked under one arm.

Scout pulled back the covers on her bed for Mary Beth and waited until she was settled before crawling in beside her. Spooning her from behind, she inhaled the scent of her hair, her baby shampoo mixed with sweat. "Do you wanna talk about what happened?"

"Lamar tried to rape me," Mary Beth sobbed. "I was so scared, Scout. I got away from him and ran to the kitchen. I grabbed a knife and I . . .I . . ." Her wild eyes darted around the room. "I jabbed it into his belly. There was blood everywhere. I freaked out. I didn't know what else to do, so I came here."

"Is Lamar still alive?"

"I'm not sure. What if I killed him, Scout? Your dad's a lawyer. Do you think he can help me? What if they send me to prison?"

"That won't happen, Mary Beth. You acted in self-defense."

Scout turned out the bedside table lamp, and they nestled together in the dark, discussing the different potential scenarios. Around midnight, when they heard voices downstairs, Scout got up and cracked her bedroom door to listen.

She heard Dad order Ford up to bed. "Dispose of your clothes. Burn them if you must. And not a word of this to anyone. Not even your sister."

Scout frowned. Why did Dad want Ford to dispose of his clothes? Unless there was blood on them too.

She returned to bed. "Dad's in a bad mood. We'll have to wait until morning to find out what happened."

"I don't think I can sleep," Mary Beth said, trembling despite the heavy down comforter.

Scout pressed her body against Mary Beth's. "Let's talk about something pleasant. Can you believe we're starting high school in a few weeks?" she said and babbled on about what teachers they might get for which subjects until she heard Mary Beth's breathing change. But Scout stayed awake for hours, her imagination wild with so many likely scenarios.

Mom called Mary Beth and Scout to breakfast bright and early the following morning. They traipsed downstairs in their bathrobes to find a platter of French toast and her mother grinning as though nothing had happened. Dad never joined them for breakfast. On workdays, he usually took coffee in a thermal cup to work. But today, he sat down across from them and helped himself to three slices of French toast and two sausage links. After they ate, he asked to see Scout and Mary Beth in his study. When he folded his hands on his desk, Scout knew they were about to have an important talk.

"There's no point in mincing words. The situation is serious. Lamar was dead when Ford and I arrived at your house. We notified the police—"

Mary Beth gasped as fear crossed her face.

Dad held up his hands. "Calm down, sweetheart. There's nothing for you to worry about. I twisted the story to our advantage."

Mary Beth expelled the breath in relief. "You mean, I won't have to go to jail?"

Dad offered her a soft smile. "Not on my watch, you won't."

Fat tears streamed down her cheeks. "I don't know how I'll ever be able to repay you, Mister Buford."

"You don't have to repay me. I'm grateful I was able to help you. I have no reason to believe they will, but if the police contact you, you are not to speak with them without me present. Is that understood?"

"Yes, sir." Mary Beth swiped at her tears. "Did you see my mom? Was she upset about Lamar?"

"I saw her. She came home from work while I was there. She's in a lot of trouble with social services. She should never have left you alone with a convicted pedophile."

"A what?" Scout asked, her eyes wide.

"A pedophile is a person who sexually assaults underage children." Dad looked from Scout to Mary Beth. "Prior to dating your mother, he'd been serving a fifteen-year prison sentence for molesting an eleven-year-old child. Your mother was aware of his conviction, but she allowed him in the home with you anyway. Social services was going to put you in a foster home, but I convinced them to allow you to live here with us."

Mary Beth appears hopeful. "Does that mean I never have to go back to that house?"

"That's correct. At some point, we'll arrange for you to get your things. June and I will be your foster parents until you're eighteen years old. If you decide to go to college after high school, I will gladly pay for it."

"That's incredibly generous of you, Mister Buford."

He smiled at her. "It's my pleasure."

As they piled out of his office, Scout said, "Did you hear that? We're real sisters now."

Mary Beth grinned at her. "Not exactly *real* sisters, but close enough for me."

Later that day, Scout interrogated Ford about the previous night's events, but he refused to talk about it. Two days later, Mary Beth was sleeping in, and Scout was eating a bowl of cereal at the breakfast counter when Mom looked up from the newspaper. "There's an article in today's paper about the incident at Mary Beth's house. According to this, a random home intruder killed Lamar." A look of admiration crossed Mom's face. "I had no idea your father had such influence over the police."

Scout remembered what Dad had said about twisting the story to his advantage. He didn't twist the truth. He flat out lied to the police.

Chapter 14

Kate

K ate changes out of her funeral clothes into jeans and a leopard print top before heading out to explore Meeting Avenue. She shops the boutiques, wanders the aisles at the old-fashioned hardware store, and stops in at the coffee shop for a pumpkin spice latte. She's responding to emails at a sidewalk table when a painting in the window at the art gallery across the street catches her eye.

Dropping her empty cup in the trash, she moseys over to investigate. The subject of the painting isn't unusual. The First Presbyterian Church, the oldest church in town, has been the object of many photographs and paintings over the years. This composition features vibrant pink crape myrtle trees in the churchyard with a glimpse of the adjacent cemetery. The style is so realistic, like a photograph taken on a camera using a vivid filter. Kate looks in the bottom right corner for the artist's name, but there is none.

She ventures inside the gallery where works of art line the walls extending deep within the building. At the reception desk, a young woman with blue hair and multiple face piercings is talking on her cell phone. Kate smiles at her, but she doesn't smile back.

At the back of the gallery, Kate's attention is drawn to a painting of a man and a little girl fly-fishing, their faces hidden by khaki-colored bucket hats. The shoreline beyond the marsh looks familiar to Kate. Is that Gulf Shores? She checks for the artist's signature, even though she knows she won't find one. The unique style belongs to the artist of the church painting in the window.

Kate approaches the reception desk and coughs loudly into her hand when the young woman makes no move to get off the phone. "Excuse me. I have a question."

"Hang on a sec," the woman says to the person on the other end and presses the phone against her chest. "I doubt I can answer it. I don't work here. The owner is out of town on a family emergency."

"Do you know who painted the piece in the window? There's no signature."

"No clue." The woman hands Kate a business card. "Check with the owner. She'll be back tomorrow."

Kate slips the card into her crossbody bag. "I'll be sure to tell the owner how helpful you've been." She spins on her heels and strolls out of the gallery.

When she enters the hotel, Kate spots Lance at the check-in counter and waits her turn in line to speak to him. "I've accepted an invitation to go to Mary Beth's house for an overnight tomorrow. Is there any chance you can have that drink tonight?" Kate's face warms. She's not used to asking men on dates.

"What a coincidence. I was just getting ready to ring your room. I, too, have to go out of town in the morning on a last-minute business trip. Is it too early for drinks now?"

She notices the time on the wall clock behind the counter. "It's five o'clock. Officially happy hour. Where should we go?"

"I know just the place. We have a rooftop bar. I think you'll enjoy seeing the town from the Starlight View." He comes from behind the desk and motions her to the elevator.

"How has your day been?" Lance asks on the way up to the sixth floor.

"Interesting. I saw a painting in Blair Gallery that really stirred me."

A smirk tugs at his lips. "Isn't that what art is supposed to do?"

Kate laughs. "This was different. I can't explain it. I'm curious about the artist. But there was no signature."

"That's odd. April, the owner, is a friend. Did you ask her about it?"

"According to the girl minding the gallery, she's out of town on a personal emergency."

Lance frowns. "That's not good. Her mother's been critically ill. I hope she hasn't taken a turn for the worse. I can give you April's number. She loves her work. She wouldn't mind you reaching out to her."

"Thanks, but I already have her number. The girl gave me her card. I may call her tomorrow."

The elevator doors open, depositing them into a garden oasis. Potted plants, containers spilling with colorful flowers, and tables of various shapes and sizes surround a covered bar in the center. A glass wall encloses the roof, offering views of Langford in every direction.

"I'm impressed, Lance. This is very upscale. I'd love to see some of your other projects."

He beams. "Maybe someday you'll get a chance."

They order two glasses of pinot noir from the bartender and take their wine over to the side of the hotel overlooking her old neighborhood. Kate's arm shoots out with a finger pointed at the Montgomery's house. "Look! What a spectacular view of the Montgomery's house. It's by far the largest on the street." She lowers her arm. "I actually had lunch there today after the funeral. I was glad to spend some time with June."

"I remember she was like your second mom. Did you lose touch with her like everyone else from Langford?" He nudges her with his elbow to let her know he's teasing.

"I'm afraid so. I needed to make a clean break." Memories flood Kate, and she sips her wine as she thinks back on those difficult years.

"I recognize that look," Lance says, startling her back to the present.

Kate tilts her head. "What look?"

"You were a million miles away. In that dark place you used to disappear to when we dated in high school."

She places her back to the wall, turning away from the past. "I was a teenager, prone to severe mood swings," she says in a joking manner.

"I'm not talking about moods swings," he says, and Kate is relieved when he doesn't push the issue.

"Have your travel plans changed now that you're going to Mary Beth's?"

"I'm still leaving on Sunday. I'm driving straight from the lake to the Mobile airport."

Lance appears disappointed. "I hope the weather holds out for you. There's a hurricane brewing in the Gulf, hence the reason for my sudden trip tomorrow."

Kate's forehead puckers. "I hadn't heard about that. When I checked the forecast earlier, they were calling for sunny skies and eighty-degree temperatures."

"As of now, they predict the storm to stay to the west. Which is bad for the folks in New Orleans. Just in case, I'm driving down to Fairhope to make certain the property manager of our shopping complex is making preparations."

"When will you be back?"

"Late tomorrow evening if all goes well."

Kate feels a pang of disappointment at the thought of not seeing him again. She'd worried a weekend in Langford would be too long. Now it doesn't seem long enough.

Lance eyes her empty glass. "Since we won't see each other again, can I talk you into another glass of wine and some appetizers? Our sushi rolls are amazing."

Kate is still full from lunch, but she's not yet ready for her time with Lance to end. "You don't have to twist my arm."

Kate follows him to a table where Lance signals for a server, placing an order for more wine and a combination sushi platter.

When the tables around them fill up, Kate asks, "Are these locals or hotel guests?"

Lance surveys the crowd. "Probably a combination of both. The Starlight View is popular with the locals."

While they wait for their order, Kate tells him about her business, and Lance talks about his family—his parents, sister, brother-in-law, and two rambunctious nephews.

"Your face lights up when you talk about them. Your love for your family is one thing I admired most about you in high school."

"There were lots of things I admired about you," he says with a twinkle in those blue eyes.

Intrigued, Kate asks, "Like what?"

"Your long legs in a tennis skirt and your lips—"

"Shh!" She glances around nervously. "Someone might hear you."

"So what if they do? What happened to you, Kate? You used to be more fun."

"I'm out of practice."

Lance laughs. "Then we'll have to remedy that."

The server returns with their wine and appetizers. Choosing a California roll from the sushi platter, Lance says, "In all seriousness, I admired your strong work ethic, your genuine concern for others, and the way you fuss over your father."

Kate smiles. "I still do. And he hates it."

"He may pretend to, but I'm sure he secretly loves it." Lance stares down at his wine. "Your aura of sadness always worried me. You and I both know it was more than mood swings. I've often wondered what made you so unhappy, and if you ever got over it."

With a sigh, Kate says, "You're not gonna let this go, are you?"

He grins. "Nope."

"I don't let it drag me down as much as I once did. But I still think about it all the time." Kate can't believe she's confiding in Lance. He, at one time, had been an important part of her life. But that was a long time ago.

He places a hand over hers. "What is *it*, Kate?"

His touch sends a feeling of warmth through her. "A secret. One that affects a lot of people. Mary Beth's call about Alice's death was an omen, a sign for me to come back to Langford. Now that I'm here, I'm second-guessing myself. This is not my secret to tell."

"What about the secret's owner? Would he or she give you permission to divulge this information?"

"I'm not sure," Kate says and looks away from Lance, watching the setting sun wash the town in a soft pink glow.

"Think about yourself for a change, Kate. Asking you to keep a secret that has made you so unhappy for so long is unfair."

His words bring tears to her eyes. No one has ever considered her feelings in this situation. She dabs at her eyes with her napkin. "I'm sorry. I'm not myself right now. All these memories are making me an emotional wreck." She pushes back from the table. "I hope you don't mind, but I need some time alone."

"I understand. I'll walk you to your room."

Lance signs the tab, and they take the stairs down one flight to her floor. When they reach her room, they exchange phone numbers. "If you're ever in New York, call me."

"If I make a special trip to see you, will you carve out time from your busy schedule for me?"

"My schedule is only busy during the week. Most weekends are free. And I'd love to spend more time with you."

When he presses his lips to hers, she hooks an arm around his neck, kissing him back. When desire stirs inside of her, she pushes him away. "You should go before I get carried away."

"Before we both get carried away." He fingers a lock of her hair. "You and I aren't over, Kate. I will see you again soon."

"I certainly hope so." She enters her room and closes the door.

Dropping her bag on the bed, Kate moves to the window and watches the lights blink on across town. Lance's words ring out in her mind. *Asking you to keep a secret that has made you so unhappy for so long is unfair.* He's right. She needs to look out for herself for a change. This secret has held her hostage for long enough. The time has come for her to take back her life.

Chapter 15

Kate

September 2003

The summer before Kate started high school, her father took her on a six-week tour of Europe. They hit all the major cities, visited most of the noteworthy cathedrals, and sampled cuisine from many cultures. The trip culminated in a weeklong visit with her father's friend at his large estate outside of London. Kate rode horses, watched polo matches, and experienced her first crush with a distant member of the royal family—an adorable young man named Benjamin Oliver Atkinson II, who had sparkling emerald eyes and a hank of dark hair that swooped across his forehead.

Kate and Phillip returned home on Labor Day. On Tuesday, the orthodontist removed her braces and a hairstylist cut four inches off and added layers to her mahogany hair. When she entered high school the next day, she felt like a new person inside and out. She was a seasoned traveler, a young woman of the world.

Kate could hardly wait to tell Scout she'd had her first proper kiss with a member of the royal family. But she didn't see her until lunchtime in the cafeteria. Scout was seated at a table with Mary Beth and some kids from middle school Kate recognized but didn't consider friends. If they saw Kate, they didn't invite her to join them. With nowhere else to sit, Kate grabbed a container of yogurt and took it outside to the courtyard.

High school underwhelmed Kate. Her teachers were boring and the academics a challenge. The first good thing happened that afternoon at tennis practice when the coach pulled her aside. "You have beautiful strokes, a strong serve, and a competitive spirit I find rare in someone your age. We'll see how the next few days go, but come next week, we may bump you up to varsity."

Kate walked home on a cloud. She could hardly wait to tell her father, who had insisted she take tennis lessons from a very early age. They played together often. The last time she'd beaten him in straight sets.

She was nearing her house when Ford appeared at her side. He'd grown taller and gotten more muscular in her absence. "Welcome home. How was your trip?"

"Amazing," Kate said, wide-eyed. "I'll show you the pictures when they come back from the developer."

"I'd like to see them. And how was your first day of high school?"

Kate flaps her hand in the so-so gesture. "I'm going to fail algebra. I have no clue how to do tonight's homework."

"I can help you." Ford started walking toward her house, and she realized he meant *now*.

She caught up with him. "Cool. But we have to sit on the porch. I'm not allowed to have friends over when Dad's not home."

"No problem."

Kate retrieved sodas from the kitchen, and they sat at the iron table on the porch.

"Who's your algebra teacher?" Ford asked, popping the top of his can.

"Mrs. Andrews," Kate said, and flipped her book open to the right page.

"There's your problem. She's the worst teacher at our school. Give me a pencil," Ford said, dragging the book across the table to him.

In thirty minutes, Ford had explained the lesson in a way Kate could easily understand. "Thank you so much. When did you get to be such a good teacher?"

"I'm not, really. But I understand math. If you can, try to change into another class. If they won't let you, I'm happy to tutor you."

"That would be great. My dad will pay you."

"Don't be silly. We're friends. I'll do it for free." Ford sat back in his chair, finishing his soda while she packed up her schoolwork. "Did you see Scout today?"

"I saw her. But I didn't talk to her. Why do you ask?"

"Mary Beth is living with us now. Her mother's boyfriend tried to rape her."

Kate gasped. "That's awful. Is she okay?"

"She seems to be. At least she's safe at our house."

Kate studied Ford's face. He wore a pained expression, as though plagued by inner turmoil. "Is something wrong, Ford? You don't seem like yourself."

Ford shrugged, as though letting go of whatever was bothering him. "I'm fine. Just tired from practice."

Kate walked him to the edge of the porch and watched him disappear inside his house. Something had just changed in their relationship. For the first time, instead of treating her like his little sister, Ford had treated Kate as a peer. And she was disappointed when she didn't see him again until Saturday afternoon.

Kate and her father were practicing casting with their fly-fishing rods when Ford arrived home from football practice. Phillip greeted him with a handshake and clap on the shoulder.

"I was only gone six weeks. How is it possible you grew during such a short time?" Her father peered at him over the top of his aviator sunglasses. "Are you drinking your mom's Miracle Grow again?"

Ford chuckled. "I don't understand it. I can't seem to stop growing."

"When's the first game?" Phillip asked.

"Next Friday night against Jackson. Coach says I'll be starting."

"Good for you! I'd like to come watch."

"That'd be great. Should be a good game." Ford gestured at Phillip's fly rod. "This looks like fun. Can I try?"

"Sure." Philip handed him the rod. "Since you're a quarterback, I imagine casting will come easy for you."

Kate watched with open mouth as Ford dropped the end of the line in the exact spot Phillip indicated. "That's not fair! I've been trying to do that my entire life."

"Some people are just naturals," Phillip said with a wink in Ford's direction. "Kate and I are making a day trip to Orange Beach next Saturday to fish for redfish. Would you like to come along? I have an extra rod you can use and an old pair of waders."

Ford's face lit up. "Really? I'd love that."

Phillip slapped his back again. "Then it's a date."

The following Friday, Kate and her father joined fans in the packed stadium and watched as Ford led his team to victory. Father and daughter waited with the student body for the team to emerge from the locker room afterward. When he spotted them, Ford squeezed his way through the crowd.

Phillip gave him a quick hug. "Excellent game, my boy."

"Thanks," Ford said. "Are we still going fishing tomorrow?"

"Indeed, we are. We're leaving at eight o'clock sharp."

A grin spread across Ford's face. "I'll be ready."

Ford was immediately enthralled with fly-fishing. And he was a natural, catching more fish than Kate and Phillip combined. They kept enough fish for their dinner, and when they got home, Phillip showed Ford how to clean them.

They watched the Alabama versus Georgia football game while they ate dinner.

"Are you considering playing college ball?" Phillip asked.

"I want to, but my dad won't let me. He thinks I'm wasting my time when I could be building my resume for law school," Ford said with a sour look on his face.

"That's tough, son. I'm sorry. But he's your father, and you should respect his wishes."

This surprised Kate, coming from a man who believed everyone should be their best selves.

Phillip went on, "Your high school and college years are mere blips on your radar of life. But your career will make or break your future."

"I get that, but I have straight As and I'm taking honors classes. If I stay focused, I can play football and build my resume. For whatever career I choose, which definitely won't be law school."

Phillip offered him a sympathetic smile. "Talk to your father. Maybe he'll come around."

"I will. I have no intention of giving up. I refuse to let him determine my future."

As fall progressed, the threesome spent every Saturday together either fishing or watching college ball on television. Ford seemed down a lot of the time, but Kate assumed his dark moods had to do with his strained relationship with his father. Ford confided in her about their horrible fights. The arguments weren't always about him playing college ball. Buford seemed to pick on his son about everything.

Phillip and Ford often talked about what college team Ford

would play for if he were to get his father's approval. Ford had his heart set on playing for Alabama, but Phillip encouraged him to look at other schools. "Keep an open mind. You'll find the right fit for you."

Over time, Ford accepted Kate into his group of friends. The guys flirted shamelessly with her, and the girls treated her with indifference. They assumed Kate and Ford were in a relationship. And Ford and Kate didn't bother to correct them.

One afternoon on the walk home from school, Kate asked Ford, "Do you realize what our friends are saying about us? Everyone thinks we're dating."

"I've been meaning to talk to you about that. I think you're seriously hot, Kate, but I don't have those kinds of feelings for you."

"Good! Me either. You're like my brother." She looped her arm through his. "I'm not interested in dating anyone right now anyway. I'd rather focus on academics and tennis."

"I agree. Maybe we should let everyone continue to think we're dating. That way, we won't feel pressured to go out with other people."

"Great idea!" Kate said, resting her head on his shoulder.

The football team made it all the way to the finals that year. Kate and her father drove to Montgomery to watch the team win the state championship.

Ford was giddy with excitement afterward. "Come with us," Ford said, taking Kate by the hand. "Coach is letting students ride home with the team on the bus."

Kate tugged her hand away. "Thanks for the offer, but I'm gonna ride with Dad."

Phillip objected, "Go with the team, sweetheart. I'll be fine."

Kate was tempted. Riding home with the team sounded like

fun. But she couldn't let her dad drive home alone. "I'm tired. The bus will stop for food, and I'm ready to get home."

Scout ran up to her brother, throwing her arms around his neck and jumping on his back. "Congratulations! You were amazing. Since I'm your sister, I get to ride home on the bus."

Ford's eyes fell on Kate. "Are you sure you won't change your mind?"

"I'm positive. Have fun," Kate said, waving at Ford and Scout as she led her father away.

On the walk to the car, her father said, "Why don't you go on the bus, Kate? A girl should be with her boyfriend at times like these."

Kate laughed. "We're not dating, Dad. Ford and I are just friends."

His face registered disappointment. "Oh. I wasn't sure. I thought maybe . . . He's such a nice young man."

Two weeks later, on Thanksgiving Saturday, the threesome gathered in the Baldwin's family room to watch Auburn play Alabama in the annual rivalry matchup. Her father left the room to order pizza. Kate didn't realize he'd come back until she noticed him standing in the doorway, staring at them.

"What's wrong, Dad? Did something happen?"

"No. I just remembered, I need to check on a patient. Listen out for the pizza while I make this call," Phillip said, retreating down the hall.

When the pizza delivery man came and went with no sign of her father, Kate tiptoed upstairs to check on him. His door was cracked, and the sound of his voice stopped Kate in her tracks outside his room. "How can you ask me to keep something so important a secret? He's my son. I have a right to be part of his life."

Kate's heart skipped a beat. *His son?* Inching closer to his door, she heard her father say, "We'll talk more tomorrow. But I'm warning you, June, I'm not letting this go."

Kate clamped her hand over her mouth to stifle a gasp. *June? Is Ford my father's son?*

She hurried back down the stairs, and a few minutes later, Phillip entered the family room, wedging himself between Ford and Kate on the sofa while they ate pizza.

When Auburn beat Alabama in overtime, Ford shook his head in disgust. "Maybe Dad's right. Maybe football is a senseless sport. You work so hard, and then you lose."

Her father got up from the sofa and poured himself a whiskey. "Losing builds character, Ford. It makes you fight harder next time. Attorneys lose lawsuits. Sadly, I sometimes lose patients. You will be the loser if you give up on football when it's your passion."

Ford jerked his head up in surprise. "But what about my dad? I'm tired of arguing with him. He's never going to come around."

Phillip tipped his glass at Ford. "You'll be eighteen when you go to college. You don't need his permission. If you get a full-ride scholarship, you don't need his money either."

Ford stood to face her father. "But you told me I should respect Dad's wishes. Have you changed your mind?"

Phillip placed a hand on Ford's shoulder. "I see how much this means to you, son. And I think it's wrong of Buford to hold you back. If you decide to proceed, I would be happy to guide you through the recruiting process."

Ford's face lit up. Kate hadn't seen that much excitement from him in months. "That would be great. You're right. Football is my passion. I shouldn't have to sacrifice it for anyone."

"That's the right attitude," Phillip said, and walked Ford to the back door.

Kate waited on the sofa for her father to return. "What's

going on, Dad? You're acting strange. Why are you suddenly encouraging Ford to go against his dad's wishes?" She already knew the answer, but she wanted to hear it from him.

Her father sat down beside her on the sofa. "I learned something tonight about Ford that I think you should know."

Chapter 16

June

June calls Buford at work late Friday afternoon to remind him about dinner. "And be on time. This might be the only chance we get to spend with Scout. She's going to Mary Beth's lake house tomorrow and spending the night."

Buford grunted into the phone. "When's she going back to Seattle?"

"I don't know. Ask her." June hangs up on him and returns her attention to making meatloaf.

June is sliding the pan into the oven when Scout enters the kitchen around six fifteen. She eyes the open bottle of pinot noir. "Do you have anything other than wine?"

"Of course. I keep the bar in the family room stocked. You should be able to find whatever you'd like."

Scout leaves the kitchen and returns a minute later with a tumbler of clear liquid on ice. "Vodka?" June asks.

"Tequila. I'm impressed you have Casamigos."

June smiles at her daughter. "We entertain a lot, honey."

Scout sips her drink and sets it on the counter. "Can I help with dinner?"

June gestures at the salad ingredients on the island. "You can toss the salad while I slice the bread."

As they work, Scout fills June in on the body that washed up in Seattle. "We won't have the autopsy results for a few days. I'm praying it's not Sally."

June saws the sourdough bread with a serrated knife. "Those poor people. I know what it's like living on pins and needles, waiting for news and praying it's not bad." She'd do anything to see her son again, even if it means—

Buford barges into the kitchen, interrupting her thoughts.

Scout raises her hand, wiggling her fingers. "Hey, Dad."

Buford raises his briefcase at her and mumbles, "Scout."

"Seriously," June says with hands planted on aproned hips. "You two haven't seen each other in sixteen years, and this is the best you can do?"

Scout crosses the kitchen to her father and gives him a stiff hug. "You're looking well."

"As are you. Let me put my briefcase away and fix a drink. I'll be right back."

June cuts slices of sharp cheddar cheese and places them on a decorative plate with hickory smoked summer sausage and crackers. When Buford returns, she says, "The meatloaf needs at least thirty more minutes. Let's go sit on the porch while we wait."

She leads them outside to the porch, and they rock in awkward silence, sipping their cocktails.

Buford is the first to speak. "So, Scout, when are you leaving?"

Scout cuts her eyes at him. "Gee, Dad. Ready to get rid of me so soon?"

"Just making conversation. Your mother and I are hosting an important political dinner party on Sunday night. You would be bored to tears with all the talk of politics."

With a tight jaw, Scout says, "Point taken. I'm not invited."

"That is not what I said." Buford cuts a hunk of sausage and places it on a cracker with some cheese. "It's just that, after sixteen years, your sudden presence would be difficult to explain. If they ask you to campaign for me, I'd be put in the awkward position of having to tell them you're not a team player when it comes to your family."

June comes out of her chair. "Buford! What a horrible thing to say. That's completely uncalled for."

"It's okay, Mom. I'm a big girl now. I can fight my own battles." She angles her body toward her father. "How am I not a team player, Dad?"

"Because you ran away after I pulled strings to get you into college. Because you haven't been home to see your mother in sixteen years. Nor have you invited her out to visit you."

Scout looks away from Buford, staring out into the yard. "I didn't run away, Dad. I left to search for my brother, the son you ran off."

Buford tosses up his hands. "So now Ford's disappearance is my fault."

Scout hunches her bony shoulders. "If the shoe fits."

"Enough bickering!" June says. "You two sound like children. Obviously, we have some pent-up anger. Let's have a civilized conversation. I'm sure we can talk it out."

Buford glares at June. "Since when did you become a shrink?"

June lets out a humph. "Now that you mention it, therapy is exactly what this family needs."

Buford pulls a hand over his face. "Not with me running for governor. Family drama of any sort will ruin my chances."

"Lucky for you, I'm leaving first thing Monday morning. No time for family therapy this visit." Scout rests her head against the chair. "Why were you so hard on us, Dad? Were we that much of a disappointment to you?"

"You were weak. Mary Beth is a poor girl from the wrong side of the tracks, and she has more backbone than you and Ford put together."

Scout's body tenses. "How were we weak? We did everything you asked of us, and we never got into trouble."

"Ford was always whining about finding himself, and your only ambition in life was to take care of people's pets."

Scout jumps to her feet. "Do you have any idea how difficult it is to get into vet school?" She looks down at her father. "I would've made a damn good vet. But I sacrificed that dream to look for Ford. Going out on my own wasn't a weakness, Dad. It took real guts. Which is more than I can say for you and Mom. You were his parents. Finding him was your job."

A pang of guilt grips June's chest.

Buford bangs his fist on the chair's arm. "How dare you? Your mother and I gave you kids everything you could ever want. And you repaid us by running away. How do you think your mother feels when her friends brag endlessly about their children's and grandchildren's accomplishments?"

"Good thing she has Mary Beth to parade around. Maybe you should ask her to your little Sunday night dinner. I'm sure she'd be happy to campaign for you."

Buford nods. "I'm sure she would. Mary Beth appreciates everything we've done for her. And look how well she turned out. She's a successful interior designer with a husband who loves her and a sweet little boy. Meanwhile, you're in a dead-end job with no prospect of a husband." He gives Scout the once-over. "Are you a lesbian? You certainly look like one, the way you're dressed."

"So what if I am? Wouldn't that just piss you off?"

Buford's lip curls. "You really are a nasty one."

"I'm a chip off the old block," Scout says with fists balled at her sides.

Contempt replaces the distaste on his face. "Was your childhood that miserable?"

"Only when you were home from Washington."

Buford stands abruptly. "I've had enough. I'm going to the club for dinner."

Scout yells at his retreating back, "Thanks for reminding me what I haven't been missing these past sixteen years!"

At the sound of Buford's car leaving the driveway, Scout collapses in her chair. "That went well."

June laughs out loud. "It's all my fault. I gave him too much control, and he turned into a monster. I should've stood up to him a long time ago."

"Why didn't you?"

"I was afraid of losing him." Truth be told, June was afraid of losing everything. But she lost it anyway. It's not too late. She can salvage her relationship with her daughter. And maybe, just maybe, she'll see her son again. The time has come for June to tell the truth. Doing so could cost June her marriage. But if she's honest with herself, her marriage has been over a long time.

"We'll talk on Sunday when you get back from the lake. Maybe, if you and I put our heads together, we can figure out where Ford is."

June feels her daughter's eyes on her. "You know something, don't you?" Scout says in a suspicious tone.

"Nothing concrete. Just a hunch."

"Why don't we talk now?" Scout suggests. "Dad obviously isn't coming back."

June needs time to prepare what she'll say. And she doesn't want to upset Scout before she heads off to spend the weekend with Kate and Mary Beth. "Let's not ruin the night by drudging up the past. We've waited this long. Two more days won't hurt. Your father can entertain his guests without me. We'll go out to dinner, just you and me."

Chapter 17

June

November 2003

June was reading in bed when her cell phone rang on the nightstand. Worried it was one of her children, who were both out with friends, she snatched it up.

"We need to talk," Phillip said in an angry tone that sent chills down June's spine. He rarely called. They either met in the driveway or he came to her back door. The moment she'd dreaded for so long had arrived.

She managed a pleasant tone despite the sick feeling in her gut. "Hello, Phillip. This is a surprise. How was your Thanksgiving?"

"Ford is my son, isn't he?" Phillip blurted.

She gripped the phone. "Maybe. I don't know for sure."

"Be real, June. Look at him. Buford is a small man, but Ford has a large frame like me."

"My brothers are both over six feet tall. He could've inherited those genetics from me."

"He has my eyes, June. He's the spitting image of Kate with the same mannerisms."

"Can we talk about this tomorrow? Buford is downstairs in his study. I don't want him to hear me."

"Then go outside. Because we're having this conversation now."

There was no point in arguing when the truth was in their son's face. "Hold on a minute." June went into her closet and locked the door, not bothering to turn on the light. "You've known Ford all his life. I'm surprised you never noticed before."

"So you admit he's my son." Phillip didn't give her time to defend herself. "I didn't notice, because I wasn't looking for it. I erased the memory of that night from my mind. It was the only way I could live with the guilt of cheating on my wife. When you got pregnant with Ford, I never stopped to consider the timing. I knew you and Buford were hoping for a baby. I assumed it was his. That was a difficult time for me. I had my hands full with Honey." He paused to take a breath. "I wanna be a part of my son's life, June."

"That's not possible. You can't tell anyone about this, Phillip. It will destroy my marriage."

"I don't keep secrets from my daughter, June."

"No? Have you told her the truth about her mother?"

"That's different. No good will come from her knowing about Honey's addiction. But Kate's relationship with Ford could become a problem. She claims they're just friends, and I believe her. But they could easily become romantically involved. For obvious reasons, we can't let that happen," he said and ended the call without saying goodbye.

Crippling fear set in as June sat on the floor in the dark closet, replaying the conversation in her mind. Her life was one secret away from being torn apart, and during the months that followed, she existed on the brink of a nervous breakdown.

She had never been a heavy drinker before, but alcohol was the only thing that took the edge off the anxiety. Throughout the day, she took swigs of vodka from bottles she hid all over the house. At night, she consumed at least one bottle of wine. Sometimes more. No one detected her drinking problem. Her family and friends didn't care what she was feeling on the inside as long as her exterior remained polished. She was a stylish woman with a magazine-worthy home. A senator's wife. The mother of the town's football star as well as a daughter who was destined to save all the animals in the world.

Ford refused to give up his dream of playing college football, and he quarreled with Buford to no end about it. After a heated argument, June summoned the courage to confront her husband. She waited until Ford and Scout had gone to bed before entering her husband's study, his sanctum, where no one was allowed without an invitation.

Lowering herself to the chair opposite his desk, she said, "We need to talk. You're missing out on a golden opportunity by refusing to let Ford play college football. Think of the bragging rights you would have with your constituents if he were to play for the Crimson Tide. And the perks, the parking passes and fifty-yard-line seats. You could invite your bigwig supporters to accompany you to the games."

He scowls, and June could tell he'd never considered this. "I'll think about it."

Much to everyone's relief, Buford softened on the issue of football, and for a few brief months, peace was restored to their home.

Phillip had kept his distance from June since learning of Ford's paternity. She'd only seen him in passing, coming and going in the driveway, and they hadn't spoken at all. Because Ford refused to make any football decisions without Phillip's guidance, June and Phillip were forced to work together to coordinate interviews with recruiters when college scouts came to Langford to watch Ford play during the fall semester of his junior year.

June finally found a moment alone with Phillip during their first college visit to LSU in Baton Rouge, Louisiana.

"Does Ford know you're his father?" June felt certain her son would've thrown a major tantrum if Phillip had told him, but for peace of mind, she needed confirmation.

"No. He already has so much going on with all this football stuff. But I will tell him when the right opportunity arises. Whether that's in a month or five years from now, I can't say." Phillip walked away before June could argue.

The University of Georgia was the last college they visited, and Ford fell in love with everything about the school, the town, and the football team. When Buford learned Georgia had taken the top spot on his list, the arguments started back up again.

He called Ford every night from Washington. And when Ford stopped accepting his calls, he wore June out on the subject. "As a senator's son, it's his duty to go to our state's flagship university," Buford argued.

June found it much easier to stand up to her husband on the phone. "He's not the senator, Buford. You are. This is Ford's choice to make. Georgia has an impressive program. Your friends will still be jealous of you, if that's what you're worried about."

June could almost feel the heat radiating off her husband through the phone when he said, "I want Ford to go to Alabama. I'm counting on you to make that happen."

In early November, Buford made a special trip home to talk to Ford in person. The fighting raged all weekend long. Buford appeared genuinely bewildered. "I don't get it. Why on earth would you want to play for Georgia when Alabama has the best football program in the SEC?"

"Actually, if you paid attention to football, you'd know Georgia is having a better season than Alabama this year."

"So? Every team has an off year. What's the real reason you want to go to Georgia?"

Ford looked him dead in the eye. "Because Athens is farther away from you."

Both schools offered Ford attractive packages, and the week before Thanksgiving, after leading his team to another state championship victory, he made a verbal commitment to Georgia. He planned to tell Buford over the Thanksgiving weekend, but Buford found out by accident before Ford had a chance to break the news.

On Friday night, Buford and June took the three kids for dinner at the country club. They were leaving afterward, when they ran into Buddy Roberts, the star running back on Ford's team.

Buddy's father, Bill, threw his arms around Ford. "Congratulations, young man. Your hard work is paying off. The whole town will cheer you on next year in Athens."

Ford looked as though he wished the earth would open up and swallow him whole. "Thank you, sir," he mumbled.

Bill gripped Buford's hand. "You lucky dog. If you ever have any extra tickets, I'd love to tag along to one of the games."

Buford pressed his lips thin, a grimace more than a smile, and ushered his family out to the car.

"What was that about?" Buford said to Ford in the rearview mirror. "Please tell me you didn't go behind my back and accept a scholarship to Georgia."

Ford locked eyes with him in the mirror. "Yes, sir, I did. I haven't officially signed yet. But I've verbally committed."

Buford glanced over at June. "Did you know about this?"

June held her shoulders back, her chin high. "Of course. I fully support his decision."

Buford white-knuckled the steering wheel as he sped out of the club's parking lot. "Who else knows about this?"

"Phillip," Ford said. "He played college ball, and he knew how to negotiate with the coaches."

"Does Kate know?" Scout asked in a meek voice. Her daughter was sitting behind Buford, where June could see her. When Ford nodded, Scout appeared crestfallen.

Mary Beth, who sat in the middle of the back seat, jabbed her elbow in Ford's ribs. "Congratulations, Ford. I'm really excited for you."

Ford's lips curved in a genuine smile. "Thanks."

"We'll discuss this in private when we get home." Buford drove like a maniac through town, and when they got home, he sent Scout and Mary Beth to their rooms. He motioned Ford and June down the hall. "Both of you, in my study now."

Closing the door behind them, Buford went straight to the bar, pouring two fingers of bourbon in a glass and gulping it down. "First thing on Monday morning, you will call the Georgia coach's recruiting office and turn down this scholarship."

Ford glared at his father. "No, I won't either."

Buford wagged his finger at Ford. "I'm not asking, Ford, I'm telling you to do as I say."

"And I'm telling you I'm going to Georgia," Ford said, crossing his muscular arms over his chest. "I'll be eighteen in July. I can go wherever I want, and you can't stop me."

"The hell I can't," Buford yelled, and threw his empty glass against the wall.

A shiver of fear ran down June's spine. "There's no need for violence, Buford."

"I'm just getting started." Grabbing her by the hair, Buford hauled June out of the chair and pinned her to the wall with one arm pressed against her throat. "Not only did you go against my wishes. You humiliated me by going behind my back."

Ford pried him off of her. "Leave her alone!"

Buford turned on Ford. "Or else what, big man?"

Ford loomed over him. "I am a big man. Bigger than you. Touch Mom again, and I'll beat the daylights outta you."

Buford attacked the bookcase like a raving lunatic, throwing books around the room and breaking crystal glasses and liquor bottles from his bar.

Ford whispered to June. "Should I call the police?"

"No! A domestic dispute will violate our agreement with social services. They could take Mary Beth away from us. Go next door and get Phillip."

Ford hurried out of the house, and minutes later, Phillip entered the family room alone, slamming the door to get Buford's attention.

"Get a hold of yourself, man! What's wrong with you?"

Buford set down the bronze statue of Lady Justice he was holding and marched across the room toward him. "Mind your own business, Baldwin. Stop interfering with my family." When Buford came at Phillip with fists flying, Phillip leveled him with a single punch in the face.

Phillip nudged Buford with the toe of his leather boot. "Now clean up this mess! June is going to lock herself in her bedroom for the night, and you're going to sleep on the sofa."

Buford slowly sat up. "Who do you think you are, telling me what to do?"

"I'm the man with the camera." Phillip pulled a small camera from his pocket and snapped several photographs of Buford surrounded by the wreckage. "If you cause any more trouble tonight, I'll share these images with the local newspaper. I'm pretty sure you don't want that."

Buford hung his head. "Obviously. Please leave my house. I promise, no more trouble tonight."

June walked Phillip to the front door. "What about Ford?"

"He'll stay at my house tonight," Phillip said, his brown eyes dark with anger.

"You're going to tell him, aren't you?"

"I can't keep it from him any longer. It's not fair to him or me or Kate."

The firm set of Phillip's jaw warned her he wouldn't change his mind. As he walked off across the yard, June had a sinking feeling her universe had shifted, that nothing in her world would ever be the same.

Chapter 18

Kate

November 2004

K ate and her father were preparing their gear for an impromptu fishing trip to Dauphin Island when Ford burst through the back door. "Phillip! Come quick! Dad found out about Georgia and went ballistic. He's tearing up our house. I'm afraid he's gonna hurt my mom."

Phillip zipped his duffel bag and straightened. "Did you call the police?"

"Mom wouldn't let me. She says social services will take Mary Beth away."

Kate's father grabbed his flip phone off the counter and stuffed the small digital camera he was holding in his back pocket. "You stay here with Kate. I'll be right back."

Ford vehemently shook his head. "No way! I'm coming with you."

"No, Ford. It may not be safe for you over there. If I'm not back in fifteen minutes, call the police."

Ford followed him to the back door and watched him through the window. Kate went to stand beside him. "How did your dad find out about Georgia?"

"We ran into Buddy Roberts at the club after dinner. Buddy's dad congratulated me."

"Weren't you going to tell him this weekend anyway?"

Ford turned away from the door. "Yes, but with Thanksgiving yesterday, I haven't had a chance to talk to him. Hearing it from someone else only makes matters worse." He opened the refrigerator and chugged milk straight out of the carton.

Kate snatched the carton from him. "That's gross, Ford. This is not your house."

"Sorry. Milk settles my stomach when I'm upset." He collapsed against the kitchen counter. "That was awful, Kate. I've never been so angry before. I literally wanted to kill my dad." He held up his hands, as though gripping a basketball. "I wanted to wrap my hands around his neck and choke the life out of him. Do you think I'm capable of murder?"

Kate looked at him as though he'd lost his mind. "What kind of crazy question is that? Of course you're not a murderer. I'm sure you were scared out of your mind, and you acted in self-defense. Is your mom okay?"

Ford's eyes traveled to the kitchen window where he could see through to his house. "I hope so. I didn't want to leave her, but she made me come get Phillip."

"Dad may be a while. Let's go sit down," Kate said, and led him to the sofa in the family room.

Ford leaned forward, burying his face in his hands. "I can't believe this. My dad is such a jerk. God may strike me dead for saying this, but I actually hate him."

Kate, at a loss for words, rubbed his back, and they sat in silence until her father returned.

Ford jumped to his feet. "Is Mom okay?"

"She's fine. She's in her bedroom with the door locked. You're spending the night here."

"How can you be so sure he won't hurt Mom?"

Phillip showed Ford his digital camera. "Because I took photographs of him in an unflattering position and threatened to share them with the press. He's currently cleaning up his mess."

Kate locked eyes with her father. "Tell him, Dad. He needs to know the truth."

"Tell who what?" Ford asked, looking back and forth between Kate and Phillip.

"Tell you the truth about your father." Phillip lowered himself to the sofa, pulling Ford down beside him. "Your mom and I have been friends for a long time."

Ford shrugged. "Yeah. So?"

"Before you were born, we both experienced problems in our marriages. During a particularly troubling time, we comforted each other in a way that was inappropriate for married people."

Ford narrowed his eyes as though letting this sink in. "Are you saying you slept together?"

"Yes, son. One time. In the heat of the moment. You resulted from our night together. Your mom and I loved each other as friends. Which, in my opinion, is the purest kind of love. You were conceived out of that love."

Ford's eyes grew wide. "So I'm not Buford's son?"

"No, Ford. You're my son. I only found out recently myself, and I promised your mother I wouldn't tell you. She's convinced this will ruin her marriage. Given what happened tonight, and your strained relationship with Buford, I believe you have a right to know the truth."

Ford was back on his feet and pacing around the room. "This is the best news ever. You have no idea how relieved I am. I don't owe him anything. I can do what I want." He threw his arms over his head. "I'm free!"

Phillip stood to face Ford. "Not entirely. We must honor your mother's wishes. I don't want to be responsible for destroying her marriage."

Ford gawked at him. "Are you kidding me? This is the best thing that's ever happened to me, and you're asking me not to tell anyone?"

"I only told you because I thought it might help you better understand who you are. This isn't just about you. It's hard on all of us."

Kate smiled at Ford. "He's right. You're the town's football hero, and Scout gets all the bragging rights. Keeping my mouth shut is torture."

"Then don't." Ford started pacing again. "Mom will have to suffer the consequences of her actions. I don't care what you say. I'm telling my dad . . . Buford . . . the truth. I can't wait to see his face."

Phillip grabbed Ford by the arm to stop him from pacing. "Think about what you're saying, Ford. Your mother loves him. If he leaves her, she'll be crushed. Then we'll be responsible for her unhappiness."

"What about my unhappiness? I'm miserable living with that man. Mom will be better off without him anyway."

"That's not for you to decide." Phillip cupped Ford's cheeks. "Look, son. We can hold out another eighteen months. Things will be better for you when you're in college. The three of us— you, Kate, and me—are already like a family. We'll go on more trips together. In fact, I was thinking of taking you two skiing in Colorado for the long holiday weekend in February."

Kate's face lit up. "Yay! I'm in. Do you want to go fishing with us tomorrow? We're going to Dauphin Island and spending the night at that cool fishing camp."

Ford looked from Kate to Phillip. "Would that be okay?"

Phillip grinned. "Of course. If you don't mind bunking with me. I booked two rooms."

"I don't mind at all. But I don't have any clothes. And I can't go home now."

"We'll worry about that in the morning," Phillip said. "For now, we should get some shut-eye. I'm planning on leaving at the crack of dawn."

After helping her father make up the sofa bed, Kate retired to her room and fell into a deep sleep. She dreamed she was in the stands for Ford's first football game as a Georgia Bulldog. After Beyoncé sang the national anthem, Ford stood on a stage in the center of the field and announced that Kate, not Scout, was his sister.

Before dawn the following morning, Kate's father stood outside the Montgomery's front door while Ford hurried inside for his fishing gear.

Ford was cheerful and relaxed all day long, making jokes and laughing while reeling in countless redfish. But his mood soured as they ate their fresh catch for dinner at the fish camp that evening.

Ford, with his large frame hunched over his plate, said, "I'm thrilled Buford isn't my father. But I feel like I've been sentenced to prison for life. I'm not sure I can live this lie. Not even for my mom."

Phillip finished chewing his food. "You were raised a Montgomery, Ford. Your life with Buford hasn't always been bad. Your childhood experiences and the valuable lessons you've learned will forever be a part of you. Now that you know the truth about your paternity, you can begin discovering your true self. You will face many paths during your lifetime. Choose the one that feels right to you."

"Going to Georgia feels right," Ford said with more certainty than Kate had seen from him in a long time. Which is why she was stunned when, thirty-six hours later, he announced to the student body at Monday morning assembly that he'd reconsidered and would play football for Alabama after all.

Chapter 19

Kate

Mary Beth's cottage is a rustic version of her home in Langford with wooden floors painted pale blue, slip-covered upholstery, and a wide-screened porch featuring a daybed and picnic table. A large main room offering both living and dining areas is adjacent to a homey kitchen where Mary Beth and Scout are sipping coffee when Kate arrives.

"What took you so long? The boat is all ready to go." Scout gestures to the window. "We're wasting this glorious weather."

Mary Beth offers Kate an apologetic smile. "Ignore her. She's had too much caffeine. I'll show you to your room so you can change." She leads Kate down a short hallway to a sunny corner bedroom. "We'll wait for you on the dock."

"I'll be down in five minutes." Kate puts on her bikini, slathers on sunscreen, and heads outside. "Where are we going?" she asks as she boards the boat.

Scout opens a cooler and removes a plastic jug filled with green liquid. "Margaritaville."

Kate laughs. "Sounds like my kinda place."

Mary Beth pushes the boat away from the dock. "I thought

we'd tour the lake first. There are some cool houses to see. And then we'll find a quiet spot to eat lunch and swim. The water is warm for late September."

Kate accepts a margarita from Scout. "Anything is fine with me. I'm just happy to be here. I can't remember the last time I spent the day on the water."

Chatting like old friends, Kate and Scout sip margaritas while Mary Beth expertly navigates the coves around the lake. When they reach the other side of the lake, she finds a deserted spot and tosses out the anchor.

Mary Beth spreads a blanket across the bow and serves paper plates with cucumber sandwiches, chicken salad, juicy slices of the summer's last tomatoes, and homemade chocolate chip cookies for dessert.

"So, Kate. I'm curious." Scout takes a bite out of a cucumber sandwich. "Were you and my brother ever romantically involved?"

Here we go, Kate thinks. "Ford and I were just friends. He was like a brother to me."

"Really? That surprises me. Everyone thought you two were dating."

"We let them think that. Ford and I were too focused on academics and sports to get involved in a relationship." Kate's face softens. "There was never anyone I wanted to date until I met Lance."

"I'd forgotten about Lance," Scout says. "Does he still live in town?"

"He does," Kate says as she forks off a bite of tomato. "We had drinks last night. He's the new owner of the hotel."

"I'd heard that," Mary Beth says. "Lance is a good guy. Everyone around town loves him." She slides her sunglasses down her nose and sets her eyes on Kate. "Tell the truth. Did sparks fly when you two reconnected?"

Heat crawls up Kate's neck. "Maybe."

"I've always wondered why you ditched us for Ford's group of friends. Why was that Kate? Did you think you were too good for us?" Scout's tone is accusatory, borderline hostile.

"Your memory is failing you, Scout. *You* ditched *me* when we started high school. I'd just gotten back from Europe, and you two had found a new group of friends while I was gone." She glances over at Mary Beth, who blushes and looks down at her plate. "I ran into Ford after school that first day. He offered to tutor me in algebra, and we started hanging out."

Scout narrows her eyes as she studies Kate. "You're lying. There was more to your relationship with Ford. Like your father's relationship with my mother."

Kate reminds herself that Scout interrogates people for a living. She has nothing concrete to go on. She's just fishing for information. "My father looked out for your mother because your father was never home. Men and women are allowed to be friends, you know."

"In my experience, there's usually more going on than friendship."

Kate glares at Scout. "Because you deal with criminals, not normal people." She notices the darkened sky behind Mary Beth. "Looks like a storm is brewing."

Mary Beth cranes her neck to look at the sky. "Uh-oh. That's not good. We should head back to the cottage."

They clean up the picnic and resume their earlier positions, with Mary Beth behind the wheel and Scout and Kate facing each other in the front. But when Mary Beth turns the key in the ignition, the engine won't start.

She palms the steering wheel. "Dang it, Jeff!"

"What's wrong?" Scout asks, her brow pinched in concern.

"We're out of gas. The gauge is broken. I've been after Jeff to fix it. We're gonna need a tow." Mary Beth shields her eyes as she looks around the lake. The only people in sight are two teenage boys fishing in a small boat a hundred yards away. Moving to the front of the boat, she cups her hands around her mouth and calls out, "Hey! We're out of gas. Can we get a tow?"

One boy yells back, "Sure thing. Be right over."

The boys speed to their rescue, fasten a line between the two boats, and tow them a quarter mile to the marina.

Mary Beth gives the boys a ten-dollar bill and thanks them for the tow. She fills the tank with gas, and they start back across the lake. The sky opens up on the way home, and the three women huddle behind the windshield to shield themselves from the sting of the driving rain. Back at the dock, they gather up their belongings and dash up to the cottage. After stowing away the leftovers from the picnic, they retire to their respective rooms to take a nap.

Kate, after a hot shower, slips on her robe and curls up in bed with a magazine. She's dozing off when her phone dings with a text from Lance. They've been messaging back and forth since parting the previous evening. *The track of the hurricane has shifted and is headed this way. Call me when you get a free moment.*

Kate clicks on his number, and he answers on the first ring. "Are we in danger?" she blurts.

"I don't think so. By the time the system makes it to Langford, it'll be downgraded to a tropical storm. The meteorologists are predicting high winds and several inches of rain tomorrow afternoon."

"Do you think this will affect my travel plans?"

"The airlines are already predicting delays and cancellations. We have plenty of rooms available if you decide to weather the storm in Langford."

The thought of returning to her hometown appeals to Kate, and she suddenly hopes they cancel her flight. "I may do that."

"If it works out, I'll cook dinner for you tomorrow night. We'll have a hurricane party, just the two of us."

Kate remembers the feel of his lips on hers when he kissed her goodnight. She could have dinner with Lance tomorrow night and track down the art gallery's owner on Monday morning. "I like the sound of that. I'll be in touch when I know more about my plans."

Kate closes her eyes and falls asleep thinking about Lance. She wakes from her nap two hours later to the sound of murmured voices in the other part of the house.

Dressing in jeans and a lightweight sweater, she pulls her hair back in a ponytail, and ventures down the hall to the main room. Scout is seated at the breakfast counter, sipping on a clear beverage while watching Mary Beth stir something on the stove.

Kate sits down next to Scout. "Did y'all nap?"

Mary Beth looks up from her pot. "Mm-hmm. For a couple of hours. Did you?"

"Same. What about you, Scout?"

"I couldn't sleep. I've been sitting on the porch, listening to the rain pound the metal roof." Scout's words are slurred. The clear liquid in her glass is obviously not water.

"Apparently the storm's path has changed," Kate says.

Mary Beth nods as she clips herbs into the pot. "Jeff says we should be fine to spend the night as long as we leave early in the morning. But I'm afraid this might impact your travel plans."

"I can always go back to Langford for a couple of days," Kate says, eyeing the platter of cheeses and crackers on the counter in front of her.

"Would you like some wine? I opened a bottle of red." Mary Beth holds up the bottle. "Or there's white in the refrigerator."

"I'll get some in a minute. My head is still foggy from this afternoon," Kate says, and spreads pimento cheese on a cracker.

Scout slides off her stool and stumbles to the bar cart, filling her glass from a bottle Kate recognizes as tequila. She returns to the counter, but instead of sitting down, she remains standing. "You know, the ironic thing about Ford's disappearance is that he went missing the same morning you and your father left for New York."

Kate looks down at her beverage and back at Scout. "We should save this conversation until you're sober."

Scout rattles the ice and takes a gulp of tequila. "Nope. I've waited sixteen years to have this conversation. I will not wait another day."

Kate stands to face her. "Fine. What is it you want to know?"

"I want to know what *you* know about my brother's disappearance."

"Very little. We were crossing the Georgia state line when your mother called. We were shocked and concerned when she told us he was missing. We had no idea where he was, and we did everything we could to help find him."

Scout's bloodshot eyes widen. "Are you kidding me? You'd only gotten as far as Georgia? If you were so concerned, why didn't you return to Langford?"

Kate thinks back to that cold December morning. She'd begged her father to go back. "Dad had to be in New York the next day for an important meeting about his new job. Besides, we were certain Ford would eventually show up. He was in college. We figured he'd gotten drunk, passed out at a friend's house, and neglected to let your mother know."

Scout stares up at the ceiling as she considers this. "That would be a logical explanation for most college students. Except Ford had never done anything like that before. And he wasn't a big drinker. He was too health conscious."

"That was true before he went to Alabama," Kate says. "But he was drinking a lot during that Christmas break."

"Really? I wasn't aware of that. Then again, I wasn't as close to Ford as you. Why do you think he was hitting the booze so hard, Kate?"

Scout's intense expression makes Kate squirm. She's clearly very good at her job. "I don't know, Scout. It's not unusual for kids to start drinking when they go to college, even if they never have before."

"That's fair," Scout says with a nod. "You were the last person to see him the night before. How was he? Did he act strange? What was his mood?"

Kate thinks back on the night before her entire world changed. "He was sad because we were leaving."

"Did he say where he was going when he left your house?"

"He told us he was going home."

Scout gets close enough to her face for Kate to smell the tequila on her breath. "You're hiding something, Kate. And I want to know what it is."

This is her opportunity, the moment Kate has been waiting for. Scout will undoubtedly be upset, her hurt and anger compounded by her drunkenness. Who knows how she'll react? She's a detective, an officer of the law. Which means she's probably carrying a weapon. Now is not the right time. This confrontation will have to wait.

Kate's phone pings with an incoming text, saving her from having to respond. "Delta just canceled my flight." She goes around the counter into the kitchen to have a word alone with Mary Beth. "I'm sorry to bail on you. But this storm is making me uneasy. I'm going to head back to Langford tonight."

"Oh, no! Are you sure?"

Kate smiles softly. "I think it's for the best. It's still early. If I leave soon, I'll be back in Langford by dark."

"I'll help you get your things together." Mary Beth wipes

her hands on a kitchen towel and follows Kate to her room. "This is about more than the weather, isn't it?"

Kate gathers her cosmetics from the bathroom. "I'm not in the mood to be interrogated about Ford all night."

"She means well. But coming home after such a long absence has been hard on Scout."

"It's been difficult for all of us." Kate drops her cosmetic bag into her duffel. "It's none of my business, but why didn't she come to your wedding?"

Mary Beth hesitates, as though deciding how to respond. "She refused to attend if I invited her parents. But June and Buford were my foster parents. I had to invite them. Scout was furious. We didn't speak for several years. You and I both know Scout is her own worst enemy sometimes."

Kate zips up her duffel and straightens. "Scout is not the only reason I'm going back to Langford early. I'm interested in a painting I saw in the gallery. The owner was out on Friday. I'm hoping to catch up with her tomorrow morning."

"I know a lot of the local artists. Maybe I can help you. Who painted it?"

"That's what I'm hoping to find out from the gallery owner. There was no signature."

Mary Beth flashes a knowing smile. "I know that artist. She doesn't sign her name. She uses a drawing as her signature."

Kate's heart skips a beat. "What sort of drawing?"

"She usually hides them in either the bottom right- or left-hand corner. But sometimes you have to search for them. All the drawings are different. But they are all of bumblebees."

Chapter 20

Scout

S cout wakes on Sunday morning with a splitting headache. When she sits up too quickly, the room spins, and she falls back against the pillows. What happened last night? Did she and Mary Beth have a fight?

She sits up again, slower this time, and swings her legs over the side of the bed. She plods on bare feet to the main room where Mary Beth is sitting at the counter drinking coffee, her overnight bag waiting beside the door.

"Morning," Scout says as she continues into the kitchen for coffee.

Mary Beth doesn't look up from studying the RADAR app on her phone. "The outer bands of the storm are approaching. We should leave as soon as you're ready."

"Give me fifteen minutes," Scout says, and takes her coffee back to her room.

Suffering through a cold shower, she tugs on a sweatshirt over a pair of faded jeans. She stuffs her belongings into her backpack, and then emerges from her room to find Mary Beth waiting by the door with key in hand, ready to lock up.

Scout waits until they're on the main highway, heading back toward Langford, before she says, "You're pissed at me."

"Mm-hmm. After what you said, I have every right to be."

"So we *did* fight. I don't remember about what."

Mary Beth glances over at Scout. "Getting drunk on tequila may be routine for you in Seattle, but I don't approve."

"It's not a regular occurrence. I won't make excuses. I'm ashamed of my behavior, and I'm sorry."

Mary Beth's shoulders sag as some of the tension leaves her body.

"Tell me, Mary Beth. What did I say that upset you so much?"

"You accused me of taking your place in your parents' lives."

"Oh. Oops." Scout inches down in her seat, wishing the seat would swallow her up.

"June and Buford were devastated after you and Ford left. I may have lessened their sadness by being a part of their lives, but I could never take your place. They're good people, Scout. They have their flaws like everyone else. But they've done so much for me, and I will forever be grateful."

"I know that. And I'm grateful for your presence in their lives." Scout absently checks her phone for text messages. "I've been thinking a lot about the past since I got home. We had some good times. But our high school years, with Dad and Ford always fighting, were awful. Despite Dad making Ford miserable, my gut tells me there was something more to his disappearance."

"I've always thought that too." Mary Beth reaches for Scout's hand. "I love you, Scout. Which is why I'm going to shoot straight with you. You've made a career out of looking for a man who doesn't want to be found. It's time for you to put Ford's disappearance in your unsolved cases' file and start living your life for you, not your missing brother. Ford isn't worried about you. Or your parents. If he were, he would've gotten in touch a long time ago."

"Unless he's dead."

"He's not dead, Scout. You and I both know that." The first raindrops splatter the window, and Mary Beth takes back her hand to turn on her windshield wipers. "I had an ulterior motive in insisting you and Kate come back for Alice's funeral. I'd hoped that getting the two of you together again would lead to you to finding Ford."

"So you think Kate's hiding something too," Scout says.

Mary Beth nods. "I'm pretty sure she knows why Ford left and where he is."

Scout stares out the window at the rain. "Of course she does. She hasn't asked if I've heard from Ford or if I know where he is. Because she knows I haven't."

"Maybe you should try talking to her, one-on-one, when you're sober."

"I will. I doubt she'll tell me anything, but it's worth a shot." Scout looks back at her friend. "How much do you remember about the night Lamar died?"

Mary Beth tightens her grip on the steering wheel. "Not much. I try not to think about it."

Scout twirls a strand of hair. "I remember something that strikes me as odd. When Dad and Ford returned from your house that night, Dad sent Ford to bed and told him to dispose of his clothes, to burn them if he had to."

Mary Beth frowns. "That's strange. Why would his clothes have blood on them? Come to think of it, your mother took the nightgown I was wearing, and I never saw it again. Maybe Ford burned mine too."

"Are you completely out of touch with your family?"

"Yes," Mary Beth says, her eyes on the road. "Last I heard, they were all in prison. Mom for assaulting her boss at the

Piggly Wiggly, two of my brothers on drug charges, and the oldest for murder."

"That's awful, Mary Beth. I'm so sorry."

They ride the rest of the way in silence. When Mary Beth drops Scout at home, she says, "Call me if you need to talk. I meant what I said. I love you, Scout. You're my sister. I only want what's best for you."

"Thanks. And I'm sorry again about my drunken behavior last night." She kisses Mary Beth's cheek and gets out of the car with her backpack.

The house is mobbed with caterers and flower people preparing for her parents' dinner party. She tries to slip up to her room without being seen but encounters her father on the stairs.

"Are you seriously having a dinner party in the middle of a hurricane?" she asks.

"Why not? Makes for a more festive occasion. Besides, they've downgraded it to a tropical storm. You can find some way to entertain yourself tonight, right? Maybe you can go to Mary Beth's for dinner."

"Don't worry. I have no intention of crashing your party. Blowhard politicians aren't my cup of tea," she says and dashes up the stairs to her room, closing the door behind her.

She flops down on the bed and clicks on Barrett's number. He answers right away. "Scout. I was just getting ready to call you."

His grave tone turns her blood cold. "The decomposed body is Sally, isn't it?"

Barrett exhales a loud sigh. "Unfortunately. The dental records matched. I'm so sorry, Scout. I know how much this case means to you."

Scout swallows past the lump in her throat. "I should be the one to notify her family."

"I figured that. How are things at home?"

"Well, let's see. My best friend just told me off. My father is having a dinner party tonight, and I'm not invited. And I'm stranded indefinitely in this godforsaken town by the remnants of a hurricane." Scout lets out a deep sigh. "But nothing is as bad as what Sally's family is facing. The Stricklands will want to claim her body. Since I won't be able to get a flight out until tomorrow at the earliest, do you mind taking care of them?"

"Of course. You can count on me."

Scout spends an hour on the phone with Sally's parents. After hanging up, she buries her face in her pillow and cries herself to sleep. When she wakes up several hours later, the wind is howling, rain is beating against the windows, and her stomach is rumbling. She splashes cold water on her face and ventures down to the kitchen where she finds her mother barking orders at the caterers.

"There you are, Scout. I peeked in on you a while ago, and you were zonked. Must've been some party at the lake last night."

"It was just Mary Beth and me. Kate left early." Scout grabs a loaf of bread from the pantry and the ingredients for a ham sandwich from the refrigerator.

"The club called to cancel our dinner reservations. They're closing early because of the storm. It's probably for the best. With this awful weather, I should help your father host his guests. Maybe we can find time afterward for our chat."

Slathering Dijon mustard on her bread, Scout says, "By *chat*, do you mean you're finally going to reveal what you've been keeping from me about Ford's disappearance?"

Her mother's smile fades. "We'll talk later."

"Since you're always asking about her, you might want to know the decomposed body that washed up in Elliott Bay

Marina is Sally Strickland." Scout ignores her mother's distraught face as she leaves the kitchen.

Scout takes her sandwich upstairs to Ford's room and sits down at his desk. She opens his wallet and fingers his identification cards. She has an eerie feeling that whatever she's missing about this case is right under her nose. She's studying the compartments in the desk when she notices a panel of wood between the cubby holes and center compartment. On closer inspection, the panel appears to be a tall, thin drawer. But there's no knob. She slides a fingernail behind the panel and eases the drawer forward. Inside are several pages of folded sheet music, the kind Ford used to write his songs, and a handful of old photographs. She studies the photographs of Ford with Kate and Phillip on their various fishing trips. If Scout didn't know better, she'd mistake them for a happy family. Her breath hitches. *Wait a minute! All three have the same deep-set golden-brown eyes and single dimple on the right side of their mouths. How did she never notice the resemblance before?*

Scout unfolds the sheet music and reads the song lyrics and then removes his driver's license from his wallet. He's smiling in the photograph. Getting a license is a big deal.

A fury like Scout has never experienced before overcomes her. She has more questions than ever, and only one person who can answer them.

Chapter 21

Kate

K ate is dressing for dinner with Lance when he calls. "Change of plans. Instead of coming to my house, how would you feel about attending a hurricane party? Our chef is worried we'll lose power. He has some food he'd like to use up and suggested we invite all our current guests for a free happy hour. Since I need to be there, I'm hoping you'll be my date."

"That sounds like fun. Tell me what time, and I'll meet you downstairs."

"How does thirty minutes sound?"

"Perfect. I'll see you soon."

Kate puts the finishing touches on her makeup and slips her feet into a pair of leopard print slides. With a few minutes to kill, she lowers herself to the edge of the bed and scrolls through missed calls and texts. Most are from her father, who is frantic about the hurricane. But there's no response from the messages she left for April Blair on her cell phone and at the art gallery. She thumbs off a text to her father, letting him know she's safely back in Langford and staying at the hotel another night or two.

She drops the phone on the bed and goes over to the

window. The gallery has been dark all day despite the sign on the door showing Sunday hours from eleven to four. She feels a strong connection to the father/daughter fishing painting. Regardless of the weather, she's not leaving Alabama until she's spoken with April and learned more about the artist. Depending on the price, she'd like to purchase the piece for her father for Christmas.

The roar of the crowd greets her when she exits the elevator in the lobby. The mood inside the bar is festive, the occupants seemingly unaware of the tropical storm currently tearing down trees and power lines outside.

Kate spots Lance socializing with a group of older men. She requests a glass of pinot noir from the bartender and strikes up a conversation with a middle-aged woman who is in town for the birth of her first grandchild.

The woman explains, "The doctor was planning to induce tomorrow, but that has been postponed another day because of the storm."

A hush settles over the room when a drenched figure appears in the doorway. Several long seconds pass before Kate realizes the young woman with soaked clothes clinging to her slim body and rivulets of water puddling on the floor is Scout.

Scout summons Kate with her finger, and Kate sets down her glass. *This is it;* she thinks. *Scout finally found out about Ford.*

She's approaching Kate when Lance appears at her side. "Scout, you remember Lance, don't you?"

Without so much as a glance in his direction, Scout says, "Beat it."

"I'll grab some towels," Lance says and scurries away.

"We need to talk." Scout turns away, her wet tennis shoes squeaking on the marble floor as she crosses the lobby.

Kate follows her to a remote windowed corner.

"Tell me the truth, Kate. Is Phillip Ford's father?"

"Yes. How'd you find out?"

Scout shoves sodden papers at her.

"What're these?"

"A song Ford wrote about being torn between his two families. About his admiration for his biological father and adoration for his secret sister. Do you have any idea how humiliated I feel right now? All these years . . . all the time I spent looking for him, and you knew."

"Keeping this secret has been the hardest thing I've ever done. But we did it for June. She was terrified your father would find out."

Bewilderment replaces anger on Scout's face, as though realizing for the first time how her mother factors into the equation. "How long did their affair last?"

"It wasn't much of an affair. They were close friends, both with troubled marriages. They got carried away one night and slept together. They kept their vow to never let it happen again."

Scout lets out a huff. "I'm not buying it. Why would Ford sacrifice his own life, his own future football and music careers, to protect Mom? She cheated on Dad. She deserves what she gets. She's better off without him anyway."

Kate has so much to say, she doesn't know where to begin. "It was more than that, Scout. Ford left to get away from Buford, who was never going to let him follow his dreams."

"You know where he is, don't you?" When Kate doesn't answer, Scout adds, "But you're not gonna tell me."

Kate presses her lips into a thin smile. "He never intended to stay away for so long. But with each year that passed, it became easier to avoid reality."

Scout's shoulders slump as she lowers her head. "I don't believe this. I've worried about him every single day for seventeen years. Not knowing if he was strung out on drugs or locked up in prison. Meanwhile, he's just fine and dandy."

Guilt grips Kate's chest. "He's fine. I wouldn't say he's dandy."

"Give him a message for me. Tell him . . . On second thought, don't tell him anything. He's dead to me. You both are." Scout spins on her heels and flees the hotel into the stormy night.

Lance arrives with a stack of towels. "Where'd she go?"

"Who knows? Probably to tell off her mother."

"Does this have to do with the secret you've been keeping?"

"Yes, but I'm done with this secret." Kate pulls Lance down to the window seat and tells him the abbreviated version of the story.

"That's an enormous burden you've been bearing. No wonder you were so unhappy as a teenager. This isn't my place to say it, but shame on Ford for leaving Scout and her mother in the dark for so long."

"Ford only cares about himself."

Through the window, Kate notices a dim light on and a shadowy figure lurking around inside the gallery across the street. "Someone's at the gallery. It might be April." She jumps to her feet and starts toward the door.

Lance calls out after her, "Wait for me! I'm coming with you. Let me grab an umbrella."

She laughs over her shoulder. "A lot of good an umbrella will do in forty-mile-per-hour winds. You stay here. I'll be right back." She slips off her shoes and leaves them near the entrance.

Lance catches up to her. "No way I'm letting you go out in this storm alone."

Bowing their heads against the rain, they dart across the street and bang on the gallery door. An attractive woman with dark hair piled on top of her head lets them in.

"Are you crazy, Lance? Why on earth are you out in this weather?"

"We came to see you about an urgent matter." Lance gestures at Kate. "This is my old high school friend Kate Baldwin. She's interested in knowing more about one of your paintings."

"I left messages for you," Kate explains. "I understand your mother is ill. I hate to hound you, but this is important."

"No worries. I apologize for not calling you back. My mother took a turn for the worst, and the girl I'd hired to look after the gallery quit on me. I drove home in the storm. I need to find someone tomorrow who can tend the gallery until . . ." April's lower lip quivers. "The end is near. We've called in hospice."

Lance takes her hand. "I'm so sorry, April. I can check with my night staff. One of them may be interested in some part-time day work."

"That would be great. One of the women at the artist colony might be interested as well."

Kate's ears perk up. "The artist colony?"

"Yes, a commune of women artists residing on a lovely stretch of land about ten miles outside of town. The women live in cottages and reserve their main structure, an old farmhouse, for aspiring art students. During the summer, they host a series of themed art weekends."

"Do you know these artists personally?"

"I do. Most are eccentric, but quite charming. Now"—April waves a hand at the artwork adorning the walls—"which painting are you interested in?"

"The one in the back of the little girl and her father fly-fishing."

"Ah, yes. One of my favorites," April says, and the three-some drifts to the back of the gallery.

Kate examines the painting closer. Now that she knows what to look for, the drawing of a bumblebee is easy to find. "When I mentioned the absence of a signature to my friend Mary Beth Fletcher, she told me to look for a drawing of a bee."

April offers an approving smile. "I know Mary Beth well. She has an excellent eye for interior design."

Lance leans in close to the painting. "Where's the bee?"

Kate points at the bee. "Right there."

Lance's blue eyes go wide. "That's unique."

"Tell me more about the artist," Kate says to April.

"She's lived at the colony for a very long time. Decades, probably. The others consider her their leader. Her works usually sell quickly. One of my established clients has made an offer on this painting. I'm waiting to find out if the artist accepts it. I probably have a message from her on my machine, along with a hundred others."

"Has she created similar works?"

"Most of her pieces are landscapes. But there was one other of this same little girl. I may have a picture somewhere." April retrieves her iPad from her desk and accesses the artist's file of works. She hands the iPad to Kate. "I really need to get a website."

In the painting, the little girl is seated on a tire swing with thin legs dangling and face hidden by a sun hat. The house in the background is unmistakably the one where Kate grew up.

Kate scrolls through the colorful landscapes. "I'm crazy about her work. What's her name?" she asks, handing back the iPad.

"She goes by Honey Bee. I doubt that's her real last name. I'm not even sure Honey is her real first name."

"Her last name is Baldwin. Like mine. I believe she's my long-lost mother."

April gasps. "That's amazing."

"Do you have a picture of her?" Kate asks.

"I believe I do, from a recent wine and cheese reception I held here at the gallery." April accesses her photos and shows Kate a picture. "She's the silver-headed lady in black."

Kate stares in disbelief at the mysterious woman she'd glimpsed at Alice's funeral. Had Honey known Kate would be there?

Looking up from the photograph, Kate says, "What else can you tell me about her?"

"She has a pleasant way about her, although she's somewhat guarded. I don't believe she has a man in her life. I've often wondered if those women are gay." April shrugs. "Honey is all about art with no other interests that I'm aware of. According to rumor, she has a history of drug addiction. But she's been clean as long as I've known her, which has been about ten years." April closes her iPad. "Would you like me to arrange a meeting?"

Kate considers how to proceed. "I'd rather pay her a surprise visit. Can you give me the address for the colony?"

"It's a little difficult to find. I have your cell number. I'll share the contact information, which includes the pinned address."

"That would be great." Kate has imagined a reunion with her mother countless times.

Is this really happening? After all these years, is she finally going to meet her mother?

Chapter 22

June

Buford is upstairs dressing when Raquel parades through the front door with her band of minions marching behind her. As they pass by, June counts at least thirty heads. She set her table for twelve.

First chance she gets, she pulls Raquel aside. "What happened to the intimate seated dinner you requested?"

Raquel nonchalantly lifts a shoulder. "Word got out you were having a hurricane party. I couldn't very well tell them no."

"You could've at least warned me."

Raquel furrows her brow, but no lines appear in her forehead. She's aged since the last time June saw her years ago. And not in a good way. She's harsh looking, way too thin with inflated lips and sunken cheeks. "I spoke to Buford earlier. Didn't he tell you?"

"Clearly not." June gestures at the dining room table, set with her best china, silver, and crystal. "I spent all afternoon on this table. My caterer has prepared a four-course dinner for twelve."

Raquel flips her black hair over her shoulder like a teenager.

"Just serve the food buffet style. No one will care. This crew is more interested in drinking anyway."

June huffs out her irritation and strides toward the kitchen. She hasn't smoked a cigarette since college, but if she had one now, she'd light right up. "We have a big problem," she says to Beth, the head caterer, and then explains the situation.

"We can make adjustments," Beth says. "We'll slice the tenderloin thin and serve it on the dinner rolls. I have tall shot glasses in the van we can use for the shrimp and grits. And I'll make a charcuterie board out of everything else. It won't be ideal. You'll run out of booze, and everyone will leave early."

June blows a strand of blonde hair out of her face. "Good! The goal is to get rid of everyone as soon as possible."

Beth gives her a gentle shove toward the dining room. "You go disassemble the lovely table you worked so hard on, and we'll take care of the rest."

"You're a godsend, Beth. There's a big tip waiting for you at the end of the night."

June spends fifteen minutes carefully putting away her tableware. When there's still no sign of Buford, she goes upstairs in search of him. As she enters their bedroom, she hears soft moans coming from his walk-in closet. She cracks the door and peeks inside. Buford's pale rear end shines like a neon globe in the dark closet. His trousers are bunched around his ankles, and he has Raquel, the source of the moans, pinned against the wall with her black dress hiked up around her hips.

June's blood boils as she flips on the light switch.

"June!" Buford turns to face her, his hands over his privates as if she hasn't seen them countless times before. "What're you doing here?"

"In case you've forgotten, I live here. This is my bedroom. How dare you have sex with your little slut in my house," June says and flees the room. She's descending the stairs when she stops in her tracks at the sight of her daughter standing inside the front door, soaking wet and dripping water on her antique oushak rug.

"Scout. What the devil?"

Silence spreads throughout the guests, and they gather closer to witness the scene unfold.

Scout jabs a finger at her. "I've spent the past sixteen years looking for my brother, and you knew where he was the entire time."

A fully dressed Buford appears behind her on the stairs. "Is that true, June? Do you know where Ford is?"

June shakes her head. "No. She's mistaken. I have no clue where he is."

"Cut the crap, Mom. Kate finally confessed the truth. Her father, Phillip Baldwin, is Ford's biological father."

The crowd erupts in low murmurs.

Scout moves closer to the stairs. "Kate, the good sister, the one Ford adores, won't tell me where he is. But she knows. She admitted he's alive and well. I'm sure Mom can get more out of her father, since they're so close."

Buford clears his throat. "Scout, honey. We have guests in our home. This is neither the time nor the place for this discussion."

Scout sets her wild eyes on him. "There's never a good time or place to air one's dirty laundry, Daddy Dearest."

Buford digs his knee into June's back. "Do something, June. Make her shut up."

June's mind reels with everything happening at once. She grips the railing. "I think these fine people should understand what they're getting into by supporting you for governor." She looks out at the people gathered in the hallway below. "I just caught my husband, your potential candidate, screwing Raquel in his walk-in closet." She cranes her neck to see her husband.

"Tell us, Buford. How long have you two been sleeping together?"

Raquel, looking like the cat who swallowed the canary, squares her shoulders. "On and off for years."

Scout claps her hands. "Good job, Dad. You can kiss the election goodbye. No one wants a governor who can't keep his pecker in his pants." She sweeps an arm at the crowd. "These people should also know what a lousy father you are. Tell them how you badgered and bullied Ford until he ran away. Mom may have slept with the neighbor. But you drove Ford to stage his own disappearance."

"Folks, I'm sorry you're having to witness this family drama. As you can see, my daughter is having some sort of mental breakdown."

Raquel presses her body against Buford. "This man's daughter's problems have nothing to do with his politics. Everyone, grab a refill and let's give them some space to talk this out."

Ignoring their leader, the minions gather their raincoats and migrate toward the door.

Buford leans in close to June's ear. "Scout has lost her mind. Call the rescue squad. She needs to be admitted to the hospital for a mental evaluation."

"I'll do no such thing. There's nothing wrong with Scout. You're the one who's insane." June continues down the stairs, fighting her way through the guests to the kitchen. She grabs her raincoat and purse and leaves the house through the mudroom.

Her world crushes down on her as she speeds off toward town. What a fool she's been. All these years, she's been terrified of losing her spouse and children and home. But she lost so much more. She lost herself.

Tears blurring her vision, she fails to notice the red stoplight overhead or the headlights bearing down on her from the left. And then her world goes dark.

Chapter 23

June

November 2004

F ord returned from his Dauphin Island fishing trip a changed young man. He couldn't bring himself to look at June, and he answered her questions with curt responses.

Late Sunday afternoon, Buford called Ford into his office. He emerged an hour later with swollen eyes and drooping shoulders. "I've decided to go to Alabama, after all." When she tried reasoning with him, Ford said, "I don't want to talk about it," and ran upstairs to his room.

June entered her husband's study. "He was dead set on going to Georgia. What did you do to change his mind?"

"I made him see Alabama is the far superior team."

"According to you. Ford feels differently. At least he did two days ago." June loomed over her husband. "What're you hiding, Buford?"

He let out a laugh that bordered on maniacal. "You have some nerve accusing me of hiding something."

June gulped down fear as she backed away from his desk. *Did he somehow find out Phillip is Ford's biological father?* "At least the decision is made, and we can move on with our lives."

When she reached the door, she ran down the hall and up the stairs to her bedroom, where she spent the rest of the evening.

On Monday morning, she caught up with Phillip in the driveway on his way to work. "You told Ford, didn't you?"

"I did," Phillip said with a curt nod. "I should've told him a long time ago."

She looked through the kitchen window at Ford, who was seated at the breakfast counter, stabbing his poached eggs with his fork. "He worships you. I expected him to be thrilled. But he's so despondent."

"Give him some time, June. His world has been turned upside down. He needs to adjust. He's not thrilled at having to keep his paternity a secret. And who can blame him, given his strained relationship with Buford?"

"To make matters worse, Buford convinced him to go to Alabama."

Phillip shot her a sharp look. "When did that happen?"

"Yesterday afternoon. They had a private conversation. Neither will tell me what they said."

His jaw tightened. "Buford is determined to destroy that boy's life, and you're enabling him. I'm disappointed in you, June. I thought you were your own person, not your husband's henchman." He strode off toward his car.

She hurried after him. "Wait, Phillip! Don't leave like this."

He slammed his car door on her and sped away without a glance in her direction.

During the months that followed, even though the football matter had been decided, the war between Ford and Buford continued to rage within their household. Buford criticized Ford about nearly everything else, from his appearance to his grades to his friends. At times, June was tempted to call the police when she feared one or the other would become violent.

She apologized to Mary Beth after one particularly

harrowing argument. "I'm so sorry. I don't know what's gotten into those two."

Mary Beth offered her a genuine smile. "Don't worry, Miss June. I put cotton balls in my ears, and I can't hear a thing."

Shame creeped up June's neck and burned her face. "Where I come from, family doesn't treat each other this way."

"Where I come from, they do. I'm much happier living here than with my mother and brothers."

June thought back to the night Mary Beth appeared in her bloody nightgown. What the poor child must have gone through with no one to keep her out of harm's way. She drew Mary Beth in for a hug. "God blessed me the day he sent you to live with us."

"I'm the one he blessed," Mary Beth said in a soft voice.

Phillip's words played over and over in her mind like a broken record. *Buford is determined to destroy that boy's life, and you're enabling him.*

She hounded her husband to let up on Ford. "Give him a break, Buford. You got your way about Alabama. Now let up. He's a good kid. He makes excellent grades, and he stays out of trouble, which is more than I can say for some of his friends."

"I'm building character," was Buford's typical response. "My father rode me hard and look how well I turned out. You need to be tougher on him. You'd be okay with him joining a rock band."

June held her chin high. "You're right. I would. If that's what makes him happy. Why don't you put the same pressure on Scout? Don't you care about building her character?"

Buford grunted. "Scout is a lost cause. She's just like my grandmother. She's gonna do whatever she wants, everyone else be damned."

In public, Buford bragged about Ford to anyone who would listen. But whenever he was home from Washington, he badgered him endlessly. He was a proud papa on graduation day, when Ford delivered the valedictorian address to his class-mates. Afterward, at a backyard reception they hosted for Ford's friends and their parents, Buford informed everyone Ford would follow in his footsteps by becoming a lawyer. When Ford got wind of it, he set everyone straight.

Standing on the back porch steps, Ford finger-whistled to get their guests' attention. "First, I'd like to thank everyone for coming today. This is an exciting time for us. As I said in my speech earlier, we will travel different paths, but I hope we will always remain close."

His friends responded with cheers and applause.

"Contrary to what my father says, my path will definitely not be leading me to law school." His audience snickered, but the contemptuous look Ford shot Buford made June's blood run cold.

Ford went on, "I'd like to take this opportunity to thank my mom for giving birth to me." He lifted his glass of sweet tea to her. "Great job on the party, Mom! Scout, you may not have my room when I'm gone, but I will leave you my marble collection."

"Forget the marbles," Scout yelled. "Send me fifty-yard-line tickets and a parking pass."

The crowd laughed.

"What about me?" Mary Beth called out.

Ford winked at her. "You're a kind soul, Mary Beth. Never change." His brown eyes traveled the crowd, landing on Phillip. "To my mentor, Phillip Baldwin, I owe you an enor-mous debt of gratitude for supporting my many endeavors." He smiled softly at Kate standing next to Phillip. "And to Kate, thanks for being my best friend. I will miss you next year."

"Come with me." Buford dug his fingers into June's arm and dragged her inside to his study. "What was that spectacle about?

Our son just humiliated everyone in this family. Most of all, me."

"You brought that on yourself. Why would you tell everyone he's going to law school when you know it's not what Ford wants?"

"What Ford wants is inconsequential. He has a duty to this family. To me. When I stand on the stage and accept the nomination for president, I need my son by my side, a respectable young man, not some guitar-playing freak."

"So this is all about your image."

"I'm a politician, June. Everything is about my image."

A sense of peace settled over the house when Ford left for Tuscaloosa in July. Those were happy times for June with Mary Beth's and Scout's friends coming and going. They seemed to enjoy having June around. They asked for fashion advice and questioned her about colleges. June even took a small group on a college tour during the long Columbus Day weekend that fall. While Scout was dead set on going to Auburn, several of the girls were interested in UNC, and June enjoyed showing them her alma mater.

Ford could not come home for Thanksgiving because of football, and a dark cloud accompanied him when he arrived for Christmas. He'd let his hair grow past his shoulders and dark bruises circled his eyes. June suspected something was bothering him, but when she tried to talk to him, he dismissed her concern. Then, out of the blue on Christmas Eve, he confided in her.

The five of them had gone to a six o'clock church service, and after a quiet family dinner, Ford had hurried off to spend the rest of the evening with Phillip and Kate. Buford and the girls had long since gone to bed, and June was putting a few Santa gifts under the tree when Ford came home from next door around midnight. He helped himself to Buford's bourbon, which he'd never done before, and sat down beside her on the sofa. "Merry Christmas, Mama."

Tears welled in her eyes. *When's the last time he called me Mama?*

"Merry Christmas to you, son."

They sat for a minute in silence. June could tell he had something on his mind, and she figured it best to let him say it in his own time.

Ford drained his bourbon and poured another. This time, instead of returning to the sofa, he stood looking at the tree. "You always do a nice job with the tree. I'm glad you still put up a real one. I'm not a fan of the artificial trees." He fingered a gold cross ornament he'd made in elementary school. "Things aren't going well with football. There are a lot of players better than me. It would've been the same at Georgia. I should've listened to Phil and gone to a smaller school."

So he's calling him Phil now? "It's not too late to transfer."

He let go of the ornament. "What's the point? I was never going to make a career out of football. But now I must figure out my future. Other than football, all I care about is fishing and music, neither of which will make me famous or earn me a lot of money."

June got up from the sofa and went to stand beside him. "Contrary to what your father says, money isn't everything. Happiness is about being successful doing the thing you love the most. You could create your own fishing brand of equipment and apparel. Or, if you choose the music route, there are many avenues in which to earn a living without being a star."

"Maybe," Ford said with a shrug. "What about your happiness, Mama? You know Phil loves you. How can you stay married to a jerk like Buford when you could be with an awesome guy like Phil?"

June was taken aback by his candor. Unsure how to respond, she tried to make light of it. "Who gave you permission to call the grown-ups in your life by their first names?"

"Don't change the subject, Mom. You need to get away from Buford. I don't trust him. He's a lying egomaniac with a vicious temper. I'm worried about your safety."

"Don't be ridiculous. Buford won't hurt me," she said with a dismissive wave of her hand.

"There are many ways to hurt someone, Mom."

June cupped his cheek. "You're sweet to worry about me, son. But I'm fine."

Ford took hold of her wrist, removing her hand from his face. "I'm being serious, Mom. Watch your back. I won't always be here to look out for you." He gulped down the rest of the bourbon, set the glass on the coffee table, and walked out of the room, leaving her standing alone beside the tree.

An eerie feeling overcame June as she watched her son trudge up the stairs. He was trying to warn her about something. But what?

June poured herself a cup of eggnog, turned out the lamps, and sat by the Christmas tree, pondering her life. Knowing her feelings for Phillip went far beyond friendship, it broke her heart to think of him moving to New York. When he professed his love for her in the driveway three days later, she was tempted to pack up her things and go with him.

"Come to New York with me, June. I love you. I've always loved you. And I believe you have feelings for me too. I can give you a good life. I can make you happy."

"Buford and I have been together since childhood. I don't know how to live without him."

Phillip took her by the arms. "All the more reason for you to leave him. You've never even been on a date with anyone else. You don't know what you're missing out on. You deserve so much better than the way he treats you."

"I would be lost in a big city like New York. My home is in Alabama. I have obligations here. I can't leave Scout and Mary Beth until they finish high school."

"You're making excuses, June." He gave her a gentle shake. "Think about yourself for a change."

"Now is not the right time, Phillip. My place is with my family."

He pressed his lips to her forehead. "I won't wait for you, June. I don't want to grow old alone."

"I wouldn't expect you to. I wish you all the best, Phillip," she said with a sad smile and walked away.

Chapter 24

Scout

S cout is packing her bags, planning to drive to the nearest airport not affected by weather and get the next flight back to Seattle, when her father bangs on her bedroom door. "Open up, Scout."

She didn't realize her dad was still home. Last she'd seen him, he was hurrying out of the house after Raquel. "I'm in the middle of something. What do you want?"

"I just had a call from the hospital. Your mom has been in an accident. It sounds serious."

Fear runs through Scout as she recalls her mom's abrupt departure from the house earlier. June had been visibly distraught, in no condition to be driving in a tropical storm. Scout had considered going after her, but she was too angry. She was afraid of what she might say or do if she caught up with her. For now, she needs to put as much distance between her and her mother as possible.

Scout drops a stack of jeans into her suitcase and unlocks the door. "What'd the hospital say?"

"Not much. Only that we should get there as soon as possible."

Grabbing her raincoat and purse, Scout follows him out of the house. Neither father nor daughter say a word on the way to the hospital in his Mercedes. In the emergency room, the nurse at the reception counter directs them to the waiting room. The awkward silence continues as they anxiously await word from the doctor about her mother. Scout has much she wants to say, so many questions to ask her dad. But she would inevitably cause another scene, and now is not the right time.

After more than an hour, a young doctor comes out to speak with them. "Your wife has suffered multiple minor lacerations all over her body and broken bones in her left arm. Our biggest concern is her head injury. We're in the process of determining the extent of damage."

"A head injury?" Dad says, his tone alarmed. "Do we need to airlift her to the trauma center in Mobile?"

"I don't believe that's necessary, sir. I'm confident we can treat your wife here. If we get in over our heads, we'll consider the transfer."

Buford stares him down. "How old are you, son?"

The young doctor puffs out his chest. "Thirty-five, sir."

"Then you're already in over your head. You're way too young for me to trust with my wife's life. I'm calling in Marcus McDermott."

"That's your prerogative, sir. Dr. McDermott has hospital privileges here. But he may opt not to take your wife's case."

"He'll take her case. Marcus and I are childhood friends," her father says, and goes outside to make the call.

Scout stands inside the emergency room, watching through the glass door as her father paces the sidewalk with his phone pressed to his ear. Marcus McDermott is the top neurologist in the state who primarily practices out of the trauma hospital in Mobile. While he spends most of his time in Mobile, he keeps a small house in Langford, his hometown, where he retreats when he needs a break from his challenging career.

"We're in luck," Buford reports when he comes back inside. "Marcus happens to be in town for a few days. He's on his way over."

"That's good news," Scout says, feeling only slightly relieved.

Many endless hours ensue as they wait for an update on her mother's condition. Scout stares blankly at the hurricane coverage on the television as she struggles to wrap her mind around everything that has happened. The idea of June and Phillip sleeping together isn't all that surprising. June belongs with a gentle and caring man like Phillip. Not a vindictive jackass like her father. Buford and that awful Raquel woman deserve each other.

When Scout gets the chance, *if* she gets the chance, she'll ask her mother why she stayed married to Buford. Although Scout already knows the answer. She did it for the sake of her family. June is a devoted wife and mother who always put her husband and children first. Truth be told, Scout and Ford would've been better off if they'd divorced.

It's almost midnight when Barrett calls to report that Sally Strickland's body is on its way home to the East Coast. With all the family drama, she'd forgotten about Sally Strickland.

"How are her parents holding up?"

"They're putting on a brave face for the sake of their other children. They understand why you couldn't be here. They promised to let us know when they've made funeral plans."

"Good. I'd like to attend if possible." In light of her mother's accident, there's no telling when she'll be leaving town now.

"Have you solved your family's problems yet?"

"My family has more problems than I ever realized," she says and recounts the events of the past few hours.

When she's finished, Barrett lets out a low whistle. "That's a lot to process, Scout. I hate for you to go through all this alone."

Scout looks at her father, who is sitting in the chair across from her with arms folded over chest and head bowed. "I'm with my dad. I wish I were alone."

"Where's Mary Beth?"

"I don't want to bother her so late. I'll call her in the morning when I know more about Mom's condition."

"I'll keep my phone on tonight. Let me know as soon as you learn more. You are not alone, Scout. I'm here for you." The sincerity in his voice warms her heart. He's the most genuine person she knows. He's her real family, the only person who always has her back.

"You're the best, Barrett. I don't know what I'd do without you."

"Good thing you won't have to find out."

Ending the call, Scout jumps to her feet and paces around the now empty waiting room. She locates vending machines and drinks enough bitter coffee to make her hands shake. Her father has fallen into a deep slumber, and she does everything she can think of to make his loud snoring stop. She shakes him, kicks at his feet, and pinches his nose. How can he sleep when his wife is potentially dying?

Around three in the morning, Dr. McDermott finally emerges from the ominous double doors leading to the examining rooms. As soon as he hears his old friend's voice, Buford stands to attention, as though he's been on alert the entire time.

"June has a fractured skull. As far as skull fractures are concerned, hers is not severe. She's unconscious, but I'm hopeful she'll wake up soon."

"Can we see her now?" Scout asks.

"We're moving her to the intensive care unit on the fourth floor, where she'll remain until she regains consciousness. You'll have more privacy and be more comfortable in the waiting room up there. A nurse will let you know when she's ready for visitors."

Scout and her father move up to the fourth floor waiting room, where Buford promptly falls back asleep. At daybreak, when no nurse has come for them, Scout calls Mary Beth.

"Mom was in a car accident last night. She's in ICU with a fractured skull."

"I'm on my way," Mary Beth says. Fifteen minutes later, she arrives, dressed in workout clothes with her blonde hair pulled back in a ponytail.

Buford wraps his arms around Mary Beth in a warm embrace. His affection might have irritated Scout yesterday. Today she could care less. Where her father is concerned, her heart has turned to ice.

Scout takes Mary Beth by the hand. "I need to get something to eat. Let's go down to the cafeteria."

Mary Beth appears torn as she casts Buford an uncertain glance. "Do you wanna come with us?"

Scout answers for him. "He's staying here in case the doctor comes back. Besides, I need to talk to you in private," she says and drags Mary Beth away.

In the cafeteria, Scout fills her plate with scrambled eggs, grits, and sausage, but Mary Beth only gets a black coffee. "I'm too upset to eat," she explains.

"I am too, actually. But I haven't eaten anything since yesterday afternoon. If I don't get something in my stomach, my blood sugar will tank."

They locate a table by a sunny window overlooking a court-yard garden. "You won't believe it, Mary Beth. Wait until I tell you what's happened."

As Scout recounts events from the past twenty-four hours, Mary Beth shakes her head, as though trying to comprehend.

When she finishes talking, Mary Beth says, "Everything about your family suddenly makes so much sense. June and Phillip were good friends. I can see her turning to him for comfort during a difficult time. But she would never have carried on a long-term affair. June worshipped your father. He was her king. She would never have betrayed him. I'm disappointed in Buford. It was easy for me to overlook his flaws after he saved me from going to prison for killing Lamar."

The mention of Lamar sets Scout on edge. Somehow, his death fits into all this. "I feel sorry for Mom. Her misguided love for my father has held her hostage all these years."

"Do you think she'll leave him now that she knows about Raquel?"

"She damn well better," Scout says, digging her fork into her scrambled eggs.

Mary Beth sips her coffee. "Where do you think Ford has been all this time?"

"In some remote destination. Otherwise, someone we know would've run into him by now," Scout says, and chomps down on a sausage link.

"True." Mary Beth's eyes drift to a little girl chasing a bouncy ball out in the garden. "Will you pressure Kate to tell you where he is?"

"Maybe eventually. When my wounded pride heals. I'm less angry at Ford than I was last night, but I'm still really hurt."

"I don't blame you. I'm sure your emotions are all over the place. We should at least call Kate. She loves June. She'll want to know about the accident."

"You call her. I'm not talking to her."

"You're going to have to at some point. Besides, hearing her perspective on the situation might help you see things differently."

"Fine. I will when I'm ready." Scout wipes her mouth and

drops the napkin on her plate. "We should get back upstairs. I don't want to miss the doctor."

As they retrace their steps through the cafeteria, Mary Beth says, "We should take some food to Buford." She hesitates. "On second thought, let him get it himself."

Scout laughs out loud. "I love you!" she says, throwing her arms around Mary Beth's neck. "I'm sorry I've been such a pain in the butt lately. You're the best thing that ever happened to my family."

"Your family, despite all its flaws, is the best thing that ever happened to me."

Scout holds her at arm's length. "All this time I've been searching for my brother when I should've been spending more time with my sister. And you are my sister, Mary Beth, in every way that counts."

Mary Beth's eyes well with tears. "That's the nicest thing you've ever said to me."

They return to the waiting room to find her father missing and an impatient-looking Dr. McDermott thumbing the screen on his phone. "Scout! There you are. I was getting ready to call your father. Do you know where he is?"

"I have no clue. We've been downstairs in the cafeteria. How's Mom?"

"I've ordered some more tests. She's no longer responding to stimuli, and I'm concerned there's another underlying problem."

Scout's brow puckers. "What do you mean, she's not responding?"

"She's slipped into a coma."

"A coma?" Scout says, her heart hammering against her rib cage.

He places a hand on Scout's shoulder. "Let's not panic yet. This may simply be her body's way of reacting to the trauma from the accident."

"Can I see her now?"

"They've already taken her down for the tests. She's likely to be a while. This might be a good opportunity for you to run any errands or go home to change," he says and leaves the waiting room.

Scout sniffs her armpit. "I could use a shower, actually. I haven't had one since we left the lake. I rode here with Dad in his car. Do you mind giving me a ride home?"

"Not at all. We can grab some of June's things while we're there. When she wakes up, she'll want a gown and robe and her favorite fussy slippers."

Scout smiles, thinking of this suggestion. Her mom has taken care of everyone else for so long and now they can take care of her. Mary Beth is so much like her, always looking out for the needs of others.

When they leave the hospital, Scout notices her father's car is no longer in the emergency room lot where he parked last night. And when they arrive at home, he's nowhere in sight. "How typical of Dad to pull a disappearing act in the middle of our family's biggest crisis ever. I'd be willing to bet my next paycheck he's run off with Raquel."

Mary Beth glances over at her. "Surely, he wouldn't do that."

"I wouldn't put it past him. At least it would make things easier for Mom. She'll have more grounds to divorce him."

Chapter 25

Kate

Kate considers calling ahead to arrange a meeting with her mother, but then decides a surprise visit is a better option. Honey can say no to a meeting request. If Kate shows up out of the blue, Honey will have no choice but to talk to her.

Mid morning on Monday, she heads out of town toward the artist colony. She gets lost once and is delayed twice by road crews clearing trees downed by the storm. When she misses the colony's small sign, she has to turn around and go back. But the beauty of the landscape as she drives down the tree-lined road takes her breath.

The silver-headed woman she suspects is Honey is the only person in sight as she approaches the farmhouse, but she's too busy picking up storm debris to notice Kate's car. The woman's mannerisms are oddly familiar, and it takes Kate a minute to recognize them as her own.

She clears her throat. "Excuse me. Are you Honey?"

"I am." Honey looks up at Kate and does a double take as the color drains from her face. "And you are?"

"I'm Kate Baldwin. I'm looking for my mother, Honey Baldwin. I believe you may be her."

"What makes you think that, other than my name is Honey?" Honey asks, tossing the storm debris into a nearby trash can.

"Your artwork, the painting of the father and daughter fishing at the gallery in town. And the older piece of the little girl on the swing."

"What about them?" Honey asks, peeling off her garden gloves.

"I think the little girl is me."

"Humph. I'm afraid that's wishful thinking on your part. The child's face is indistinguishable, and lots of little girls have dark hair."

"But the house in the background of the swing painting is the house where I lived as a child."

"I'm sorry, dear, but you're mistaken. I don't have any children," Honey says, but she cannot meet Kate's eyes.

Kate has no doubt this woman is her mother. The determined set of her jaw is the same one she's seen in the mirror countless times.

She hands Honey a business card. "I'm visiting from New York. I'll be in town for a couple more days. If you think of anything that might help me, I'm staying at the Meeting Inn. I'm not looking to cause trouble, nor to judge anyone for something they've done in the past. I just want to know my mother."

Slipping the card into the back pocket of her jeans, Honey pulls her gloves back on and returns to picking up sticks. Kate watches her work for a minute longer before getting in her car and driving away. She refuses to get discouraged. She blindsided Honey with her surprise visit. Now she'll take a step back and let her mother come to her. So what if she has to stay in town a few extra days? It'll give her more time to spend with Lance.

Kate parks her rental at the hotel and wanders across the street. The gallery is closed, but she stands at the window admiring Honey's painting. How many times has Honey painted this landscape? Does she ever get tired of the same scenery?

Kate understands how a drug addiction could drive a young mother away from her baby and husband. But what has kept her away all these years? Why did Honey lie to her just now? Does she think Kate is a threat to the peaceful life she's created for herself?

When she senses someone behind her, Kate cranes her neck to see Lance. "How'd it go with Honey?"

Kate turns to face him. "She claims she's not Honey Baldwin. But I'm certain she is. I gave her my card and told her I'll be at the inn a few more days."

His brilliant blue eyes light up. "So you're staying?"

"Looks that way. Although I have no clue how I'll spend my time. What're your plans for today?"

"Yard work. Cleaning up from the storm. Care to join me?"

Kate snickers. "As much as I would enjoy spending this glorious day outdoors, I have a black thumb. I pay someone to take care of my balcony garden."

"You don't need special skills to pick up sticks and rake leaves, Kate. I'll reward you by buying you lunch and cooking you dinner."

"Well then, that's an offer I can't refuse." She looks down at her gray slacks and white silk blouse. "But I need to change first. Do you live nearby? I can walk over."

"Just a few blocks. I'll text you the address."

He walks her back across the street to the inn. "I'll see you in a few minutes." He kisses her goodbye, his soft lips lingering on hers, stirring something deep inside of her she hasn't felt in a long time.

She touches her finger to his lips. "Forget lunch and dinner. I'll have more kisses like that as my reward."

He chuckles. "Do a good job, and you'll get both."

Her head is in the clouds as she rides the elevator to her floor. She's walking down the hall to her room when Mary Beth calls. "I have bad news. June was in a car accident last night."

"Oh no! Is she okay?" Kate says as she swipes her key card and enters her room.

"Her injuries don't appear to be life threatening, but she's in a coma, which has the doctors concerned there might be something else going on."

"That's awful. I'm so sorry," Kate says, tossing her bag on the bed and going to the window.

"Now would be a good time for Ford to come home. I assume you know how to reach him." There's an edginess to Mary Beth's tone Kate has never heard before. She isn't suggesting Kate call Ford. She's insisting.

"Scout told you about our confrontation."

"Of course. But I'm not surprised. I've always assumed you knew more than you were saying about his disappearance. It's Ford's loss if he doesn't want to be part of their lives. But the least he can do is visit his mother on her deathbed."

The hairs on the back of Kate's neck stand at attention. "Deathbed? I thought you said her injuries didn't appear to be life threatening."

"The doctors can't explain her coma. In my book, that's serious."

"I'll call him, Mary Beth. But I'm not making any promises. There's more to Ford's disappearance than Scout knows."

"I assumed that as well. Will you at least try?"

"I'll let you know what he says. I'm staying in town a few extra days. I'd like to visit June if possible."

"She's not ready for visitors. Scout hasn't even seen her yet. But I'll text you updates as we get them."

"Please do." Ending the call, she places another to her father and tells him about June's accident, promising to let him know when she finds out more.

"By the way," Kate says. "I'm extending my stay."

"Because of June?"

"And because I found my mother."

Silence passes between them. Finally, he asks, "Was it the reunion you'd hoped for?"

"Not exactly. I'll tell you about it later." Kate inhales a deep breath. "Scout and Buford found out you're Ford's father. It's over, Dad. It's time for this charade to end."

"You don't mean that, Kate. If Buford finds out you know the truth, your life could be in danger."

"He won't find out. I would never divulge Ford's secret. But Scout may insist I tell her where Ford is. I can't keep his whereabouts from her any longer."

She's surprised when her father doesn't argue. "I understand, sweetheart. You do what you must do."

Her call to Ford goes straight to voice mail, and she leaves a detailed message about June's accident and Scout finding out Phillip is Ford's biological father. He often takes days, even weeks, to get back to her. Especially during his business season, which he is in the middle of now. Ford lives his life on his own terms, in his own time. He won't drop what he's doing and rush down to Alabama for anyone. Not even his mother.

Chapter 26

Kate

December 2005

U nexpected tears had streamed down Kate's face as her father backed his SUV out of their driveway for the last time. Why was she crying when she was excited about the move, ready for a fresh start in a new life? Because no matter where life took her, a piece of herself would always live in this house in Langford, Alabama.

When they drove past Lance's house, he was on the front porch holding up a sign that read Big Apple Here She Comes. Fresh tears filled her eyes as she waved goodbye. She regretted ending their relationship, but she needed to make a clean break. He'd understood how unhappy she was, and had been supportive of her decision to move to New York instead of finishing out her senior year in Langford. Kate's love for him felt like the real deal, but they were too young to be so serious. They needed to experience the world before they made the forever commitment. If it was meant to be, they would find their way back to each other.

Kate and Phillip, each lost in their own thoughts, talked little during the first two hours of the trip. Instead of stopping at a hotel along the way, they'd agreed to take turns driving the seventeen-hour trip in order to meet the movers at their new apartment at nine in the morning. They'd just crossed the state line into Georgia when June called with the news that Ford was missing.

Here we go again, Kate thought as she listened to her father's end of the conversation. In recent months, she'd grown weary of Ford's drama, his sullen mood and her father constantly trying to placate him.

"We should turn around," her father said when he hung up.

Kate seethed with anger. "We can't. We have to meet the movers in the morning. Ford will show up. He was upset about us leaving. I'm sure he got drunk with some of our friends and crashed on someone's sofa."

"You're probably right." He loosened his grip on the steering wheel. "I told June you'd text your friends to see if anyone has seen him. Do you mind doing that?"

"Not at all." Kate pulled out her phone. "I'll send a group text, but I'm sure they're all still asleep."

Phillip's concern grew when they stopped for lunch in South Carolina, and he read the message from June that Ford was still missing. "We should go back," her father said. "I'll delay the movers."

"But you have that important meeting at the hospital on Friday. We can't postpone our lives because of Ford. He will have shown up by the time we get back to Langford, and we'll have to start our trip all over again."

Phillip hung his head. "I guess you're right. I was worried something like this would happen. He hasn't been himself in months."

"Since he found out you are his father," Kate mumbled.

With Kate behind the wheel, they continued north on the interstate. She perked him up by making plans for their first few days in New York before she started school, and her dad his new job on January second. They would unpack enough boxes to feel settled, and then see the sights and shop to their heart's content.

Thirteen hours into the trip, they stopped in Fredericksburg, Virginia, for dinner. Kate exited the highway and pulled into a Waffle House parking lot. "I'm starving," she said, turning off the engine.

"So am I," said a voice from the cargo area of the SUV.

Kate's neck snapped as she turned to see Ford peering at them over the top of the back seat. "What're you doing? Are you out of your mind? Everyone in Alabama is looking for you right now."

Her father unbuckled his seat belt and turned around to see his son. "Ford! Thank heavens you're safe. You should call your mother right now though. She's worried sick about you."

"No way!" Ford said with a vehement shake of his head. "I refuse to go back to that life."

"But it's cruel not to let your mother know you're safe."

"It's cruel of her to make me pretend Buford is my father," Ford said, his face set in steely determination.

"What about football?" Phillip asked.

"I'm done with football. I'm ready to start my real life. I've saved some money, and I've made a plan." He climbed with his backpack over the back seat. "I didn't intend to drag you into my problems. My goal was to stay hidden in the back until we got to New York and then take off without you seeing me. But I have to pee something awful, and I ran out of protein bars in Georgia." He unzipped the front pocket of his backpack and removed a handful of empty wrappers.

Kate looked at the wrappers and then glared at Ford. "Looks like you failed the first part of your plan."

Her father gave her a warning look before reaching for his

door handle. "Let's go inside. We'll talk this through over dinner."

Inside the restaurant, Ford headed straight to the restroom while Kate and Phillip located an empty table. Over cheeseburgers and fries, Ford told them his plan to become a fly-fishing guide in Alaska. While Kate thought the idea ludicrous, she was impressed with his knowledge of the state and industry. He'd clearly done his homework. Not only did he know the best places to fish, he knew which guides were the best to work for.

Kate said little while Phillip peppered Ford with questions, most of which he answered intelligently.

"What about college?" Phillip asked.

Ford dragged a french fry through a puddle of ketchup. "I understand the value of a college education, and I'll eventually get my degree. Putting myself through school may take longer than four years, but once I'm settled, I'll figure out a way to make it work."

"If you make college a priority, I will support you financially. You can fish in your free time until you graduate," Phillip said and stuffed the last bite of burger in his mouth.

Kate stared at her father with her mouth agape. "You're not seriously considering going along with him, are you?"

"I'm giving him the benefit of the doubt. I would do the same for you. Now, if you'll excuse me, I need to use the restroom," Phillip said and got up from the table.

Ford watched him go and then locked eyes with Kate. "Why are you so mad at me?"

"Do you really have to ask? What kind of pie-in-the-sky dream is fly-fishing in Alaska? Grow up, Ford. Finish college and get a real job like everyone else."

"That's easy for you to say. You're using your artistic talent to become a fashion designer. My track to career bliss is less conventional. I'm good at fly-fishing and I love being outdoors. I'm suffocating in Langford. I need space."

"You'll certainly get plenty of that in Alaska," Kate said in a sarcastic tone.

"Can't you just be happy for me?"

Kate banged her fist on the table. "What about our happiness? Dad and I left Langford to get away from the lies. And now you're roping us into an even bigger one. Call your mom. She deserves better than this."

"I'll call her when I get to Alaska. But I have no intention of telling her where I am. I'm sorry I've been such a burden to you. Just forget you ever saw me." Ford got up from the table and left the restaurant.

"Where's Ford?" her father asked when he returned.

"He left. He said for us to forget we saw him," Kate said, sucking the last of her iced tea through a straw.

"Why didn't you go after him?" Phillip asked, freeing his wallet from his back pocket and dropping three twenties on the table.

"Because I don't want to be a part of his disappearing act. And you shouldn't either."

"He's my son. I'm already a part of it, whether or not I like it. We have to find him. Come on." Taking her by the arm, Phillip hauled Kate to her feet.

"Let go of me, Dad. You're hurting me." Kate jerked her arm free and walked ahead of him out to the car.

"Keep your eyes peeled for him," her father said as they drove toward the interstate.

A half mile down the road, Kate pointed to a tall figure hitchhiking. "There he is."

When Phillip pulled over to the curb, Kate jumped out of the SUV and forced her brother into the passenger seat. She climbed into the back seat and leaned over the console so she could see him.

"What gives, Ford? I'm not buying any of this. You're eighteen years old. You don't have to stage a disappearance. You're free to leave home anytime you want. There's something more going on, and Dad and I deserve to know what it is."

Tears filled Ford's eyes. "There's more. A lot more." What he said next shocked the hell out of Kate, and she willingly vowed to never tell another living soul.

Chapter 27

Scout

Scout spends the afternoon watching her mother's motionless body for any sign of movement, but June's condition remains unchanged. Dr. McDermott, who can find no scientific explanation for the coma, surmises this is June's body's way of healing. Mary Beth has cozied up her mother's hospital room with her favorite fake fur throw and battery-operated candles. While Scout thinks her efforts are frivolous, Mary Beth seems to take joy in making June feel at home.

When Mary Beth leaves at four o'clock to relieve the babysitter, Scout walks her to the door. "You should try talking to your mama," Mary Beth says. "I'm sure she can hear you. After everything that happened last night, she probably needs to know you're not upset with her."

Scout stares down at the floor. "But I am upset with her."

"Then you need to move past your anger. You will forever regret it if something happens, and you haven't made your peace with her."

"I won't lie, Mary Beth. This family has had enough lies to last a lifetime."

"Tell her how you feel, Scout. Get everything off your chest. Whether or not she hears you, it will be good therapy for you."

Scout sits for another two hours without uttering a word. Every time she opens her mouth, nothing comes out.

At six o'clock, she takes a break for dinner. She gives the nurses her number and makes them promise to call her if anything changes. She's exiting the waiting room when the elevator pings, the doors open, and out walks Barrett.

"Barrett!" Scout jumps on him, her arms around his neck and legs hugging his torso.

He spins her around. "Ah. It's so good to see you. I've been so worried about you."

She unwraps herself from him, and he lowers her to the ground. "What're you doing here?"

"I figured you needed a friend."

His smoldering dark eyes send an electric current through her. She's missed him more these past few days than she realized. "Not just any friend. I need you."

"Well, I'm here now. How's your mom?"

"She's in a coma. Her neurologist thinks it's her body's way of healing. I've been here all day. I was getting ready to go home and grab some dinner." She notices the duffel bag slung over his shoulder. "I assume you flew into Mobile. Did you rent a car?"

"I took an Uber. The fare was cheaper than a rental."

Scout loops her arm through his. "Then you can ride with me. You're staying with us. We have a spare guest room, and my father is currently MIA, so we have the house to ourselves."

"What do you mean, your father is missing? Where'd he go?" Barrett asks on the drive to her house.

"Probably to see his girlfriend. He left and didn't tell anyone where he was going. If we're lucky, he won't come back."

Barrett's eyes grow wide when she pulls into their driveway.

"Damn, Scout. This house is enormous. Why did you ever leave Langford?"

She parks in front of the detached garage. "A home's pretty facade does not make for happy occupants, Barrett."

He brushes a strand of hair out of her face. "Was your childhood that horrible?"

"My childhood was as normal as they come. Everything went south during my teenage years when my father and brother turned our home into a war zone."

Scout opens her car door. "I'm starving. I'm sure you are too," she says because he's always hungry. She leads him through the mudroom to the kitchen, where she finds a note on the counter.

"Is that from your father?" Barrett asks, eyeing the cardstock note with her mom's pink monogram.

"No, it's from Betty, our housekeeper. Mom's friends have brought over some food." She drops the notecard on the counter and surveys the contents of the refrigerator, peeling back the foil on a chicken tetrazzini casserole.

Peering over her shoulder, Barrett says, "Looks like chicken mash?"

She looks up at him. "What is chicken mash?"

"My mother's go-to dinner when money was tight. We called it chicken, but the protein could've been anything from chopped hot dogs to canned tuna."

"Sounds gross." Scout peeks inside a foil-wrapped log. "Yum! Beef tenderloin. Set this on the counter," she says, handing the log to Barrett.

"Your mom's friends bring over beef tenderloin when someone has an accident? What do they bring when someone dies?"

"Don't ask. They compete to see who can outdo the other."

She locates a batch of ham biscuits and a container of homemade potato salad. Barrett slices the tenderloin while she heats up the ham biscuits and opens a bottle of red wine.

"Since when do you drink red wine?" Barrett asks.

"Since it's free. There are several cases left over from Dad's disastrous hurricane party." She holds her glass up to his. "Thanks for making the trip. Your support really means a lot."

"You would do the same for me." He touches his glass to hers.

"You're right. I would," she says, and they sit down at the pine table to eat.

"I'd offer to show you the town, but the nightlife in Langford is lame. We can watch a movie later," Scout says, shoveling a forkful of potato salad into her mouth.

"Or we can take a walk. I've been sitting all day. I wouldn't mind stretching my legs."

Scout smiles. "A walk sounds nice. I'll show you downtown."

Barrett takes a bite out of a ham biscuit and then shoves the rest of the biscuit in his mouth. "Do you need to go back to the hospital tonight?"

"I should. But I'm not. I'll check in with the nurses later."

When they finish eating, they clean up the kitchen, and Scout shows Barrett to the guest room to freshen up. "I'm gonna change my shoes, and I'll meet you back downstairs."

Ten minutes later, they leave the house and head toward downtown. A full moon brightens up the night sky, and crisp fall air has replaced the humidity of the tropical storm.

Barrett marvels, "It's so quiet here without the traffic and sirens. I could get used to small-town living."

"Ha. You wouldn't be able to support yourself. There's no crime here. The murder rate in Langford is in single digits."

"I could run for sheriff. How cool would that be?"

Scout laughs out loud. "Even as sheriff, you'd be bored out of your mind."

They continue on Meeting Avenue all the way through town. When they hear loud music beating from inside The Tavern, Barrett cups his eyes to look through the window. "They have pool tables. One appears to be opening up. What do you say?"

"I'm game. I'll grab the table if you get us some drinks."

For the next three hours, Scout and Barrett consume several rounds of drinks and play pool, beating every local challenger. On the walk home, Scout calls the hospital, and a pleasant-sounding nurse informs her there's been no change in her mother's condition.

They are two blocks from her house when Barrett places a hand on her shoulder. "How come you never hit on me?"

"Ha. You mean like every other woman in your universe?"

He flashes a devilish grin. "Something like that."

"Your fan club is big enough. You don't need me in it. Besides, I don't fit the mold. Look at me. I'm built like a boy." She sweeps a hand down her thin body. "I can't compete with the gorgeous, big-busted blondes you date."

He stops walking and turns her toward him. "Big boobs are overrated, Scout. Most of the women I date are shallow and self-centered. But you're different. You've got guts and a high moral standard I admire."

"Tell my dad that," she says and walks on ahead of him.

Barrett catches up with her. "How come you never talk about your love life?"

"Because I don't have one. I don't have time to date."

"Are you gay?" He nudges her with his elbow. "You can tell me. I won't judge you."

She casts a sideways glance at him. "Do I look gay?"

"Gay no longer has a *look*, Scout. Some of the most feminine girls I know are gay."

"You're the closest friend I have. Don't you think I would've told you something so important?"

"There's a lot about you I don't know. A lot you don't seem to wanna talk about."

"Well, I'm not gay. I just suck at relationships."

He smiles over at her. "Like me, you haven't found the right person yet."

"In your case, it's not for lack of trying."

They arrive back at the house to find her father's silver Mercedes in the driveway. Scout groans. "Our luck just changed. The dictator's home."

"What will he think of me? Will he like me?"

Her father will hate everything about him, but she doesn't tell Barrett that. "He's very conservative. He'll have a problem with the hair." She tugs on a hank of his shoulder-length wavy hair. "He's liable to insult you. Don't let it bother you. He's a jerk."

Barrett's face tightens. "Don't worry. I know the type. I can handle him."

When they enter the house, Buford is standing at the breakfast counter eating cold chicken tetrazzini straight out of the dish.

"I've been texting you, Dad. Mom slipped into a coma. Where have you been all day?"

"I had some out-of-town business I had to take care of."

Scout rolls her eyes. "Yeah, right? Business relating to Raquel Ramsey."

Buford's eyes drift to Barrett. "We have rules in this house, Scout. Bringing home strange men is strictly forbidden."

Scout glares at her father. "He's not a stranger. This is my coworker and close friend, Barrett Nunez. He flew in from Seattle today."

"Is he your boyfriend?"

Barrett pulls her in for a half hug. "I'm trying, sir. She's playing hard to get."

Scout pushes Barrett away. "He's joking, Dad."

Buford's lip curls as he gives Barrett the once-over. "You need a haircut, young man."

Barrett flashes his winning smile. "Don't tell my hairstylist that. She cut two inches off just the other day."

Scout and Barrett burst into laughter as they leave the kitchen. From down the hall, Scout calls, "In case you're wondering, Dad, Barrett is staying in the guest room."

Outside her bedroom, Barrett surprises her by kissing her on the lips.

"What was that for?" she asks, her blue eyes wide.

"I wanted to see what you taste like. You're sweet, like Christmas sugar cookies." He touches his finger to her lips. "Goodnight, Scout."

"Goodnight, Barrett. Thanks again for coming. I'm glad you're here."

Scout studies her rosy complexion in the mirror as she washes her face. Something has shifted in her relationship with Barrett. He's never flirted with her before. Did he miss her? Is that why he flew to Alabama? She experiences a pang of guilt. How can she be thinking about romance when her mother is in a coma, fighting for her life?

Chapter 28

Kate

Lance prepares a simple, delicious dinner of grilled steaks, roasted potatoes, and mixed green salad tossed in champagne vinaigrette. They dine at the table on the porch and then move to the comfortable lounge chairs on the patio by the fire pit to finish their wine.

"I don't know when I've spent a more pleasurable day," Kates says, slipping off her shoes and tucking her feet beneath her.

"Are you kidding? We worked like dogs. You should be exhausted."

She laughs. "I am, but in a good way. My muscles ache, and my hands are covered in blisters, but I feel like we accomplished a lot."

"Yard work is gratifying. You'll have to plan another trip to Alabama to water your pansies."

"Don't you dare let my pansies die." She eyes a nearby container of citrus-colored Johnny-Jump-Ups. "This may sound silly to you, but I enjoyed picking out the pansies and arranging them in your containers. I haven't created anything in so long. In too long."

He tilts his head to the side. "That surprises me in your line of work."

"My team of fashion designers is in charge of creatives while I manage the business side of the company. Although truthfully, my administrative assistant is better at that than I am. I miss the artistic aspect of my career."

"Maybe you should get back into it."

She runs a thumb around the rim of her stemless glass. "Actually, I've been thinking of launching a clothing line."

"That sounds exciting." Lance sits back and crosses his long legs. "Tell me about your life in New York. Do you have many social obligations associated with your stardom?"

"Ha ha. I'm not a star. At least I don't think of myself as one. I go to my share of work-related social events, most of which I'd rather skip." Lately, Kate has been moving through her life like a robot. She's lost interest in everything. She smiles over at Lance. Until now.

He sets down his drink and reaches for her hand. "I've been thinking a lot about us these past few days. About the *us* in high school. I've had a few serious girlfriends over the years, but I never felt about any of them the way I felt about you."

"We were good together, but our timing was all wrong. Remember the sign you made for me when I moved. I can still see you standing on your front porch when we drove by your house on our way out of town."

"I tried so hard to be brave, but I was a mess after you left." He brings her hand to his lips. "I've never been in a long-distance relationship before. But I'm willing to try it if you are."

"I'd like that. We've been given another chance, an opportunity to find out what might have been. We owe it to ourselves to take it."

"I agree." Letting go of her hand, he fidgets with his phone until soft music plays from outdoor speakers. He pulls her to her feet and takes her in his arms. He's leaning in to kiss her when her Apple Watch vibrates her arm with a call from her father.

"I'm sorry, Lance. This is Dad calling. I should take it."

"You go ahead." A mischievous twinkle appears in his blue eyes. "I'll bookmark our place for later."

She retrieves her phone from her purse. "Hey, Dad. What's up?"

"I just arrived in Langford."

Kate's jaw drops. "You're here? In Alabama? Why didn't you give me a heads-up you were coming?"

"Because I knew you'd try to talk me out of it. I'm worried about you, sweetheart. You have a lot going on with finding your mother and June's accident."

"You could've called," Kate says. "You didn't need to fly all the way down here."

"Well, I'm here now. Are you staying at the Meeting Inn?"

"I am." Kate locks eyes with Lance, who is listening to her side of the conversation. "I was having dinner with a friend. Go ahead and check in. I'll leave now and see you in a few."

She ends the call and drops her phone into her purse. "I'm sorry, Lance. I must cut our evening short."

"I heard," he says, turning off the music. "I'll walk you back to the hotel."

"You don't have to. I'm a big girl. I can find my way on my own."

He thumbs her cheek. "I realize that, but I don't want to miss out on spending a single minute with you."

She gathers their empty glasses and takes them to the kitchen. Lance follows her, turning out lights as he goes.

As they head toward town, Lance says, "I'm excited to see your father again. Do you think he'll remember me?"

"Dad never forgets a face." At the end of Lance's block, Kate notices a For Rent sign in front of a gray bungalow. "How cute is that house? I didn't notice the sign earlier."

"She just put it up this afternoon. The owner, Robyn, is a freelance writer. She travels all over the world. When she's gone for extended periods of time, she finds a tenant to help pay the bills and take care of the yard in her absence."

Kate stops to admire the cheerful window boxes and bench swing on the front porch. "Have you been in the house? What's it like inside?"

"Robyn and I are friends. She's invited me over for dinner several times. The house is tiny but updated. She recently converted half of her screened porch into a sunny office."

"I assume she rents it furnished."

He nods. "Aside from her clothes and personal items, which she puts in storage."

They arrive at the hotel to find her father standing in the lounge doorway, staring at the posted menu. "Hey, Dad. I'm sure you remember, Lance Reid."

"Of course, son." Phillip gives Lance's hand a firm shake. "You're all grown up. How's life treating you these days?"

"Very well, sir. I'm a commercial real estate developer. The hotel is one of my properties."

"Excellent. I was just admiring the improvements you've made." Phillip gestures at the lounge. "The bar is open for another hour. Can I buy you two some dinner or dessert or a drink?"

"Thanks, but I should get home. I have an early day tomorrow." Lance kisses Kate's cheek and whispers near her ear, "I'll call you in the morning."

Kate watches Lance disappear through the rotating door. When she turns back to her father, he's watching her with a suspicious look on his face. "What?"

"I haven't seen that dreamy expression since you and Lance dated back in high school."

Kate presses her lips thin. "You're being ridiculous."

"I call it like I see it. Let's sit down," Phillip says and leads her over to a table for two by the window.

From the server, he orders a grilled chicken Caesar salad with a glass of red wine, and Kate asks for a cup of chamomile tea.

"Why are you really here, Dad?" Kate asks when the server leaves.

Phillip sighs. "I came because of June. I feel the need to be close to her. I won't be able to bear it if something happens to her."

Kate places her hand over his. "I know. I'm worried too. Hopefully, we'll get to see her tomorrow."

The server arrives with their drinks, and Kate blows on her tea to cool it. "Why do you think my mother lied about her identity? Do you think she doesn't want to know me?"

"Honey does things in her own time. What exactly is it you want from her?" He holds up a hand. "You don't have to answer that. It's none of my business. You have a right to meet your mother."

Kate sips her tea. "I just want to know her, to learn more about her art, and hear about her life. June told me about her drug addiction. Maybe Honey did us a favor by leaving."

"Maybe so. Life with Honey was difficult. I probably should have told you about her addiction. But I didn't want you to have a negative image of her."

The pain on his face tugs at Kate's heartstrings. "I know that, Dad. You were looking out for me." She reaches for his hand. "I'm honestly glad you're here. I need your support. These past few days have been difficult, and my emotions are all over the place right now. I have no clue how to make things right with Scout, and I'm terrified June will die. I came here hoping to find a clue about my mother, only to learn she's been here this whole time. Her painting in the gallery is so obviously you and me, fishing in our favorite spot in Gulf Shores."

Phillip furrowed his brow. "How would she know? She must have been spying on us."

Kate bobs her head. "I assume so. It's like she's been waiting for me to find her, but now that I have, she says she doesn't have any children. I don't get it."

"Honey doesn't like surprises, and you threw her off guard when you showed up out of the blue. I'll pay her a visit tomorrow. I want to confirm it really is her before we decide how to proceed."

"That's a good idea. I guess there's always a chance it's not her, although I doubt it."

The server delivers her father's salad, and he picks up his fork to eat. "Tell me about Lance."

Kate stares down at her tea. "Reconnecting with him was a pleasant surprise. He's pretty amazing."

Phillip smiles at her. "I always thought you two had something special."

Kate sits back in her chair. "This town has a hold on me I can't explain. Seventeen years ago, I couldn't get out of here fast enough, but now, I don't want to leave."

"Is that because of Lance?"

"Partially. Since moving to New York, I've done my best to forget about my past life in Langford. But I've forgotten all the good things too. The stately homes and manicured lawns. The friendly people with their gracious manners. The live oaks draped with Spanish moss. The domesticity, people taking care of their homes and working in their yards. It's just so different from New York City."

Phillip jabs his fork at her. "I recognize that look. You've got it bad."

Kate crinkles her nose. "What look?"

"The same look I had decades ago when I moved to Langford. The idea of living in a small town enamored me. Despite my failed marriage, you and I had many happy years here together."

"Yes, we did." The *look* her father is talking about mostly has to do with Lance. A part of her was genuinely happy while she was dating him in high school. Until now, she didn't realize she's been carrying him around in her heart all these years. He's the most important of the unfinished business she has in Langford.

Chapter 29

June

June hovers near the ceiling while doctors and nurses fuss over her. Their expressions are grim, but she can't hear them. She's grateful not to feel the pain from her fractured skull and broken arm. She should reclaim her damaged body and fight for her life. But she's not ready yet. Her attraction to the ethereal light is too great.

As she floats around her altered state of consciousness, she experiences the most important moments of her life for a second time. She drops in at the country club for her wedding reception, a grand affair with every influential member of Alabama society in attendance. She and Buford have been friends since childhood, dating since middle school, and now they will finally be husband and wife.

A light flashes, and June is in a hospital room. She's a mess after giving birth to Ford, with hair in disarray and no makeup on her face. But she's blissfully happy. And Buford is the proud father of the son he's always wanted. He insists on naming the baby James Buford Montgomery IV.

"He'll have big shoes to fill. It's good to set the bar high early on."

June goes along with him, even though she fears the baby might be Phillip's. As they promised each other, she and Phillip haven't spoken about their night together. He's too preoccupied with Honey's problems to give June and her baby another thought. As June looks down at her sleeping infant, she vows to never tell a soul the truth.

June blinks, and she's in another hospital bed, this time with a pink bundle in her arms. "What kind of name is Scout?" she asks when Buford suggests calling the baby Scout after his grandmother.

"A name our child can live up to. My grandmother was a woman of strong character. She had a heart of gold, but she kept everyone in line with a firm hand and high expectations. Including my grandfather."

June readily agrees, not because of his grandmother but because she's a fan of the little girl character named Scout in *To Kill a Mockingbird*.

She takes the elevator down three floors and six years to the emergency room where a young female doctor is setting both the ulna and radius in Scout's wrist, two of many broken bones her tomboy daughter suffered as a child. She incurred most of her injuries while rescuing stray or wounded animals. On this occasion, she'd crawled out on a tree limb and was attempting to peek inside a bird's nest when the limb broke and crashed to the ground.

Scout, like her father, is often misunderstood. June chuckles to herself now, thinking about how little her daughter has changed over the years. Her gruff exterior still throws people off. But deep down inside, she's as tender-hearted as they come.

June hears loud arguing as she's flying over their home during the kids' teenage years. She chooses not to stop. Those days are better off forgotten.

June arrives at her proudest moment, the day Ford signs to

play football for Alabama. Other parents congratulate June on a job well done. But she refuses to take the credit. Ford has done it all himself. He's made his dreams come true. He was disappointed about Georgia at first. But he's come around as she knew he would. Kids are resilient that way. At least that's what she'd thought at the time.

She attends both children's high school graduations, stands at the window watching Phillip and Kate drive away on a gloomy December morning, and lands on the sofa in front of a roaring fire the January night Buford returns home from Washington at the end of his senate term.

"I'm taking a break from politics," Buford says out of the blue.

June looks up from her needlepoint in surprise. "How long of a break?"

"I'm not sure. I may never go back." He drains the last of his bourbon and gets up for a refill.

"Have you given up on running for president?"

"Washington is a cesspool. Two senate terms are enough." When he returns to the sofa, he sits down closer to her. "I may run for local office down the road. For now, I want to spend time with you."

"That would be nice. We've grown apart while you were away. Maybe we can remedy that." She rolls up the pillow canvas she's working on and stuffs it in her needlepoint bag.

"We've been through some difficult times these past few years. I've made some mistakes, but so have you." He pauses, and she wonders what mistakes he's referring to. Is it possible he knows about Phillip? When she doesn't defend herself, he goes on, "But we've been given an opportunity to make a fresh start. We're empty nesters now. We can travel and entertain, be the fun-loving couple we once were."

"I'd like that," June says softly.

After so many years, June is thrilled to be her husband's primary focus, and they fall in love all over again. He brings her elaborate bouquets of flowers home from work and buys her expensive jewelry. They travel to Europe and Costa Rica and go on safari in South Africa. June is as happy as she could ever hope to be. She misses her children, but Mary Beth's presence in her life lessens the constant ache for Ford and Scout.

On a Wednesday afternoon five years after Ford ran away, June finds herself at the stove in their old kitchen, preparing dinner for Buford. Her cell phone rings, and it takes a minute to locate it at the bottom of her purse. She doesn't recognize the area code or the number, but she answers it anyway, in case it's one of her children. She hears loud crackling, followed by Ford's faint voice. "Hey, Mom. It's me."

Gripping the phone tighter, she leans against the counter for support. "Ford. How are you? I've missed you something terrible."

"I'm fine. I followed your advice. I found success doing the thing I love the most."

"That's wonderful, son. I'm thrilled for you. Where are you?"

"I'd rather not say. It's better for our family if I stay away."

"I don't—"

"I need to go, Mom. I just wanted you to know I'm okay."

June hears a click, and the crackling disappears as the line goes dead. She stares at the phone in her hand. At least she knows he's alive.

Her last stop on her journey of life is at a hospital room on the labor and delivery ward where Mary Beth and Jeff cuddle with their newborn son. Images from the past two years flash before her eyes. Billy's birthday parties. Rocking him to sleep while singing him lullabies. Taking him on long strolls on chilly afternoons. Since Jeff's mother is deceased and Mary Beth's is in prison, June is the only grandmother he'll ever know. At least Mary Beth will miss her if she never recovers from the accident.

June is soaring through the skies like an eagle when suddenly she's spiraling downward toward the earth. A parachute breaks her fall, and she drifts slowly to her hospital room, where Buford is pouring his heart out to her.

"I made a terrible mistake, June. Things were going so well between us, and I screwed it all up. I've never been able to resist Raquel's charms. You're my rock, my wife, the love of my life. But she's my obsession." Buford gets up and walks to the window. "You were my ticket to the White House. Unfortunately, I ruined my own chances of becoming president. I'm not surprised you never heard about the scandal. We covered it up like so many other things. Someone was always throwing a wild party in Washington with drugs and underage prostitutes. But this one time, one of my peers made the drastic mistake of inviting an undercover journalist. Of course, the journalist had her price. Everyone does."

So that's why he suddenly lost interest in politics. How could he sleep with an underage prostitute? A child?

Shame on you, June. You were so naïve and gullible and afraid that you completely missed all that Buford was doing.

The earth opens up and sucks her in like a vacuum.

Chapter 30

Scout

S cout and Barrett arrive at the hospital to find the intensive care unit in chaos with alarms sounding, doctors being paged, and her father being shooed from her mother's room by a sour-faced nurse.

"What's happening?" Scout asks her father.

Buford appears shaken. "I don't know. I was talking to your mom, and her heart monitor flatlined."

"Flatlined? Is she . . ." Scout stops short, unable to say the word.

Her father shakes his head. "I don't know. The doctors are working on her now."

Scout grabs her father by the arm. "What did you say to Mom? Did you upset her?"

Buford wrenches his arm free. "None of your business, Scout. That's between your mother and me."

"Mom's in a coma, Dad. She can't hear you."

They've just sat down to await news of her mother when Kate and her father appear in the doorway. Dr. Baldwin has changed little in the years since Scout last saw him. Aside from a few gray hairs and laugh lines around his eyes, he's the same pediatrician who treated her aches and illnesses as a child.

Barrett leans in close and whispers, "Is it my imagination or did the temperature just drop twenty degrees in here?"

Scout cups her hand around her mouth. "That's Kate and her father."

"That explains it," Barrett says and gets up to greet the Baldwins.

The threesome is standing close enough to Scout for her to hear their conversation. "I'm Barrett Nunez, Scout's friend and coworker from Seattle."

Kate introduces herself and her father. "Why the long faces? Did something happen with June?"

"I'm not sure. We're waiting for more information from the doctor."

Buford jumps to his feet and strides over to Barrett. "What do you mean *we*? You've never even met my wife. And you . . ." —he shoves Kate's father—"are not welcome here."

When Phillip shoves him back, Barrett grabs a fistful of both men's shirts and holds them away from each other with arms stretched wide. "Easy there, tigers. We're in a hospital."

Buford, his face dark with anger, says to Barrett, "Let go of me, punk."

Barrett laughs out loud. "I interact with hardened criminals daily, and I've been called every name in the book. You'll have to do better than *punk* to get under my skin." He releases Phillip, but continues to grip Buford's shirt as he walks him backward to his seat. "Now sit down and cool your jets."

Scout tucks her chin to her chest to hide her smile.

When her father sits down next to her, Scout gets up to speak to Kate's father, who engulfs her in his large arms. He pulls away, bestowing upon her the warm smile she remembers so well. "If you can spare a minute, I'd like to clear the air. I know this might not be the best time to talk, but while we're waiting for an update on your mom, I'd like to say a few things now."

"Okay," Scout says, and allows him to lead her over to the window.

"Do you have children, Scout?"

"No, sir. I hope to one day, though."

"A parent always tries to do right by their child. Sometimes they hurt their other children in the process. That's what happened with Ford. He was desperate to chart his own course, away from your domineering father. He felt the only way to do that was to make a sudden exit from your lives, and I was able to help him. The situation has been the hardest on you and Kate. She got caught in the middle, and you got left hanging. She hated keeping his secret. She's begged him many times to come out of hiding."

Scout studies Phillip's kind face. It's hard to be mad at a man who genuinely cares so much about other people. She can totally see how her mother might have once been attracted to him. "If I asked you where Ford is, would you tell me?"

Phillip hesitates, as though considering her request. "I don't want to break my promise to Ford. I'd rather he tell you himself."

"But he's not here now, is he?" Scout says, unable to keep the anger out of her tone.

Before Phillip can respond, Dr. McDermott emerges from the examining rooms. Their small group huddles around him for an update. "June went into cardiac arrest. We defibrillated her, and she is currently stable. I've called in a cardiologist, and we're running more tests to determine what happened. I don't expect we'll find any major heart conditions. June is a healthy woman. Her recovery is in her hands."

"What does *in her hands* mean?" Scout asks.

"She should've woken up by now. Your mother's will to live may be the only thing that can pull her through. Science defies this notion, but I've seen it many times."

When the doctor leaves, Scout turns toward Phillip. "I've heard of this, but it seems hard to believe. Is that true? Can a person's will to live save them?"

Phillip gives her a solemn nod. "I, too, have witnessed it many times."

Buford snorts. "Hogwash. You can bring in a fortune teller, but I prefer to listen to the medical professionals."

Phillip stares down at him. "I am a medical professional, Buford."

"You're a pediatrician. Your patients are children. That doesn't count," Buford says and storms out of the waiting room.

Kate watches him go and turns back to her father. "Is there anything we can do to help June?"

"You can talk to her. Tell her how much you love her. She needs all of us right now."

"My mother needs Ford," Scout snaps, her angry glare shifting from Phillip to Kate. "Can one of you at least try to get in touch with him?"

"He can be difficult to reach. I left him a detailed message yesterday, but I haven't heard from him." Kate's fingers graze her father's arm. "Maybe he'll listen to you, Dad."

"I'll try. If he can't get away, maybe we can set up a Zoom call with him. I need to take care of a few things this morning. When I come back this afternoon, I'll bring my laptop." Phillip looks down at his daughter. "I'm going to head out. Are you staying here, or do you want me to drop you at the hotel?"

"I'll stay here. I want to find out more about June."

Barrett turns to Scout. "I may go back to your house while your mom is having these tests run. I need to check my email and makes some calls."

212

"I don't blame you. Take my rental." Scout hands him the key. "Do you mind bringing us lunch when you return? Langford Market has made-to-order sandwiches. They're about a half mile from our house in the direction opposite town."

"Got it," he says, taking the key. "Text me your order."

The others exit the waiting room, leaving Kate and Scout standing alone. "You've been holding out on me," Kate says. "Barrett is seriously hot. Are you two in a relationship?"

"We're just friends. But he's a good guy." Scout smiles at Kate as though they were ten years old again, discussing a boy in their grade.

She thinks about what Dr. Baldwin said. *The situation has been the hardest on you and Kate. She got caught in the middle, and you got left hanging.* Scout has never thought about the situation from Kate's perspective. Keeping Ford's secrets must have been difficult for her. First about him being her half-brother and then about his whereabouts.

Harboring feelings of anger toward Kate is exhausting. They're adults now. And they should act like it. For her mother's sake, if for no other reason.

"Looks like it's just you and me," Scout says. "Wanna grab some coffee and a breath of fresh air while we wait for Mom to come back? The staff knows how to reach me if anything happens."

Kate grabs her purse. "Sure! Why not?"

An awkward silence accompanies them in the elevator on the way down. When the doors open in the lobby, they exit to find Mary Beth waiting for the elevator to go up.

"How's June this morning?" Mary Beth asks, pulling them out of the line of traffic.

"She went into cardiac arrest a short time ago, but she's stable now," Scout explains. "The doctor is having more tests run."

Mary Beth's chin falls to her chest. "I was afraid of that. I woke up this morning with a bad premonition."

Scout's heart sinks. "Uh-oh. That's not good."

Kate's fingers graze Mary Beth's arm. "We're going for coffee. Wanna come?"

Mary Beth looks up, sniffling and wiping at her eyes. "Thanks, but I'm going home to cook. I always feel better when I'm working in my kitchen. Let me know if anything changes," she says and heads toward the exit.

Scout and Kate continue to the cafeteria. They take their coffees out to the angel garden and sit down on an iron bench beside a bronze water fountain of two children—a little girl pumping water from a well and the little boy cupping his hands under the stream.

Scout sags against the bench. "I'm scared, Kate. Mary Beth's premonitions almost always come true. What if Mom dies?"

"Don't give up on her, Scout. Your mama is the strongest woman I know. You heard Dad. We have to boost her spirits, offer her encouragement."

"Maybe it'll help if Mom knows you and I made peace. Do you think that's possible, Kate?" She looks up at her oldest friend. "I'm sorry for treating you so unfairly, not only these past few days but when we were growing up. I've said and done some awful things. Would you accept a blanket apology?"

Kate smiles. "As long as you'll accept one from me."

"We know so much about each other, yet we hardly know each other at all. What say we start over with a clean slate?" Scout holds a hand out to Kate.

"I'm all in." Kate shakes her hand, and they sit in silence for a minute while they sip coffee. "Tell me the truth about Barrett. And don't lie about being just friends. I can tell by the way he looks at you, he has feelings for you."

Scout's heart skips a beat. "You think so, really? I've had a crush on him since forever. But I'm not his type. He prefers beautiful dingbats."

Kate laughs. "Your type is way more intriguing."

Scout lifts an eyebrow. "Oh, really? What type is that?"

"You were a feisty little girl with a heart of gold. As far as I can tell, you haven't changed."

Scout laughs. "And you were poised and sophisticated, wise beyond your years. You don't appear to have changed either."

"I take that as a compliment."

Scout twists her body toward Kate. "Your Dad refused to tell me about Ford. He promised Ford he would keep his secret, and I respect that. But now I'm asking you. What can you tell me about him?"

Kate hesitates before responding. "Ford's situation is complicated. Because it involves your family, it's better for you to hear it from him. Just be patient for a bit longer. If we can't get in touch with him, then I'll tell you."

Scout nods. "That's fair."

They remain on the bench, talking about old times, for a long time after they've finished their coffees. Before heading back upstairs, they stand and wander around the garden admiring the bronze statues of little children in various forms of play—throwing a ball, jumping rope, and carrying a bouquet of balloons. The last statue is of a little boy in a raincoat and wellies with his plump puppy at his feet. A plaque announces the dedication of the angel garden to the town's beloved pediatrician—Dr. Phillip Baldwin.

"Did you know about this?" Scout asks, her mouth agape.

"I did. But this is the first time I've seen it. The parents of one of Dad's patients spearheaded the project. The kid had leukemia, and Dad, as he does with all his patients, went above and beyond the call of duty to seek treatment. Fortunately, the little boy survived. Each statue was donated by parents of a sick child whom Dad helped."

"That is so touching. Does your father's healing wand work for adults? Maybe he'll wave it at Mom."

"In this case, the wand is in June's hands."

Barrett is waiting for them when they return to the fourth floor. Scout plops down in the chair next to him. "We went downstairs for coffee. Any word about Mom?"

"I asked at the nurses' station. She's back from her tests and sleeping peacefully."

"That's good. I'll go see her in a minute."

"I met Betty. She packed us a picnic." Barrett gestures at the picnic basket at his feet. "But she had some disturbing news. Your father packed up all his clothes and took off without telling her where he was going."

"That's actually the best news I've had in a while. I'm starving. What did Betty make for us?" Scout lifts the basket onto her lap and peeks inside. "Ooh, Kate! All our favorites are here. Fried chicken legs, pimento cheese sandwiches, deviled eggs, and those miniature cream-filled brownie cupcakes she always made. You're obligated to help us eat it."

"For sure," Barrett says. "I watched Betty pack the basket. There's enough food in there to feed the staff."

"I'm tempted. But I should see what Dad's doing for lunch first." Kate pulls her phone out of her pocket. "He's calling me now," she says and takes the phone over by the window.

Barrett sinks his teeth into a pimento cheese sandwich. "What happened between you and Kate while I was gone? The frostiness between you two has melted."

"We apologized and agreed to make a fresh start," Scout says and takes a bite out of a chicken leg.

"That's great news." Barrett stuffs the sandwich half in his mouth and reaches for a deviled egg.

Scout gnaws the chicken down to the bone, drops it into the trash can, and wipes her hands with a napkin before squirting them with Purell. "I'm going to see Mom. Wish me luck."

Barrett gets up and walks her to the automatic doors. "Okay. Good luck. But why do you think you need it?"

"Because I have no clue what to say to bring Mom back to us."

Barrett takes hold of her arms. "Don't put that kind of pressure on yourself, Scout. You are not responsible for saving your mom."

"Really? Because it feels like I am. Ford isn't here, and Dad has left town. I'm the only one in the family she has left."

Her burden weighs heavily on Scout as she continues through the double doors.

Chapter 31

Kate

"Did you see Honey?" Kate blurts when she accepts her father's call.

"I did, and I'll tell you about it when I see you. Any word on June's condition?"

"Only that she's back from her tests." Across the waiting room, Kate notices Scout talking to Barrett in front of the entrance to the ICU. "Scout's going in to see her now. Were you able to get in touch with Ford?"

"Nope. I left him an urgent message, and I'll keep trying. I'm out in front of the hospital. Can I interest you in taking a walk and grabbing a bite of lunch? We can come back later to see June, since Scout is in with her now."

"That sounds great. I'll be down in a few."

Pocketing her phone, Kate stops to speak to Barrett on her way out. "I'm going to grab lunch with my dad. We'll be back later to visit June. Please tell Scout that Dad could not reach Ford, but he'll keep trying until he does."

"Will do. I'll make sure Scout texts you if there's any change in June's condition while you're gone."

Kate leaves the waiting room and takes the elevator down to

the first floor. Locating her father's rental car in front of the hospital, she slides into the passenger seat.

"Tell me about Honey. Was it her?"

"Oh, yeah. It's definitely her. She's still the same free-spirited girl I married." He chuckles. "We're so different. I'm not sure how we ever ended up together. You were the one good thing that came out of the marriage." His expression grows serious. "Honey is burdened by shame, sweetheart. I assured her you're not a vindictive person, that you just want to know her. I'm sure she'll come around in time."

"By *time*, do you mean days, weeks, or months?"

"I have no clue. Honey does things on her own terms. She could be waiting for us at the hotel when we return from lunch, or she's liable to show up at your office in New York six months from now."

"Or I might never hear from her again."

Her father glances over at her. "I doubt that. She obviously loves you very much. She admitted to keeping tabs on you all these years."

Kate wonders what *tabs* her mother has been keeping. "On a brighter note, Scout and I have declared a cease-fire," she says and tells him about her visit to the angel garden with Scout.

"I'm thrilled to hear it. As little girls, you two got along beautifully despite your very different personalities. You were happy digging in the sandbox with her, and she let you dress her up in June's clothes."

Kate laughs. "I remember. I was an aspiring fashion designer from an early age."

Phillip makes a right-hand turn onto Meeting Avenue. "When you share a long history with a friend, you naturally encounter bumps in the road. In yours and Scout's case, they were craters. But it adds depth to your relationship. You may

219

have to work harder to get along because you are so different. But I believe your friendship is one worth nurturing."

"I think so too, Dad."

They leave Phillip's car in the hotel garage and walk a mile and a half to Langford's Market. They order sliced chicken on whole wheat wraps with the market's signature tangy sauce and take their sandwiches outside to the sidewalk terrace. While they eat, Phillip finally opens up, after all these years, about the difficulties in his marriage to her mother.

On the way back to the hotel, Kate guides her father on a detour past the gray bungalow. "I'm considering renting it. What do you think?"

He smiles down at her. "I knew it. You *do* have the small-town bug."

"Maybe. Do you think I'm crazy? You know how I've always wanted to expand my business into clothing. According to Lance, the house has a sunny office in the back that sounds perfect for a design studio. Who knows? A quiet retreat from New York might boost my creativity."

"Then go for it! You have nothing to lose. Renting is the best way to test the waters, to find out if living in a small town is a good fit for you."

"I think so too. I'll at least call about it." Kate snaps a pic of the sign with the owner's phone number. "A one-year lease will give me plenty of time to sort out my life."

"And for you and Lance to get engaged."

"You're incorrigible." She loops an arm through his, dragging him down the street.

They're nearing the hotel when Mary Beth calls. "I've been cooking all morning, and I'm inviting everyone over for dinner to help eat all this food. At a time like this, we should all be together. We have to eat anyway."

"You don't need to convince me, Mary Beth. I would love to come to dinner. But my dad's in town."

"Bring him! Lance too! Tell your dad I can't wait to see him. Six o'clock and dress casually."

"We'll be there," Kate says and drops her phone in her purse. "That was Mary Beth. She invited us to dinner. I hope you don't mind."

"That suits me fine," Phillip says. "It'll be good to see Mary Beth again. She was always one of my favorites."

Kate smiles. "She's a truly genuine person. How long are you planning to stay in Langford, Dad?"

"Until June comes out of the coma," he says with certainty and without hesitation.

"You don't sound worried."

"I have faith in June. She's strong, and she has all of us rooting for her. She's going to pull through."

"I hope you're right," Kate says, but she lacks her father's confidence. June's world has crashed down around her, and after all she's been through, she may very well have lost her will to live.

On the sidewalk in front of the hotel, Phillip says, "I need to return some emails, and you need to call the woman about the rental house." He glances at his watch. "Why don't we meet in the lobby at four. That should give us plenty of time to stop by the hospital on the way to dinner."

"Sounds like a plan."

When they enter the hotel, Kate spots Lance at the front desk. "Go ahead up, Dad. I'm going to invite Lance to dinner."

"Tell Lance I look forward to catching up," her father says, and kisses her cheek in parting.

Lance smiles when he sees Kate heading his way. "I checked your reservation, and I was glad to see you haven't checked out yet."

She gives him a scolding look. "I wouldn't leave without saying goodbye. I'm staying until June is out of the woods anyway. Mary Beth has invited everyone to dinner. Are you free?"

Lance frowns. "I am. But it sounds like a family affair, and I'd hate to impose."

"You're not imposing, although you may be bored. June will undoubtedly be the topic of conversation."

He grins, and his blue eyes twinkle. "I could never be bored in your presence."

Her face warms. "Stop! You're making me blush."

He leans across the counter and whispers, "I can think of other ways to make you blush."

"You're a naughty man," she teases as she backs away from the counter. "Dad and I are going by the hospital first. Meet you at Mary Beth's at six? I'll text you her address."

"It's a small town, Kate. I know where everyone lives."

The notion of small-town living continues to grow on Kate in the elevator. As soon as she reaches the privacy of her room, she places a call to Robyn Hart.

"I'm sorry. You're thirty minutes too late. I just rented the house to a young couple. I have your number, though. I can call you in case it doesn't work out."

Kate's heart sinks. "That would be great. My name is Kate Baldwin."

"Wait! Kate Baldwin the fashion designer?"

Kate smiles. "One and the same."

"Oh my gosh! I'm a huge fan. I heard you were originally from Langford. I have your suede driving moccasins in nearly every color. I've worn out my black ones. Will you ever make them in black again?"

"Actually, black is back in stock this season. Text me your

size and address, and I'll have a new pair shipped to you." Giving away free products is Kate's favorite part of the job.

"Really? That'd be awesome." Robyn pauses a beat. "I probably shouldn't say this, but I hope the couple changes their mind about the house. I'd love to rent it to you."

Kate's heartbeat quickens. "Is that a possibility?"

"Maybe. They seemed concerned about the small size. They're hoping to start a family soon."

"Well, definitely keep me posted if anything changes."

Kate spends an hour communicating with her New York office, arranging to stay through the upcoming weekend. She showers, takes extra care in applying her makeup, and dresses in jeans and a soft pink oversized silk blouse.

Because her father gets tied up on the phone with a patient, they don't leave the hotel for the hospital until five o'clock. When they arrive, a nurse informs them that June isn't allowed visitors but refuses to provide any additional information.

Phillip pulls Kate away from the nurses' station. "I see June's doctor in the room with her now. Marcus is an old friend. I'm going to see if I can have a word with him about her condition. I'll be right back."

From the bustling hall outside June's room, Kate watches her father's face as he converses with the doctor. His grave expression gives her cause for alarm. When he finally emerges, Phillip takes Kate by the arm and leads her into the waiting room.

"What's going on, Dad? You're scaring me."

Her father hangs his head. "June's numbers are deteriorating. Her doctor is experimenting with some different meds and wants to keep her quiet while they wait for her reaction."

Kate narrows her brown eyes. "Shouldn't Scout be here?"

"Apparently, she's been here most of the day and is planning to return after dinner. Marcus isn't concerned enough to call her back yet. He asked if we'd seen Buford. He hasn't spoken to him since this morning."

"I forgot to tell you. According to Betty, the Montgomerys' housekeeper, Buford packed up all his clothes and took off."

Her father shakes his head, as though disappointed in Buford's behavior. "Poor Scout shouldn't be alone at a time like this."

"She's not alone, Dad. She has us. And Barrett. It's probably a good thing Buford is gone. Whatever he said to June this morning sent her into cardiac arrest."

"In that case, I say good riddance." He motions Kate toward the door. "We might as well head out since there's nothing we can do for June here. Marcus promised to call me if anything changes."

On the drive over to Mary Beth's, Kate presses her father for details about June's decline. He says little, but his mood is pensive. She fears they could be in for a long night ahead.

Chapter 32

Scout

Scout returns from a long run to find Barrett seated at the kitchen counter nursing a beer. She grabs a bottled water from the refrigerator and sits down beside him. "For Mary Beth's sake, I feel obligated to go to this dinner, but I'm not planning to stay long. You can stay here and order takeout if you'd like."

Barrett jumps to his feet. "Are you kidding me? I can't wait to meet Mary Beth."

"Are you sure? I feel bad. I'm not doing a very good job of entertaining you."

Barrett pulls her off the stool to her feet. "I didn't come to Alabama looking for a wild time. I'm here to support you, Scout."

Scout tears off a sheet of paper towel and wipes the sweat from her face. "But we spent the whole day at the hospital."

"And we'll go back tonight after dinner. Your mom's in a coma. She needs her family and friends right now." He spins her around and marches her out into the hall. "Now go get ready or we'll be late."

Scout takes a cold shower and dresses in jeans and a button-up black blouse with a flared hem. Twenty minutes later, when she returns to the kitchen, she retrieves a case of wine from the pantry and deposits it in Barrett's arms. "Here! Carry this. More leftover wine from Dad's political dinner party."

Barrett's brow hits his hairline. "You're taking Mary Beth a whole case of wine? How many people is she having tonight?"

"It's a hostess gift. There's several more cases left. I assume Dad doesn't want it, since he left it behind when he moved out."

Barrett tucks the case under one arm as he follows her outside. "Oh. I see how it is. You're giving away his wine out of spite."

"Exactly," Scout says over her shoulder.

Scout and Barrett are the last to arrive at Mary Beth's. Barrett takes the case of wine to the kitchen, leaving Scout and Mary Beth alone at the door.

"We'll eat soon," Mary Beth says. "I know you're anxious to get back to the hospital."

"Please don't rush on my account. Dr. McDermott promised to call if Mom's condition changes."

"How did your visit with her go today?" Mary Beth asks.

"I spent most of the afternoon in her room. I talked about everything I could think of. My runaways and dreary apartment in Seattle. I relived old times, holidays when my grandparents were still alive, and our beach vacations. Sadly, nothing I said elicited a response from her. I'm really worried, Mary Beth. She's gotta wake up soon."

"She was in a serious accident, Scout. You can't expect her to just sit up in bed as though nothing happened."

"I guess you're right."

Barrett returns with two tequilas on the rocks, and Mary Beth excuses herself to go in the kitchen. Ten minutes later, she announces dinner, and they move to the round table on the terrace.

Scout and Barrett sit down together with Kate and Lance to her right, Mary Beth and Jeff to his left, and Phillip directly across from them. Scout drops her napkin in her lap. "This is lovely, Mary Beth. Mama would be proud."

"I cut the roses from her garden," Mary Beth says as she nods toward the enormous centerpiece. "I don't think she'd mind. She's with us in spirit."

The table goes silent with all eyes on Mary Beth.

Mary Beth stills. "What? Did I say something wrong?"

Jeff drapes an arm around her. "If she's with us in spirit, that means her spirit has left her body. Which is obviously not what we want."

Mary Beth appears flustered. "Oh gosh! I'm so sorry."

"Don't worry about it," Scout says. "We knew what you meant."

Jeff delivers a touching blessing, and Scout sinks her fork into the gooey lasagna. "This is delicious, Mary Beth."

"Thank you. I experimented today by using both hamburger meat and ground Italian sausage. I made the sauce from scratch with canned summer tomatoes and the cheeses . . ." She giggles. "There's nothing low-fat about these cheeses."

"Well, you outdid yourself." Scout takes another bite and levels her gaze on Phillip. "Have you had any luck reaching Ford?"

Phillip gives his head a grave shake. "Not yet. He lives in a remote area and is often out of cell service range. I left several messages. I'm not sure why he hasn't called me back. Except that this is his busy season."

Kate drops her fork on the plate with a clatter. "Tell them, Dad. It's not fair to any of us to keep his location a secret any longer."

Phillip looks uncertainly at the faces eagerly watching him. "I don't think Ford would—"

"I don't care what Ford wants," Kate says, her face tight with anger. "We both left messages for Ford, explaining the gravity of the situation, and he can't even be bothered to call us back. The world doesn't revolve around Ford. Scout and Mary Beth love him too. They have a right to know where he is."

Phillip hesitates. "I don't know . . ."

"Then I'll tell them." Kate's brown eyes leave her father and settle on Scout. "Ford is in Alaska. He lives in a remote area and owns his own adventure fly-fishing tour company."

Phillip lets out a reluctant sigh. "Kate is right. You all deserve to know the truth. I'm proud of Ford. He's done well for himself. He pilots his own floatplane and takes his clients deep into the wilderness."

Scout sits back in her chair, her appetite vanished. She's not sure whether to feel relieved or angry. "Typical of Ford. He's off fishing, and we're down here in the lower forty-eight holding vigil while Mom fights for her life."

"Ford would be here if he could. He may not have gotten our messages." Phillip's tone falls short of convincing Scout.

"Is he married?" Mary Beth asks, forking her salad.

Phillip chimes in, "No. He's a bit of a recluse. He lives in the middle of nowhere with a pack of Alaskan huskies. But he's close friends with his veterinarian. I think she's sweet on him." Phillip chuckles. "He likes her too. He just doesn't know it yet."

"He's still really into his music," Kate says. "He writes songs in his spare time. He's sold several to famous country music singers. Have you heard that current top hit by Rex Bell?"

Mary Beth's face lights up. "'Sunshine?' I love that song!"

Scout's heart sinks as the song's lyrics about a brother's love for his little sister come back to her. Ford undoubtedly had his beloved Kate in mind when he wrote the song.

Barrett chimes in. "I'm not much of a country music fan, but even I like that song."

Phillip continues, "Ford's success has restored his self-confidence. He's found himself, and he's pursuing the life he wants to live. He knows how to show his clients a good time, and has a long waiting list for his tours."

"What makes his guided trips adventurous?" Lance asks, which leads to a lengthy discussion about the many opportunities to explore the Alaskan wilderness.

Scout eats in silence as she processes this new information about Ford. The words *restored his self-confidence* ring out in her mind and make her soften toward her brother. Her father destroyed Ford's confidence like he destroyed their family. If it's the last thing she does, Scout will make him pay.

Phillip removes his cell phone from the inside pocket of his sport coat. "Excuse me. I need to take this." He leaves the table, and with the phone pressed to his ear, he wanders to the back corner of the yard. When he returns, his face is grave. "Scout, we need to get you to the hospital. Your mother has made a turn for the worst."

Scout's heart pounds against rib cage. She checks her phone. "Why didn't Dr. McDermott call me?"

Phillip helps Scout up from her chair. "I spoke with him earlier when I stopped by the hospital. I told him I was having dinner with you. He thought it best for you to hear the news from me."

"What exactly did he say? What's wrong with Mom?" she asks, her eyes wide with fear.

"Her organs are shutting down, Scout. The medical professionals have done all they can. The rest is up to June."

Chapter 33

Kate

Kate says goodbye to Lance on Mary Beth's front porch.

"I'll be praying for you all," Lance says, taking her in his arms.

"What if she dies?" Kate cries. "I've never lost anyone close to me before. I had no idea it could hurt so much."

Lance kisses her hair. "June will pull through. How can she not when she's surrounded by so much love and support?"

Kate buries her face in his chest. "I don't want to leave you, Lance. I feel safe in your arms. It's so familiar, like we're back in high school again and the last seventeen years never happened." She looks up at him. "I wanted you to know how I feel, even though now is not the appropriate time to be talking about us."

"I disagree. In times of crisis, when a loved one's life is in jeopardy, it's the right time to be expressing our emotions. Once June is on the path to recovery, I'm treating you to a fancy dinner out, and then I'm taking you home to my bed," he says in a husky voice.

Kate smiles. "Let's skip the dinner out and eat in. We'll be closer to the bedroom."

"I like the sound of that." Lance looks past her to the street. "Your father is waiting." Taking her by the hand, he walks Kate down the sidewalk to the curb and tucks her into the car.

"How bad is it, Dad?" Kate asks on the way to the hospital.

"I only spoke with McDermott briefly. He'll tell us more when we get to the hospital. But it's not good."

Kate and Phillip arrive at the same time as Scout, Barrett, and Mary Beth. They've no sooner entered the waiting room than McDermott emerges through the familiar double doors.

"I'm extremely concerned. She's not responding to any of the treatments. There's no apparent reason for the coma and organ failure. I'm consulting with more specialists to make sure I haven't missed anything, although I don't think I have."

"Can we see her?" Scout asks, biting down on a quivering lower lip.

The doctor's gray eyes travel the group. "Of course. One at a time, and please keep your visits short. Be encouraging. Don't say anything that might upset her. She needs her loved ones right now." His eyes land on Scout. "I've been trying to reach your father. He's not returning my calls. If you can get in touch with him, please let him know what's happening."

Scout watches the doctor's retreating back before looking down at her phone. "I'll send Dad a text that'll get his attention." Her thumbs fly across the screen. *Where are you, Dad? Mom is dying. You should be here.*

Mary Beth places an arm around Scout's shoulders. "I'm so sorry, Scout. I don't know what's gotten into Buford."

"Nothing's gotten *into* Buford. This is him. He's a real jackass. You should know that, Mary Beth. You lived with us for half your life."

"I admit he can be a jerk. But I've also known him to be very generous and compassionate."

"Maybe to you," Scout mumbles as she drops to a chair.

"You all can go ahead in to see Mom. I spent most of the afternoon with her."

Kate gives Mary Beth a gentle shove toward the double doors. "You're up first."

"I won't be long," Mary Beth says and hurries off.

As she awaits her turn, Kate eavesdrops on the other occupants in the waiting room. They appear to be one large family. Their loved one's days are numbered. There's talk of sending her home and calling in hospice. But at ninety-four, she's lived a good life. She's not even dead yet, and they're already making plans for her funeral and discussing the disbursement of her property.

June is still so young, with so much life ahead of her. She can't die on them now.

Mary Beth returns to the waiting room, but instead of taking a seat, she goes to stand by the window, her shoulders heaving as she cries into a wad of tissues. When Scout gets up to comfort her, Kate slips away to see June.

Kate is taken aback by June's deathlike pallor. She'd been so healthy, so alive, when she'd seen her the day of Alice's funeral.

She pulls a chair close to the bed and forces herself to sound cheerful. "So, I'm thinking of moving back to Langford. Part-time, of course. I need some creative space to work on my new clothing line. The first piece will be a thigh-length cashmere wrap coat. Powder blue like the one you had when I was little. I loved that coat. You always looked so pretty and feminine in it. We'll make the coat in the same soft shade of blue and call it The June."

Kate takes June's cold hand in hers. "Growing up without a mother wasn't easy. But you treated me like one of your own. I will always be grateful for the love and compassion you showed me. I'm sorry we lost touch after I moved to New York. I didn't realize just how much I missed you until now. You are one reason I want to spend more time here.

"Lance Reid is another reason. Do you remember him? He was my high school boyfriend. I'm going to marry Lance." Kate snickers. "I can't believe I just said that. But it's true. I love him. I never stopped loving him. I'm going to have his children, and I want you to be their surrogate grandmother.

"Please come back to us, Miss June. We all need you. Don't give up the fight. We're all here waiting for you. Dad is coming in to see you soon. He still loves you, and I think you have feelings for him. After all you've been through, you two deserve happiness. Don't let go of life yet."

Kate squeezes June's hand before letting go. "I love you, Miss June," she whispers as the first tears spill from her eyelids.

Her father is waiting outside the double doors. Not trusting her voice, she nods at him, and he kisses her cheek before disappearing down the hall to June's room.

Kate finds a seat and scrolls through her emails with one eye on the double doors. When Phillip emerges some forty-five minutes later, he passes through the waiting room and out the other door without speaking to anyone.

Kate overhears Barrett say to Scout, "Even though I've never met your mom, I feel like I know her. Would it be okay for me to say a few words to her?"

Scout's lips curve in a tender smile. "She'd like that. If anyone can get through to her, you can."

Barrett is smiling when he returns, but his dark eyes are sad. "She's as lovely as her daughter."

He pulls Scout to her feet and pats her bottom, sending her off to see her mother. But she's back in a flash, offering no explanation about her brief visit.

The night wears on at a snail's pace. Just after midnight, a young female doctor appears, and the family of the ninety-four-year-old huddles around her. Some cry openly while others listen with faces set in stone. After the doctor delivers the sad news, they collect their belongings and file out of the waiting room.

Her father returns with swollen eyes and sits down next to Kate. When she notices him checking his phone repeatedly, she asks, "Do you have a patient in crisis?"

"No. I'm still trying to get in touch with Ford."

Kate rolls her eyes. "Why bother? He's not coming."

"He might. You never know," Phillip says, dropping his phone in his lap.

"Why don't you go back to the hotel?" she suggests. "I'm going to stay here, at least until we get an update. There's no sense in both of us missing out on sleep."

Phillip shakes his head. "I'm not leaving. Not until . . ." His voice trails off.

"Are you sure? I could call you if something happens."

Her father pats her arm. "I appreciate that, sweetheart. I just feel the need to be here."

"Suit yourself." Kate excuses herself to use the restroom and takes the elevator down to the chapel on the first floor. Flickering candles on the altar cast a soft glow on the wood-paneled room. Making her way to the front pew, she sits down and bows her head. The silence calms her as she prays for June's recovery.

Kate nearly jumps out of her skin when she feels a hand on her back. Turning around in her pew, she's stunned to see Honey. "Geez! You scared me to death!" she says with a hand over her pounding heart.

Honey, her blue eyes misty with tears, says, "I've imagined this moment many times, but now that we're here, I have no idea what to say."

Kate softens as her heart rate slows. "You don't have to say anything. I'm just glad you're here."

Honey moves to the front pew beside Kate. They study each other for a long minute. Kate has her father's eyes and dimple, but her upturned nose and round face are her mother's.

"I was furious at your father for making me leave California. I was a wild child, not yet ready to be a wife or a mother. I felt like such a failure, unable to live up to your father's expectations. Having June Montgomery living next door didn't help. She was everything in a wife and mother I could never be."

"I understand. Dad sets the bar high."

"That's what you want from your parent. He did a lovely job with you," Honey says, fingering a lock of Kate's hair. "I often felt like his child. Sometimes his patient."

A faraway expression crosses Kate's face as she remembers the past. "He treats all his patients like his own children."

Honey's face hardens. "He loved June from the beginning. I saw it in his eyes."

Kate nods. "He'll be devastated if she doesn't make it."

"June will pull through," Honey says with confidence, as though she knows more than the doctors.

Kate shifts on the pew toward Honey. "I'm curious. Why didn't you go back to California if you missed it so much?"

Honey tugs a small glass vial with a cork top out of her pocket and rubs it between her palms. "I go to California every year for a couple of weeks. When I left your father, I was in no shape to go anywhere. I moved in with some women at the artist colony. Those women are now my sisters. They saved me from myself. With their support, I was able to get off the drugs. I've been clean now for twenty years."

"Good for you," Kate says, feeling no animosity toward her mother for her drug addiction.

"I visit New York for a few days every year as well."

This surprises Kate. Her mother doesn't seem like the big city type. "Why New York?"

"Because that's where you live, sweetheart."

"I'm flattered. Were you ever tempted to speak to me?"

"Every single time I saw you."

Kate smiles at the thought of her mother watching her from behind every street corner. "I'm thinking of renting a house in Langford. I'd like to get to know you. I want to hear about the past, but I'm more interested in you as a person."

"That would be lovely." With a naughty twinkle in her eye, Honey asks, "Does this potential move have anything to do with a handsome young man with dark wavy hair and shocking blue eyes?"

Kate's face warms. "How do you know so much about me?"

"I'm an expert at making myself invisible while eavesdropping on people's conversations. I never approached you because I assumed you resented me for abandoning you. And I don't handle rejection well."

Kate pauses while she considers her response. "Dad would never let me feel sorry for myself because I didn't have a mother. He never said an unkind word about you to me. Now that I know about your addiction problem, everything makes more sense. As you said earlier, you did me a favor by leaving me in Dad's very capable hands." She lowers her gaze. "While I don't harbor any animosity, I regret all the years I could've known you."

"It's not too late. We're both here now. We can make up for lost time," Honey says, inching close enough to Kate for her to feel the warmth of her thigh. She's a living, breathing woman, her own flesh and blood. They can't change the past. But they can build a relationship for the future.

Kate smiles. "I'd like that very much." She eyes the glass vial. "What's in there?"

"A lock of your hair that I cut the day I left." She holds up the vial for Kate to see. "I put it in here to preserve it. I always keep it with me. Somehow, it makes me feel closer to you."

The gesture touches Kate. She wishes she'd had a relic of her mother's to treasure over the years. She reminds herself not to criticize. Her father did his best as a single parent. And his best was good enough for her.

Kate and Honey sit together in comfortable silence. Lowering her head, Kate closes her eyes and praises God for bringing one mother back to her and pleading with him to save the other.

Chapter 34

June

The sweet sound of Mary Beth's voice draws June away from her warm cocoon and back to her hospital room.

Seated on the edge of the bed, Mary Beth strokes June's thigh through the blanket. "Thank you for everything you've done for me over the years. You've been a true mother in every sense of the word. I'm not ready to lose you. I need you. And Billy needs his grandmama. You nurture us every single day in so many ways, ways you're not even aware of."

Mary Beth moves from the bed to the chair. "I understand you're hurt. Buford fooled me too. I remember our turbulent teenage years when he was so awful to Ford. But he never treated me with anything but kindness. Better that you found out the truth now. You're young and fit and beautiful. You'll find happiness again. True happiness with someone more deserving than Buford."

Rummaging through her purse, Mary Beth removes a spray bottle and spritzes the air with magnolia scented oil. "Since you're not allowed to have candles, I experimented with some products and came up with a spray form of your signature scent. Isn't it nice?" She sniffs the air. "I think you should market your candles. Maybe even expand to diffusers and plugins. I'll help you develop your brand. You'll need a website and packaging and an advertising campaign. Starting your own business would give you something to focus on and help you forget about Buford." She sets the spray bottle on the bed table. "We can talk more about it later, when you're feeling better."

Mary Beth places her warm hand over June's. "Did Scout tell you she and Kate called a truce? Isn't that wonderful? I have a hunch they'll both be spending more time in Langford from now on. Phillip's here too. He's in the other room, waiting his turn to visit you. He seems to really care about you, June. Maybe he's your ticket to happily ever after." She presses her lips to June's cheek. "Please, come back to us, June. You've done so much for us. Now it's our turn to help you."

The mention of Phillip's name sends June back to the safety of her cocoon. She can see Kate when she enters the room, but because she's so far away, she has to work hard to hear her. Kate talks of designing an article of clothing in June's honor. June remembers that powder blue wrap coat well. It may still be in the back of her closet. Who knows? Maybe they will bury her in it.

When Phillip visits her bedside, June fights the strong desire to be near him. But wait. He's talking about Ford's disappearance. She gives in and ventures a little closer.

"Ford stowed away in the back of my car. We were more than halfway to New York before he made himself known. When I insisted he call you, he refused. He threatened to run away from me, and I couldn't let that happen."

Phillip sits back in his chair, crossing his long legs. "Ford was desperate to put as much distance between himself and Buford as possible. I helped him change his name. He goes by Jay Baldwin now. I bought him an airline ticket to Anchorage and paid for his college. He's become one of the most sought-after fly-fishing guides in Alaska. You would be proud of him, June. He's really made a name for himself. He gives you credit for encouraging him to make a success out of the thing he loves the most."

Phillip pulls his phone out of his pocket. "I've been trying to reach him. He would want to be here." He drags a finger down the screen. "He's hard to get in touch with when he's out in the wilderness. Sometimes it takes days to reach him. As soon as he's available, I'll arrange for a Zoom call. I want you to hear his voice."

He places the phone in his lap. "I'm sorry I stayed away for so long. But I couldn't stand to see you with Buford. I never stopped loving you, June. Not a day has passed when I haven't thought of you. I've lost count of all the women I've dated, but none of them hold a candle to you." Phillip chokes back a sob. "Don't leave me now. If you give me another chance, I can make you happy. I'll resign from my position at the hospital and move anywhere with you. To Seattle to be near Scout. Or we can retire to sunny Florida. Or we can grow old together right here in Langford."

Slowly rising from his chair, Phillip kisses her lightly on the lips before trudging out of the room.

June is hovering near the ceiling, replaying Phillip's one-sided conversation, when a young man with shoulder-length hair, a scruffy beard, and dark soulful eyes enters the room.

He introduces himself as Barrett Nunez, Scout's coworker and friend from Seattle. "I hope you don't mind me being here. We've never officially met, but I've heard so much about you, I feel like I know you already." He leans in to study June's face. "I see where your daughter gets her good looks." He brings a finger to his lips. "Shh! Between you and me, I'm crazy in love with your daughter. I have been for some time. Problem is, she's stuck in the past. Or she has been until now. God willing, her recent discoveries about Ford will provide the closure she needs to move on with her life."

Moving to the edge of his chair, Barrett plants his elbows on his knees and picks at a loose thread on her blanket. "Whether or not you realize it. Scout admires you. I get the impression she'd like to be more like you."

June thinks he's lying, but she appreciates his efforts. This young man gives her a warm and fuzzy feeling.

"I personally think Scout is perfect the way she is, the spirited girl who has stolen my heart." He stands to go. "Thanks for letting me drop by. I look forward to seeing you again soon under more pleasant circumstances. I have a feeling you and I will be good friends."

June is disappointed when he leaves. She suddenly wants to know more about this young man who might one day be her son-in-law.

Instead of returning to the light, June drifts up to the clouds. She's floating around in the sky when a powerful force snatches her back to her hospital room, where a new visitor is seated beside her bed. He's changed drastically since the last time she saw him. He's no longer a muscular football player, but a lean young man with hair past his collar and a full beard covering his face. But his golden eyes are the same. His name is on her lips. "Ford."

He shivers, as though he hears her. "Hi, Mom. I'm long overdue a visit, and I'm sorry it's under such dire circumstances."

He removes a flask from the pocket of his windbreaker and takes a swig. He doesn't appear drunk. Does he need liquid courage to face her?

"I . . . um . . . I'm not sure what to say. I live in Alaska now," he says and talks for a few minutes about his life as a fly-fishing guide. "I couldn't take it anymore, Mom. Buford was making all your lives miserable because of me. I had to get out of the way so you, Scout, and Mary Beth could live in peace."

Ford begins to cry. "I never meant to hurt anyone, most especially you. That was such a confusing time for me. Buford is a despicable man. It was my responsibility to protect you from him, and I failed you." He wipes his nose with the back of his hand. "I told myself if I ever came home, I would turn myself into the police. I kept postponing my trip, knowing I would likely go to prison. I came here to make it right. It is time for me to own up to my sins."

Leaning in close, what Ford says next stops June's heart.

Chapter 35

Scout

Alarms sound in the intensive care unit, waking Scout from a light sleep. The double doors open and out walks a modern-day Grizzly Adams. Her mouth hits the floor. Peering over the top of his dark beard are her brother's frightened brown eyes.

Scout marches over to him. "What's going on in there?" she asks, pointing through the still opened double doors where nurses and doctors swarm their mother's room.

"I tried to tell her the truth about my disappearance, and a monitor over her head let out a loud beeping noise. A nurse came in and kicked me out. I have no clue what happened."

"She's dying is what's happening. Her organs are shutting down for no apparent reason except that she's lost her will to live. And your sudden reappearance may have driven her over the edge."

"I'm sorry, Scout. I didn't know."

Scout brushes past him. "Stay here while I find out more."

She hurries down the hall and slips unseen into her mother's room. From the conversation between nurses and doctors, she confirms that her mother flatlined again, but they revived her.

A young doctor in blue scrubs scrutinizes the monitors. "She's going downhill fast. I'll notify the family. I'm not sure she'll make it to morning."

Scout waits for the room to clear before crawling into the hospital bed and nestling up close to her mother's lifeless body. The wall she's built around her all these years crumbles, and the words she's been searching for find the way to her lips.

"Please don't die, Mama. I need you here with me. I was wrong to cut you out of my life, and I'm so very sorry. If you'll give me another chance, I promise to make it up to you. I'll come home for long visits, and you can fly out to Seattle to see me. I'll rent a new apartment, one that feels like a home with two bedrooms, so you don't have to stay in a hotel. I want you to meet Barrett, and my other friends, and the runaways. And I want to get married and give you grandchildren so you can be proud when you show their pictures to your friends.

"I don't care what happened in the past. None of that matters anymore. I only care about the future. Our future, Mama. Yours and mine. Mother and daughter together at last. We're survivors. We're strong women who don't give up without a fight. Fight, Mama, fight."

She bursts into tears. "I can't bear it if you leave me. Don't go, Mama. Please don't go."

Scout sobs herself to sleep. When she wakes, rays of sun are streaming through the window, and her mother's blue eyes are watching her. She sits bolt upright. "You're alive!"

"Thanks to you, I am. Your heartfelt speech brought me back."

Scout's eyes grow wide. "You mean you heard me?"

June nods. "Every single word."

She throws herself onto June's chest. "Never do that to me again. You scared the hell out of me."

June strokes her hair. "Now that I have you back in my life, I'll have no reason to."

Scout climbs out of bed. "I need to tell the doctors you're awake."

"Not yet, Scout. Please go find your brother. If he hasn't run off again. He has something important to tell us about his disappearance."

"Yes, ma'am." Scout hurries out of the room. Finally, at long last, she's going to get her answers.

"Mama's awake!" she announces to the waiting room, jolting five sleeping heads awake. They jump to their feet and surround her with faces eager for more information.

"That's amazing," Kate says, her face alive despite having just woken up.

"That's wonderful news. How is she?" Phillip asks.

"She seems fine, but I haven't called in the doctor yet. She asked to speak to Ford first." Scout's steely glare lands on her brother. "She claims you have something important to tell us about your disappearance."

Ford strokes his beard. "Wow. So she heard me. Incredible."

Concern crosses Phillip's face. "Are you sure about this, Ford?"

"I'm positive. It's way past time for everyone to know the truth. Most especially the two of you." Ford looks first at Mary Beth and then Scout.

Barrett's fingers graze Scout's arm. "Are you okay?"

She smiles at him. "I'm fine. But you look tired. Why don't you go back to my house and get some sleep?"

Barrett shakes his head. "I'm not leaving without you. I'll go down to the cafeteria and get coffee for everyone."

"Coffee would be awesome."

Scout ushers Mary Beth and Ford back through the double doors. They enter June's room to find her sitting up in bed, looking fresh and alert.

"Hey, Mom. I've missed you so much." Ford kisses her cheek. "I understand you heard what I said to you."

"Every word." She places a hand on his bearded cheek. "It wasn't your responsibility to protect me, son. I'm the parent. It's my job to protect you. If only I'd known. I can't believe what was happening right under my nose."

"Ugh!" Scout pulls at her hair. "Start talking, Ford. I can't stand the suspense a moment longer."

Ford laughs out loud. "You haven't changed a bit." He motions Scout and Mary Beth to the two available chairs. "Y'all should sit down. This might take some time, and what I have to say might upset you."

Mary Beth takes a seat, but Scout remains standing. "I'm too worked up to sit."

"Suit yourself." He locks eyes with Mary Beth. "It started the night you stabbed Lamar. When we arrived at your house, Lamar was still alive, despite having a knife in his chest."

Mary Beth presses her hand to her mouth as she remembers.

"Buford ordered me to finish him off. I argued with him. I told him he was out of his mind, but he badgered me." A pained expression crosses Ford's face. "I can still hear him yelling at me, calling me every name in the book—sissy and crybaby and coward. He said real southern men protect their women. And Mary Beth was part of our family." Ford swipes at his wet eyes. "He wouldn't let up, and I couldn't think straight. He reminded me that he was a successful United States senator, and that he knew what he was doing. He said he'd make it right with the police, and no one would ever know. I squeezed my eyes shut and jabbed the knife in farther. Blood gushed from his chest and trickled from his mouth, and his body went still. There was so much blood. It was all over me."

"I heard Dad tell you to dispose of your clothes," Scout says.

"I burned them the next day in the fireplace, along with Mary Beth's nightgown." Ford snatches a tissue from the box on the bed table. "When I tried to call for help, Dad took my phone and sent me out to the car. He told me to pull my sweatshirt hood over my head and try not to let anyone see me. I sat in that car for hours, watching police cruisers and rescue vehicles. I was freaking out. I felt certain the police would arrest me, and I would spend the rest of my life in prison. But when Dad finally came back to the car, he told me he'd taken care of everything. He didn't elaborate, and I didn't ask questions. I didn't want to know."

Ford blew his nose and tossed the tissue into a nearby trash can. "Buford had saved me from a murder charge, and I felt grateful. But when the shock wore off, I realized I'd fallen into his trap."

Everything about those years suddenly makes sense to Scout. "And so he blackmailed you. Is this why you went to Alabama after you'd verbally committed to Georgia?"

"Yep. He held this over my head about everything. My grades were awful that first semester. I begged Dad to let me take a year off from college to figure out my life. But he refused. That's when I realized I had to get away. Phil's move to New York presented the perfect opportunity for me to disappear." Ford's shoulders slump. "In hindsight, I was running from myself as much as from Buford. Fear of going to jail has kept me away all these years. But I can no longer live with my guilty conscience." He lowers himself to the edge of the bed. "I came home for you, Mom. But I'm also here to confess to the police."

"Scout is the police," Mary Beth says, and Scout adds, "I'm a detective with the Seattle Police Department."

Ford's lips form an O. "I didn't realize that. So you traded in your stethoscope for a handgun?"

Scout smiles. "That's a story for another day."

A nurse bustles into the room, stopping in her tracks when she sees June sitting up in bed. "You're awake. I'll call the doctor." Spinning on her heels, she heads out of the room.

June calls after her, "Tell him I don't want to be disturbed. I'm having a private discussion with my children."

Scout waits for the nurse to leave. "How did he blackmail you? Did he have any evidence against you?"

"He threatened to go to the police. He said they'd believe a senator over a 'punk kid,'" Ford says using air quotes.

Scout paces in a small circle, raking her hands through her matted hair. "Dad convinced the police that a random home intruder killed Lamar. The newspaper confirmed his story. Question is, Where's the knife?"

Ford shrugs. "I assume the police have it."

Scout shakes her head. "I doubt it. Why would he give it to the police with yours and Mary Beth's fingerprints all over it?"

Ford folds his arms over his chest. "All right then, detective, you tell me. Where's the knife?"

"My guess is Dad took it and lied to the police. He told them the victim was dead when he got there. Lamar was a convicted pedophile who tried to rape Mary Beth. They wouldn't have much incentive to investigate the case."

Mary Beth, who's been quietly listening, chimes in, "Jeff's Uncle Merle has been on the police force for forty years. He might know something about what happened that night if you want to talk to him."

"Maybe I should," Ford says.

Scout is torn between following the law and protecting her brother. "There is no statute of limitations for murder. If you go to the police, by law they'll be obligated to reopen the investigation. In my opinion, this can of worms is better off unopened. You've served your time. The years of hell Dad put you through were your sentence."

Ford gazes over at June. "What do you think?"

"I agree with Scout. Jail is for criminals. And you were just a kid following your father's orders." She reaches for his hand. "You've just come back to me, Ford. Please don't go away again."

Ford looks over at Mary Beth. "Do you agree?"

She bobs her head. "This is all my fault. Too many years of your life were ruined because of me. I couldn't live with myself if you went to prison."

When she begins to cry, Ford gets up and takes her in his arms. "My years in Alaska weren't ruined. They were just different than they would've otherwise been. Buford would've eventually run me off. Blackmailing me for Lamar's death just made things easier for him."

"Then it's settled. Nothing we said leaves this room." Scout places an arm around her brother. "If your guilt continues to torment you, find yourself a good therapist."

"I've been seeing a therapist for years, Scout. She hasn't done any good."

"Then find a new one," Scout says, and squeezes his shoulder.

The nurse returns. "The doctor is on his way in. He insists on examining the patient. I'll have to ask the rest of you to please leave."

"We're going!" Scout says. But as they file out of her mother's hospital room, she has a sneaking suspicion the issue of Lamar's death is far from over.

Chapter 36

Kate

Kate and Phillip have a brief visit with June before she begins to nod off.

"We should let you get some rest," Phillip says, slowly rising from his chair. "We have much to talk about. Would it be all right if I come back in a couple of weeks and spend a few days?"

June smiles. "Come for Thanksgiving! Both of you. I'll go all out. We'll have an old-fashioned family reunion."

"Count me in." Kate relishes the idea of spending Thanksgiving in her hometown with family, friends, and Lance.

"Me too." Phillip kisses June's forehead. "I can't think of any place I'd rather be."

On the way to the parking lot, Kate asks her father, "Will she be all right?"

Phillip unlocks the car and opens the passenger door for her. "Physically, yes. Adjusting to life without Buford will present challenges."

"She has some dark days ahead, for sure. Learning Buford blackmailed her son is a tough pill to swallow. Not to mention that he was having a long-term affair with Raquel. I hope she was serious about having everyone for Thanksgiving. Having the holiday to focus on will give her life some purpose."

"True. Maybe I'll come back a few days early to help her prepare. It'll be like old times. Correction! Better than old times because Buford won't be here."

Kate slides into the passenger seat, and her father goes around to the driver's side. He starts the engine and exits the parking lot. "I need to head back to New York. I have a couple of patients I should check on this afternoon. There's a twelve thirty flight out of Mobile. If I hurry, I can make it. Do you want to come with me?"

"I think I'll spend one more night. I'd like to see Lance again, and I want to look for a rental house."

Phillip glances over at her. "So you're going through with it? Good for you. Have you told Lance you're thinking of renting?"

"Not yet. I want to surprise him. Besides, this isn't about Lance. This is about me making a change I didn't realize I needed until I came down here."

"Will you see Honey again before you leave?"

"Not this trip." During the wee hours of the morning, while the others slept, she'd told her father about her encounter with Honey in the chapel. She'd been unable to gauge his reaction. Phillip had been her sole provider as a child, and she can see where he might be jealous of her relationship with Honey. Grateful for the sacrifices he's made for her, Kate will make certain he knows he'll always be her number one.

Instead of pulling into the parking deck, Phillip parks in the valet circle. He turns off the engine and angles his body toward her. "You belong in Langford, Kate. I haven't seen you so alive in years. Maybe it has to do with a certain young man. Or maybe you're inspired by starting your clothing line. Or maybe it's finding your mother. Whatever it is, hang on to it."

"I will, Dad. And I could say the same about you. This rosy

glow in your cheeks is new." She affectionately pats his cheek. "This is your big chance with June. Don't blow it."

They get out of the car, and her father hands his key to the valet attendant. "I'll be back in ten minutes, tops," he tells the valet.

Kate and Phillip ride up in the elevator together. When her dad gets out on the third floor, she wishes him safe travels and continues to her room on the fifth.

She takes a long, hot shower and rummages through her clothes for something clean to wear. She's smoothing the wrinkles out of a wine-colored tunic when her phone rings with a call from Robyn Hart.

"If you're still interested, the house is once again available for rent. The couple decided it was too small for them after all."

Excitement flutters in Kate's chest. "That's excellent news. I'd love to see it. I can be there in half an hour."

"I'll see you then."

Kate pulls on faded jeans with her tunic and heads out on foot to the rental house.

Robyn, a fresh-faced young woman with a shock of red hair and freckles across her nose, answers the door in exercise clothes. "I apologize for my appearance. I've had a crazy morning," she says and motions for Kate to enter.

The clean gray and white decor appeals to Kate, as does the simple floor plan. On the street side are small living and dining rooms. At the back of the house, an eat-in kitchen opens onto a screened porch large enough for a round iron table, two chairs, and a bench swing. They pass through a paned glass door into the office where a standing desk is positioned in front of windows overlooking the well-tended fenced backyard. Off the office, a short hallway leads to two bedrooms that share a bath with a walk-in shower.

The tour ends in the yard where Robyn explains her situation. "I'm leaving at the end of the month for an extended trip to Europe, the Middle East, and Asia. I'll be gone for at least a year, potentially longer. I'm looking for a twelve-month lease with an option to extend."

"Twelve months is ideal." At the end of that time, Kate will have a much better outlook for her future.

"I'll provide you with towels and sheets and a fully equipped kitchen. All my clothes and personal items will be moved to storage. You'll take care of the yard. I have a lawn mower in the shed out back. But there's a teenage boy who lives two doors down who will cut the grass if you get in a jam."

The idea of spending long hours working in Robyn's tidy yard thrills her. "I'll take it," Kate says and writes a check for the deposit and first month's rent.

Instead of walking back to the hotel, she strolls in the opposite direction toward Lance's house. She'd called him earlier about June, and they'd made dinner plans. But she can't wait another second to share her news.

She's relieved to find his car in the driveway, and when she rings the bell, he comes to the door in jeans, a worn Crimson Tide T-shirt, and bare feet. "Kate, this is a surprise. I didn't expect you until six."

Kate grins. "I have something exciting to tell you that can't wait."

"I'm intrigued." He steps out of her way. "Come in. I just got off a long conference call and was getting ready to fix some lunch."

She follows him into the kitchen.

Over his shoulder, he asks, "Can I interest you in some homemade chicken and rice soup? I picked it up yesterday from Langford Market."

"I don't want to intrude."

"You're not intruding at all. I'd appreciate the company.

And I have plenty of soup," he says, removing a large plastic container from the refrigerator.

"In that case, I'd love some." Kate, suddenly nervous about breaking the news, lowers herself to a stool. Is it presumptuous of her to assume he'll be happy about her living here part-time?

"So what's so exciting that can't wait?" he asks, dumping the soup into a pot on the stove.

"Actually, I have two exciting things to tell you. I saw my mother last night. She visited me at the hospital. We had a long heart-to-heart, and we've decided to get to know each other."

"That's wonderful, Kate." He smiles as he removes two bowls from an upper cabinet. "I'm so happy for you. I know how much you wanted this reunion."

"Since I'll be spending more time with Honey, and because I need a quiet place to create my new clothing line, I've rented Robyn Hart's house. I'll be living in Langford part-time. At least for the next year."

His brow hits his hairline. "Are you kidding me? That's the best news ever." Crossing the kitchen in three easy strides, he pulls her to her feet and swings her around.

When he puts her down, she says, "I'm glad you approve. I wasn't sure. This thing between us is happening fast."

He leans in, his mouth close to hers. "It's not happening fast enough for me. I know what I want, Kate. Do you?"

"Absolutely." She touches her finger to his lips. "I want you. I've always wanted you. These past few days, I've come to realize why I'm still single at age thirty-four."

"And why is that?" he asks, his breath on her lips.

"Because I subconsciously compared every man I've ever dated to you. And none of them have come close to measuring up."

"I've been doing that too. Only not subconsciously. All these years, I've been very much aware of how incomplete my life was without you." Pinning her against the counter, he presses his lips to hers. The feel of his body against hers sends a jolt of electricity to the pit of her stomach and down her legs.

She pushes him away. "We should wait. I don't want to spoil our romantic evening."

He goes over to the stove and turns off the soup. "Our romantic evening is starting early. I've waited seventeen years to be with you. And I'm not waiting another second." Lance sweeps her off her feet and carries her upstairs to his bedroom where they spend the afternoon making love.

Chapter 37

June

While she can barely keep her eyes open, June doesn't want to miss out on a single moment with her son, daughter, and Barrett. The threesome has been camped out in her room since just after lunch, when she was moved from intensive care to a private room on the second floor. If her numbers continue to improve, Marcus will release her first thing tomorrow morning. How can she be ready to go home when she was so near death a few hours ago? Her bloodwork may be fine, but June is mentally unprepared to face the difficult road ahead.

Ford jabs a finger at the notepad in Barrett's hands. "Add sweet potatoes to that list. Out of all Mom's Thanksgiving dishes, I've missed sweet potato casserole the most."

Thanksgiving is the one bright spot on June's otherwise bleak horizon. Everyone has agreed to come, including Barrett, and they have all eagerly volunteered to help with the cooking. Barrett will fry a turkey. Ford will smoke a salmon. And Scout, who claims she can't boil water, will contribute specialty items from Seattle as appetizers.

June has grown quite fond of Barrett in the short time she's known him. She remembers his declaration of love from when she was in a comatose state. *I'm crazy in love with your daughter.* And June can tell Scout has feelings for him as well. She hopes Barrett acts on his feelings soon. He's easy to be around with a wonderful sense of humor. And when he smiles at Scout, his obvious adoration of her melts June's heart.

June smiles up at her son. She still can't believe he's here. But she suspects something is troubling him, that he's putting on a happy face for her benefit. Then again, maybe somber is his normal demeanor. She hasn't seen him in seventeen years, when he was an eighteen-year-old boy. She knows little about the grown man he's become.

"Ford, tell us about your Thanksgivings in Alaska? Do you cook, or have dinner with friends? There's so much about your life I don't know."

"We'll have to remedy that," Ford says, squeezing her hand. "As for Thanksgiving, every year is different. Sometimes Phillip and Kate make the trip out. Last year, I had dinner with Charlie's family."

Scout nudges Ford with her foot. "Who's Charlie? Have you been holding out on us? Are you gay?"

Ford smacks her leg with the back of his hand. "As gay as you are. Charlie is short for Charlotte. You would like her, Scout. She's a veterinarian."

"Right. I remember Phillip mentioning her. Is there something going on with you and Charlie we should know about?"

"Is there something going on with you and Barrett we should know about?"

Scout's face beams red, but there's no hesitation in her comeback. "We've only just been reunited, and we're already bickering like siblings."

June pulls her blanket up under her chin. "Don't you three have something better to do than hang out in hospitals?"

Scout looks at her watch. "You're right. We've been here a long time. We should let you rest. What are your plans, Ford? Can you stay in town a few days?"

"I wish I could. But I'm in the middle of my busy season. I haven't looked at the airline schedule, but I need to catch a flight out sometime tomorrow."

June's heart tumbles in her chest. She just got him back, and he's leaving already. "But you promise to come back for Thanksgiving?"

"I will be here, Mom. I'll stay a few days afterward, so we can spend some quality time together."

Scout stands to give him a hug. "You're staying at the house tonight, right?"

Ford deflates as he lets out a sigh. "I guess. I'll have to face the ghosts sometime."

"You've got Barrett and me. We won't let you face them alone." Scout tucks the blanket around her mother. "Can we bring you some dinner later?"

"Thanks, sweetheart. But Mary Beth already volunteered. I want the three of you to enjoy your time together. Have a nice dinner out somewhere."

Ford leans down and kisses her cheek. "Goodnight, Mom. I'll stop by in the morning before I leave."

June smiles softly at her son. "I'd like that." Then turning to Scout, she says, "Can you spare a minute? I'd like to have a word alone with you."

"We'll wait for you downstairs in the lobby," Barrett says to Scout and then leaves with Ford.

June waits until the door closes behind them. "That man has it bad for you."

Scout blushes. "Do you really think so?"

"I know so. He seems like a super nice young man." June

pats the bed, and Scout sits down beside her. "Have you heard from your father?"

"Nope. He's been missing since yesterday morning. According to Betty, he packed up all his clothes and left the house without a word. Good riddance, as far as I'm concerned." June doesn't respond, and Scout gives her a skeptical look. "Please tell me you're not thinking about taking him back."

"Not at all. I learned a lot about myself while I was in a coma. I convinced myself I was happy, that our marriage was solid. But truth be told, I stayed with Buford because I was afraid of being alone." June looks away. "Now, though, I'm literally afraid of being alone. What he did to Ford was pure evil. Buford needs me to smile pretty for the cameras during his campaign. He won't take it well when he finds out I plan to divorce him. If he feels backed into a corner, who knows what he'll do?"

"I'm a trained law enforcement professional, Mom. I'll take care of you." Scout lifts her shirt, revealing a holstered handgun tucked inside her waistband. "If it makes you feel better, we'll buy a gun for you, and I'll teach you how to shoot it."

"But won't you be leaving for Seattle soon?"

"I'm staying at least a week. Longer if necessary. I've already cleared it with my boss. I have plenty of vacation time built up. You're my priority right now."

Relief overcomes June. "That means so much, sweetheart. Thank you."

Scout slides off the bed to her feet. "I'm having the locks changed first thing in the morning, and I'll help you find a divorce attorney. If you're still uncomfortable being home alone when it's time for me to leave, we'll hire a private security service to patrol the house."

June hates the idea of being a prisoner of fear in her own home. "I hope it doesn't come to that. I can't believe I'm saying this, but I hope Buford has run off with Raquel. Let them live happily ever after someplace else."

"Wouldn't that be nice?" Scout takes hold of June's hand. "You're not alone, Mom. You have an entire village on your side, a whole waiting room full of people who spent the night here last night, praying you wouldn't die."

June's eyes glisten with tears. "I wouldn't have pulled through without them. I wanted so badly to go toward the light. I'm shocked at how ready I was to give up on my life."

Scout brings June's hand to her lips. "But you chose life instead of death because you're a survivor. And strong women don't give up without a fight."

Recognition crosses June's face. "You said that to me last night."

Scout's grin reaches her twinkling blue eyes. "I did. I was testing you, to see if you remembered." Her daughter's expression turns serious. "You've been given another chance at life, Mom. I have faith you'll find true happiness this time around."

June nods. "This experience has been a wake-up call. I need to make some changes to find what fulfills me."

"You will." Scout lets go of her hand. "I should go. I have some things I need to take care of." She crosses the room to the door. "And Mom, after you're settled at home, I want to hear more about *the light*."

"Oh, Scout. I can't wait to tell you. It was amazing." A warm feeling overcomes June as she rests her head against the pillow and falls into a deep sleep.

Chapter 38

Scout

Scout stops by the nurses' station on the way out of the hospital. She flashes her credentials at the charge nurse, a serious-looking woman with black hair pulled back in a severe bun on top of her head. "I'm Detective Scout Montgomery with the Seattle Police Department. My family is involved in a domestic dispute. Please notify security that my father, Buford Montgomery, is not allowed anywhere near my mother, June Montgomery, in room 202," she says with a thumb over her shoulder.

The nurse, whose name tag identifies her as Martha Craig, reaches for the phone. "Understood. I'll alert security now and notify the other staff members."

"Thank you." Scout slides a business card across the counter. "If anything comes up, you can reach me on my cell phone."

Scout continues to the lobby, where she finds Barrett waiting near the main entrance. "What took you so long? I was getting worried. Is something wrong?"

She breezes past him. "Mom needed to talk. Where's Ford?"

Barrett hurries to keep up with her. "He went on to the house. Is June okay?"

Scout longs to tell Barrett about Lamar's death, but she knows he'll insist she go to the police. And she *should* go to the police. Her initial gut reaction was to protect her brother. But now her conscience is bothering her. She's not sure she can keep this secret. Or if it's in Ford's best interests for him to have to live with it. "Mom's experiencing a lot of changes at once. She needs a lot of support right now."

Barrett grabs her arm. "I know you, Scout. What aren't you telling me?"

She averts her eyes from his intense gaze. "I'll explain later. I need to figure a few things out first."

Scout drives home in silence, her mind racing as she searches for a solution to this mess. If only she could find a way to implicate her father. Buford is the one who lied to the police, the one who covered up the crime. He should be the one facing charges.

She parks in the driveway beside Ford's rental car and kills the engine.

"Let's go for a run," Barrett suggests. "It'll help clear your mind"

"You go ahead. I have something I need to take care of here."

Inside the house, when Barrett goes upstairs to change into running clothes, Scout enters her father's study, locks the door, and closes the blinds. She attacks his bookcases, looking for the key to the fireproof filing cabinet that houses his important documents. She finds it hidden in a pewter cup on the top shelf.

Opening the safe, she combs through the files one by one. At the back of the bottom drawer, she discovers an unmarked file folder. She removes the folder from the cabinet and opens it on his massive mahogany desk. Inside is a blood-crusted knife, sealed in a plastic bag, and a copy of the police report regarding Lamar's murder.

Scout scans the report and then reads it more thoroughly. *Based on his account of events of the night in question, Senator Buford Montgomery drove Mary Beth Nance home from his house following a study date with his daughter, Scout Montgomery.*

Scout knows this to be a bold-faced lie. Mary Beth never left their house that night.

Senator Montgomery claims he walked Mary Beth to the door and made certain she got inside safely. He was returning to his car when he heard the screams. He entered the house to find Mary Beth hovering over her mother's boyfriend's dead body. The report names Mary Beth's mother as Colleen Nance and the boyfriend Lamar Beckman. The victim had apparently died from a stabbing wound to his chest. No weapon was found.

When the police asked to interview Mary Beth, the senator told them she was waiting in the car and was too shaken up to be questioned by the police.

Except it wasn't Mary Beth in the car. It was Ford.

Senator Montgomery offered to bring Mary Beth to the police station the next day. Apparently, that interview never took place.

The report goes on to talk about how social services got involved and Colleen Nance agreed to the Montgomerys fostering Mary Beth. All subject to court approval, of course.

Scout lets go of the report and watches it float down to the desk. She imagines what might have happened if her father had done the right thing—if he'd called 9-1-1 when Mary Beth showed up at the door in her bloody nightgown. First responders would've gone to her house and potentially saved Lamar's life. Which is neither here nor there because he was a dirtbag pedophile who, in Scout's opinion, deserved to die. The stabbing would've been ruled self-defense, and Mary Beth would've come to live with them.

Instead, her father intentionally dragged his teenage son to a crime scene for the sole purpose of forging a situation from which to blackmail him. Buford told the police a bag of lies, paid them a whopping sum of money to make this case go away for the sake of the minor, Mary Beth, and insisted they report Lamar's death to the media as a random act of violence, an innocent man killed by an intruder in a home invasion gone wrong.

Returning the empty folder to the safe, Scout takes the knife and police report to the kitchen, stuffing them in the tote bag she left on the counter.

She's retrieving a cold beer from the refrigerator when Ford enters the kitchen. She hands him a beer and closes the refrigerator door. "What're you up to?"

"Just poking around, checking out all the changes. The new kitchen is amazing." He pops the top, gulps some beer, and wipes his mouth with the back of his hand. He circles the room, pausing at the porch door to look out at the backyard. "She didn't touch my room."

Scout grunts. "Meanwhile, she gave mine a complete facelift, wiping every trace of me from the house."

"That's not fair, Scout. Mom never played favorites."

"Ha. So says the favorite."

He turns toward her, placing his back to the porch. "What happened to your dream of becoming a vet?"

"I was on my way to Auburn when I took a detour to find my missing brother. After meeting hundreds of runaway kids, I made a career out of it."

His brow furrows. "Wait. I thought you were a detective?"

"I'm a detective who specializes in runaways. We have a large population in Seattle. I try to help the kids as much as possible and convince them to go home whenever I can. Preferably alive."

A smile tugs at the corner of his lips. "So you traded in stray animals for runaways?"

She laughs. "Yes! That's a good way to look at it."

His lanky body slumps. "I'm sorry, Scout. I had no idea my disappearance would affect your life so profoundly. I was so desperate to get away. I saw my chance, and I took it."

"Now that I know the truth, I would've done the same thing in your shoes," Scout says, and takes a swig of beer.

"Coming home was harder than I expected. The awful memories overpower the happy ones from our childhood. Despite what you said earlier, I can't just pretend like Lamar's death never happened. I can't live with this guilt any longer, Scout. I have to do something."

"I understand. Earlier, when I tried to convince you to let it go, I was thinking like a sister, not a detective. As a law enforcement officer, I can't keep your secret. However, I can help you. We need to make Dad pay for what he did. If we play our cards right, the police will go after him instead of you. He's the guilty one. You were a kid, just doing what your father told you."

Ford appears surprised. "You'd do that for me?"

"And for Mom. I'm worried about her safety. Now that she knows what Dad did to you, she's terrified of how he'll react when she files for divorce. And rightly so. She belongs to him, like this house, his Mercedes, and his country club membership."

The mention of the country club brings an idea to mind. Scout pulls out her phone and keys in the number she still remembers after all these years.

Ford closes the distance between them. "Who are you calling?"

She holds up a finger to Ford. When the club receptionist

answers, she asks for the grill room, and makes a reservation for three people at eight o'clock.

"Done," Scout says, dropping her phone on the counter. "You, Barrett, and I will have an expensive dinner on Dad while we come up with a plan to take him down."

Ford offers her a high five. "I like your way of thinking. Do you seriously think I can avoid going to prison?"

"There's a good chance. I'm going up to shower." She leans in close to him and sniffs. "You should too. You stink."

He gives her a gentle shove. "I'd forgotten what a little brat you were."

She shoves him back. "The little brat grew into a big brat. Now that I've found you, I'm not letting you go."

"You'd better not."

Scout marches out of the kitchen and up the stairs. She's on a mission. When she's finished with Buford Montgomery, he'll never again hurt someone she loves.

Chapter 39

June

June can't hide her apprehension from Mary Beth. She knows her too well, and she easily detects something is wrong. "What is it, June? You can tell me anything."

June shivers despite the several layers of blankets covering her body. "I don't trust Buford, and I can't shake this sense of dread that something bad is about to happen."

Mary Beth tucks the blankets tighter around June. "You'll have Scout, your personal bodyguard, with you for the first few days. After she leaves, you'll come stay with us. At least at night until you feel more comfortable being in the house alone."

"I may take you up on your offer."

Mary Beth brushes June's hair off her forehead. "Don't worry. We love you, and we're not going to let anything happen to you."

"And I love you too. I just hate being an inconvenience."

"Stop! You could never inconvenience me. You know how much I enjoy your company." Mary Beth chuckles. "Heck! After we almost lost you, I may never let you out of my sight again."

"I'm sorry I worried everyone so much."

"We're just glad you're going to be okay." Mary Beth removes items from a picnic basket and sets them on the bed table—a dinner plate in her everyday china pattern, stainless eating utensils, slices of warm sourdough bread, a small casserole dish of lasagna, and a plastic container full of mixed salad greens.

"This is a feast, Mary Beth. You outdid yourself."

"You know I like to cook when I get stressed. These past few days have been pretty darn stressful." Mary Beth sits down in the chair beside the bed while June eats.

"Let's talk about this new business you mentioned while I was in a coma."

Mary Beth shakes her head as though bewildered. "It's a miracle you heard us."

June sinks her fork into the lasagna. "Heard every word. I'm totally intrigued."

Mary Beth sits back in the chair and crosses her legs. "I've been telling you for years you should market your candles. I'll help you. We'll develop your brand." While June eats, Mary Beth shares her ideas for expanding June's product line, website design, and marketing efforts.

"I must admit, the idea of running my own company intrigues me. I haven't felt this excited about anything in years. And it'll help take my mind off my problems with Buford."

"Good! We'll get started right away." When June finishes eating, Mary Beth places everything back in her picnic basket. "I wish I could stay longer. I hate to leave you alone, but I need to help Jeff get Billy ready for bed."

"Go." June shoos her away. "I've monopolized enough of your time these past few days."

After Mary Beth leaves, June eases out of bed and plods across the room to the built-in lockers where her belongings are stored. She finds her phone in a plastic bag with her torn and bloody clothes from the accident. The battery is dead, and the screen cracked, but when she plugs it into the charger she locates in her suitcase, she's relieved to see the battery icon appear.

Climbing back in bed, June pulls the covers up to her chin, closes her eyes, and falls into a deep sleep.

She wakes sometime later. Her mind is groggy, and her eyes are slow to focus in the dimly lit room. Fear grips her chest when she sees Buford sitting in the chair beside her bed. She reminds herself not to panic. She's in a hospital. Nurses and doctors are right outside her room.

Buford moves to the edge of his chair. "Sweetheart! You're awake. I've been so worried about you."

"You have a funny way of showing it. I came out of the coma early this morning, and you're just now getting here?"

"I had campaign business to take care of in Mobile."

"Your wife is in the hospital after a serious car accident, and you're conducting campaign business?" June raises the bed's head to a sitting position. "Was Raquel helping you conduct this campaign business?"

"About Raquel . . ." Buford moves from the chair to the bed. "I realize what you might think after finding us together in the closet, but we're not having an affair. It was just one time. We got carried away."

Anger overcomes her fear. This man has been lying to her the entirety of their marriage, and she's had enough. "You're lying. You admitted you've never been able to resist Raquel's charms. She's your obsession."

The color drains from his face. "You heard that?"

"Yep." She looks him dead in the eye. "I'm divorcing you, Buford."

His face tightens. "You don't mean that. I realize you're upset, honey, but we can work through our problems. We'll see a marriage counselor. I have a real shot at becoming governor, but I need my beautiful wife by my side. You'll be the most stylish first lady Alabama has ever seen."

She glares at him. "I have no interest in being first lady. What I want is to be rid of you."

Buford jumps to his feet. "I'm the most respected attorney in this town. None of my peers would dare go against me to represent you."

She hunches her shoulder nonchalantly. "Then I'll find a divorce lawyer in Mobile. I'm sure they have a better crop to pick from anyway."

"You won't get a red cent from me. Are you willing to lose your precious house?"

June's home is an extension of her. She can't imagine living anywhere else. Scout's words rush back to her. *Fight, Mama, fight.* "We'll see about that. You've been having a long-term affair. That's strike one against you."

Buford lets out a *humph*. "I'm not the only one. What about your little affair with Phillip? You had a son with another man. A son you passed off as mine."

June's heart races, and the room spins. She rests her head against the pillow, staring up at the ceiling until the dizzy spell subsides. "How long have you known?"

Buford drops back down to his chair. "Years. I'm not stupid, June. His resemblance to Phillip is uncanny. Every single time I looked at him, I saw Phillip."

"So that's why you bullied him," June says in a meek voice.

"I wanted to kick him out of my house. But I knew you would never stand for it, and I couldn't afford to lose you. Just like I can't afford to lose you now." He reaches for her hand. "I'm begging you, June. Please give our marriage another chance. We're good together, a power couple with the social network to put us in the governor's mansion."

June holds his gaze. "Ford's in Langford. He came home when he found out I was in a coma. He told me an interesting story about the night Lamar died."

A flush creeps up Buford's neck. "I don't know what you're talking about."

"Oh yes, you do. You're a monster, and I want you out of our lives for good. Either give me a divorce or I'll tell the press every dirty little detail about that night."

Buford's jaw hits the floor. "Are you blackmailing me?"

She smiles sweetly at him. "What goes around comes around, Buford."

"You little bitch," Buford says and jumps on top of her with his hands around her throat.

Groping for the bed railing, June presses the nurse call button. Nurses swarm into the room, one of them shouting out for someone to call security.

Buford lets go of her neck. "This isn't over yet, June," he says, his foul breath assaulting her nose. He shoves his way past the nurses and flees.

A nurse punches in a number on the room's landline. "Seal off the exits. We have a domestic dispute situation in room 202," she says, and then provides Buford's description to the person on the phone.

Security appears a few minutes later. "The perpetrator got away. But our officers are on alert in case he returns."

With trembling hands, June unplugs her phone from the charger and calls Scout. When she doesn't answer, she tries three more times before leaving a message and typing out an urgent text for Scout to call as soon as possible.

Because of her, Buford knows Ford is in town, and he knows Ford ratted him out. June has put her son's life in danger, and she doesn't even know his number to warn him.

Chapter 40

Scout

Scout orders enough food for an army. Ford repeats his story to Barrett as they devour platters of crispy calamari and tangy buffalo wings for appetizers. While they feast on strip steaks and sip expensive red wine, they discuss Ford's predicament from every angle. Scout and Barrett agree his best option is to tell his version of the story to the police.

"Preferably to Jeff's Uncle Merle if we can get in touch with him," Scout says over dessert. "*If* the prosecutor presses charges, and the case goes to trial, I doubt a jury will convict you. You were only sixteen years old at the time. A minor. And the man you thought was your father provoked you into committing the crime." She fishes the police report out of her tote bag and hands it to her brother. "This is Dad's statement to the police."

Ford's eyes grow wide as he scans the page. "This is all a lie. Dad didn't drive Mary Beth home that night. She stayed at our house with you while I went with him."

"Exactly. Mary Beth's testimony will prove Dad was lying about the incident."

A glimmer of hope flickers across Ford's face. "You're right. I never thought of that."

Barrett takes the report from Ford and reads it. "Where'd you get this?"

"I found it in Dad's file cabinet while you were out running." Scout tilts her wineglass at her brother. "First thing in the morning, you and I will go down to the police station. You'll make your statement, and then you'll get on the next plane back to Alaska."

Ford shovels in the last bite of pecan pie and pushes his empty dessert plate away. "What if they tell me I have to stay in Langford?"

"Let me worry about that. I know how to handle the police," Scout says, and summons their waitress.

When she brings the check, Scout and Ford both sign their names, including a crude drawing of the middle finger in case Buford asks for a copy of the bill.

When Barrett offers to drive home, Scout climbs into the back seat, letting Ford ride shotgun. "I'll get Uncle Merle's contact information from Mary Beth and reach out to him." Removing her phone from her bag, she notices several missed calls and texts from her mom.

Fear crawls up her back when Scout listens to June's voice message. "We have a problem. Dad just visited Mom at the hospital. She told him everything. He knows Ford is in town and that Ford told us the truth about Lamar's death."

Barrett locks eyes with Scout through the rearview mirror. "Is he still at the hospital?"

"No. He took off when the nurses called security. He probably went to the house to get this." Scout holds up the plastic bag with the bloody knife.

Barrett squints at the mirror. "What is that?"

"The knife that killed Lamar," Ford says, his face white as a sheet. "Where'd you find it?"

"With the police report in Dad's file cabinet. I assume yours and Mary Beth's fingerprints are all over it. I'm surprised he never showed it to you when he was blackmailing you."

Ford sinks down in his seat. "He didn't need to. I was already so afraid, I willingly did whatever he wanted."

Anger surges through Scout. "He's a monster!"

"He may go after the knife. In which case we can catch him in the act," Barrett says and presses on the gas pedal.

As they approach the house, Scout notices a light on in her father's study, but when Barrett pulls into the driveway, her father's car isn't there. "I'm sure I turned out the light in his study. He's either here now, or he's come and gone."

Barrett turns off the car. "We have to assume he's still here. You stay in the car, Ford, while your sister and I check things out."

Ford produces a Glock from a hidden belt holster. "Seriously? And miss out on all the action?"

Scout eyes the gun. "Do you have a concealed carry permit for that?"

"Duh, Scout. I wouldn't be carrying it otherwise. I live in the Alaskan wild. I never leave home without it. Not that I expect to encounter any grizzly bears in Langford."

"Stay in the car," Scout orders. "If you hear gunshots, call 9-1-1."

Scout draws her own weapon as she and Barrett enter the house. They clear the mudroom and kitchen before crossing the hall to Buford's study. The door is partially cracked, and she can see a shadow moving around inside. She nudges the door open with the toe of her cowboy boot until she has an unobstructed view of her father tearing through the contents of his file cabinet.

She clears her throat. "What's going on, Dad?"

Buford startles at the sound of her voice. "Geez, Scout! You scared me."

"Are you looking for this?" She holds up the bag with the bloody knife.

The color drains from his face. "Give me that," he says, lurching toward her.

Barrett trains his pistol on him. "Stop! Put your hands in the air!"

Buford's hands go up. "We can work this out. What is it you want?"

Through gritted teeth, Scout says, "Justice for my brother. I'm going to make you pay for what you did to him, to our family."

Ford appears behind them in the doorway. "You ruined twenty years of my life, you rotten bastard. And you deserve to die for it." He levels his gun on Buford. "I should put a bullet in your ugly face right now."

"Don't do it, Ford," Scout says in a warning tone. "He's not worth it."

Sliding past Scout, Ford walks over to Buford and presses the gun's barrel against his forehead. "Prison is too good for you. After what you did to me, you deserve to die."

"Please, son. Don't shoot."

"I. Am not. Your son," Ford says, his finger now on the trigger.

"Ford! Put down the gun!" As the words leave Scout's lip, a police siren sounds outside.

Her brother lowers his pistol. "Ammunition is scarce these days. I wouldn't waste a bullet on you." He stuffs his gun back in the holster. "I called the police. We are going to tell them the truth about what happened to Lamar."

The doorbell sounds, followed by loud knocking. "Police! Open up!"

"I'll get it," Barrett says, and goes to let them in.

Buford thumbs his chest. "I'm a powerful man in this state,

and you're a nobody. If you think the police will take your word over mine, you're sadly mistaken."

Scout says, "You're forgetting something, Dad. There was a third party involved that night. Mary Beth will corroborate Ford's story."

"But—" Buford's response is interrupted by the appearance of two uniformed officers, one older and one a baby-faced rookie.

Scout shows the officers her credentials. "I'm Scout Montgomery. The senator's daughter. We're having a domestic dispute relating to an incident that happened nearly twenty years ago." She hands him the police report. "We have new developments in the case."

The older officer takes the report from her. "I remember this case. Merle Fletcher was the officer on duty that night. He'll want to know about this. Let me see if I can get him over here."

"That would be great. Thanks." Scout corrals the others into the kitchen, planting Ford and Buford at the table with Barrett standing guard over them. "I'll be right back."

She goes outside to the porch to call Mary Beth. When she answers, Scout quickly explains the situation. "I realize it's late, and I wouldn't ask you if it weren't important. But can you please come over? The police need to hear your version of that night's events."

Without hesitation, Mary Beth says, "I'll be right there."

Merle, a burly man with a bald head and beady eyes, arrives at the same time as Mary Beth. He listens with rapt attention as she explains her connection to this case.

With a disbelieving shake of his head, Merle says, "So you're that little Nance girl. I can't believe I never made that connection. Your brothers were a handful. We were called to that house countless times. Everyone on the force was worried for your safety. I even reported your mother to social services more than once. It was a crying shame the way she left you kids to fend for yourselves."

"I wouldn't have survived if not for the Montgomerys," Mary Beth says, her expression a mixture of gratitude and remorse as she locks eyes with Buford.

Merle motions Mary Beth to the table. "If you feel up to talking about it, I'd like to hear what happened the night Lamar died."

Avoiding the empty chair next to Buford, Mary Beth goes around to the opposite side of the table and sits down next to Ford. When she tries to speak, a sob catches in her throat.

"Take your time, sweetheart," Merle says, his concern for his nephew's wife etched in his face.

Mary Beth takes several deep breaths while she composes herself. "Other than the Montgomerys, I have never told anyone what happened. Not even Jeff." Her expression is pained as she relives that night. "I'd finished unpacking from my trip to the beach with the Montgomerys, and I was getting ready for bed when I heard someone in the kitchen. My brothers had all moved out by then, and since Lamar wasn't allowed in the house with me alone, I assumed Mom had come home early from work. I saw him cutting an apple at the counter, and I tried to back out of the kitchen without him hearing me, but he turned in time to see me. He attacked me before I could call for help. He grabbed a handful of my hair and pinned me against the counter with his hand in my underpants. He was wild-eyed drunk, and I knew he was going to rape me. Somehow, I got my hand on the knife he'd been using to cut the apple, and I jammed it into his chest." Tears spill from her eyelids. "There was blood everywhere. I panicked and took off. I ran in bare feet, all the way to the Montgomerys."

Merle looks up from his iPad where he's been typing notes. "But that's over five miles."

"I know." Mary Beth reaches for a napkin to wipe her eyes. "Scout's father told me to stay here with Scout and Miss June while he and Ford went back to my house to investigate. We heard them come home a couple of hours later, but we didn't see either of them again until the next day when Mr. Montgomery . . . Buford informed me Lamar had died. He told me he'd twisted the story to our advantage, that he'd convinced the police Lamar was killed by an intruder. While I knew lying to the police was wrong, I was so relieved not to go to jail."

"So that wasn't you waiting in the car that night?" Merle looks from Mary Beth to Ford. "It was you."

"That's correct," Ford says, and recounts his version of the story.

Merle looks at Buford with disgust. "You're a piece of work. Why would you blackmail your own son?"

Buford glares at Ford. "He's not my son. He's my wife's bastard child."

"That's a problem between you and your wife, not a sixteen-year-old boy." Merle waves the other officers over. "Cuff him and take him to the station."

Scout looks away. Despite everything her father has done, watching him being taken away in handcuffs is more than she can handle.

"What will they charge him with?" Ford asks.

Merle closes his iPad cover. "That'll be up to the prosecutor. I can think of several charges, accessory to murder being top of the list."

"What about me?" Ford asks, his knuckles white as he clasps his hands together on the table.

"I honestly don't know, son. The case is complicated. Mary Beth was acting in self-defense, and you were a minor, following your father's orders. We'll have to leave that up to the prosecutor as well. How can we get in touch with you?"

Ford hands him a business card. "My cell service can be spotty. If I don't answer, leave me a message, and I'll call you back as soon as I can."

Merle studies the card. "Alaska, huh? Under normal circumstances, I'd tell you not to leave town—

"I'll vouch for him," says Scout. I'm a detective with Seattle PD. If you need him to come back, he'll be here. But this is his busy season. His clients are counting on him."

"All right then," Merle says, reluctantly.

Everyone at the table stands at once, and Merle shows himself out.

"I'm going to the hospital," Ford announces.

Scout looks at her watch. "Now? But it's almost eleven o'clock."

Ford shrugs. "I fly out early tomorrow, and I won't have time to stop by the hospital in the morning. Besides, I want Mom to know what happened tonight, and she should hear it from me."

"Do you mind dropping me at home on your way?" Mary Beth asks him. "I walked over. But it's late now."

"Of course. Let's go," Ford says, motioning for her to follow him.

Ford and Mary Beth exit through the mudroom, leaving Scout and Barrett alone in the kitchen.

Scout rakes a hand through her hair. "I need a minute to process what just happened."

"I know what will help." Barrett leaves the kitchen and returns a minute later with a bottle of her father's expensive brandy. He locates lowball glasses in the cabinet and pours two fingers in each, handing one to her. "Let's go outside. I could use some air."

They cross the porch to the yard and walk over to the dark hole where the magnolia tree used to be. "I miss that tree. As a child, I climbed its branches and built forts at its base." Scout sips her brandy. "Before Mom comes home from the hospital, I'm going to buy a magnolia sapling and plant it for her."

"That's a thoughtful gesture." Barrett turns toward Scout, brushing a strand of hair out of her face. "You're something else, Scout Montgomery. Since tonight is all about confessions, I might as well make mine. I'm crazy about you. I fall harder for you with each passing day. Is there any chance you have feelings for me?"

Scout, who's waited an eternity for this very moment, takes a quick breath and says, "As long as we're confessing, I've had a crush on you for years. But your friendship means everything to me, Barrett, and I'm terrified of ruining it with romance."

Taking her empty glass, Barrett sets both their glasses in the grass at their feet. He places his hands on her hips and pulls her close. "Many solid relationships start out as friendships. I suggest we give it a shot. If there's no chemistry or we end up fighting all the time, we'll go back to being just friends."

"Stop talking and kiss me." She hooks an arm around his neck and pulls his face close to hers. When their lips meet, her knees go weak, and she tightens her grip on his neck.

When the kiss ends, Barrett blinks his eyes hard. "Wow! Is it my imagination or are those real stars?"

Scout tilts her face to the sky. "There are no stars out tonight."

"I told you we have chemistry."

Scout's breath is a whisper against his lips. "Is this the part where you sweep me off my feet and make crazy love to me on the kitchen floor?"

Barrett laughs. "Not when your brother could walk in on us at any minute."

Scout presses her body against his. "He'll probably be gone a while."

"I'm not taking that chance. I'm sorry, Scout. But I'm old-fashioned in some ways and having sex in your family's home is inappropriate. We'll have to wait until you get back to Seattle."

Scout moans in frustration, but she'd wait forever for him. He's her guy, her soul mate, her future. She feels it deep down in her core.

Chapter 41

June

During the weeks since her release from the hospital, June has spent countless hours on the phone with Phillip. They've discussed everything—the past, the future, and the years they spent apart. They've rediscovered the closeness they once shared when he lived next door, and she considered him her best friend. But as she waits for his arrival on Monday of Thanksgiving week, she's a teenage girl again getting ready for her first date. It dawns on June that she'd never had a proper first date, one of the many things she missed out on by being true to her childhood sweetheart.

She stirs whipping cream into the chicken poblano chowder and transfers the pot to the back burner. She walks through the house, turning on lamps and lighting her signature candles. Her home has never looked so lovely, so warm and inviting, with every surface gleaming in anticipation of Thanksgiving.

Phillip volunteered to come early to help prepare for the big day. But June suspects that's an excuse to spend time with her alone before the others arrive. Their two families have much to be thankful for this year. The prosecutor decided not to charge Ford or Mary Beth with any crimes. He threw the book at

Buford, who somehow weaseled out of most of the charges. Her soon-to-be ex-husband sold his law firm and left town for good. According to the local gossip mill, he'd moved to New Orleans with Raquel.

June hired the most reputable divorce attorney she could find, a female barracuda from Montgomery. Meredith's exorbitant fee paid off. She negotiated ownership of the house and a generous settlement that will provide for June well into her old age.

Darkness has fallen by the time Phillip finally arrives. When she opens the door, his striking good looks steal her breath. He kisses her cheek, and she catches a whiff of his citrusy cologne. "I'm sorry I was late. My flight was delayed leaving Atlanta."

She palms his cheek. "No worries. I'm just glad you're here."

June shows him upstairs to the guest room, and while he freshens up, she fills two glasses with cinnamon maple whiskey sour, a recipe she found on the internet.

He holds his glass to hers. "To us. At long last."

She smiles and clinks his glass. "To us."

"The house looks wonderful," Phillip says as they mosey around the large rooms.

"Thank you! Betty and I have nearly killed ourselves getting everything ready."

His face grows serious. "You're kind to include Honey. It means a lot to Kate. I hope it's not too much."

"Not at all. The more the merrier." She straightens a lampshade in the hallway. "I probably should've discussed it with you first, but Kate seemed so excited about spending her first holiday with her mother. I hope it won't be awkward for you two."

"Honey is now a part of Kate's life, and we need to find a

way to get along. So much has happened since our divorce, it seems like we were married in another life."

"I already feel that way about Buford, and we're not even officially divorced yet. Did Ford tell you he's bringing his veterinarian friend?"

Phillip appears surprised. "He did not. But that's great news. I hope this means they've finally moved beyond friendship."

June places a hand over her heart. "All my children are discovering their significant others. Kate and Lance. Scout and Barrett. Ford and Charlie. I can't leave out Mary Beth and Jeff, even though they discovered each other a long time ago."

"You and me." Phillip hooks and arm around her waist, pulling her close.

"You're not my child," she says, laughing as she pushes him away.

Phillip pokes his head in Buford's study. "Whoa. What happened in here?"

"I packed up all his stuff and put it in the garage with his clothes. He's made no effort to get it. Maybe he wants a fresh start."

"You shouldn't have to house his belongings indefinitely. Give him a deadline. If he doesn't come get it by the specified date, have the junk people haul it away."

June considers the idea. "I may very well do that."

They continue to the dining room where the table is set with her best crystal and china. "This looks lovely. But did you leave anything for me to help with?"

"Actually, I'm thinking of making a drastic change. They're predicting the weather on Thursday to be unseasonably warm. I'm considering having dinner on the porch." He follows her back through the kitchen to the porch.

Phillip eyes the small rectangular table. "Can you fit everyone?"

"Not that table, silly. We'd have to rent one. But there are only twelve of us, including a toddler." June pinches her chin in thought. "It means a lot of extra work. We'll have to remove all this furniture and give the porch a good scrub. Maybe it's too much."

"It's only Monday. We have plenty of time. Everyone will appreciate the informal atmosphere out here."

June straightens. "I think so too. Let's do it. We'll get to work first thing in the morning."

Over dinner, they create a to-do list that will keep them busy until the big day. After cleaning up the kitchen, they retire with cups of licorice tea to the gas fire in the family room.

June blows on her tea and takes a tentative sip. "I'm thinking of making a lifestyle change. I haven't mentioned it on the phone, because I wanted to talk to you about it in person."

Phillip turns to face her. "Tell me about it."

"I may sell the house," she says, a smile twitching at the corners of her lips.

His jaw slackens. "But you love this house."

"June Montgomery loved this house. I'm no longer a senator's wife and socialite. I'm not even sure who that person was. I feel like I was playing a role in a movie, and the movie has ended. I'm taking back my maiden name and reinventing myself as June Calhoun."

"Good for you!" He offers her a high five. "Normally, I would say it's too soon after to make such a drastic move. But I sense a renewed strength and determination in you."

June stares down at her teacup. "I'm not sure I ever had either of those things."

"Oh, you had them all right. When I first moved in next door, you were so in love with Buford and eager to start a family.

285

You were ready to take on the world. Will you move to a different town?"

June shakes her head. "Langford is my home. Being closer to my children would be my only reason to move, but I can't see myself living in Seattle or Alaska." She tucks a strand of hair behind her ear. "I'm considering making an offer on a small farm just outside of town. I've scheduled a second viewing with the Realtor for tomorrow. Would you come look at it with me?"

"I would be glad to. Tell me more about this farm."

Her face lights up. "Wait until you see it, Phillip. It's so charming. Magnolias line the long driveway leading to a small Dutch colonial house. It was built in the early nineteen hundreds, but the bathrooms and kitchen have all been updated. The best part of the farm is the rustic barn I plan to convert into a candle workshop and business offices for Southern Essence."

Phillip appears surprised. "So, you finally settled on a name for your company? Southern Essence. Very sophisticated. I like it."

"Thanks. It will work if I decide to branch out into fragrances beyond magnolia."

Phillip finishes his tea and sets his cup down on the side table. "Sounds like you're already sold on this property."

An image of the farm comes to mind, bringing a smile to her face. "Maybe I am. Do you think I'm crazy?"

"I think you're wonderful." He rests his arm on the back of the sofa, inching closer to her. "Tell me, June. Where do I fit into your new life?"

June considers her response. While she doesn't want to hurt his feelings, she needs to establish expectations from the start. "I hope you'll play a major role. But I will never again allow any person, man or woman, to be the center of my world like I did with Buford. I'm counting on my new business to provide the focus I'm looking for." She touches her fingers to his cheek. "How do I fit into *your* life?"

"I'm several years away from retiring. But I'd like to spend as much time with you as possible. I'm thinking of buying a share in a private jet charter. Since Kate is living here part-time now, I figure I'll be coming to Langford at least every other weekend. If you'll have me."

"I'll definitely have you." He goes silent, and June can tell something is bothering him. "What's wrong, Phillip? Are you worried we're getting ahead of ourselves?"

"Not at all. Having you back in my life is my dream come true. It's just that I haven't been with a woman in a long time."

"I'm scared too, Phillip." She gets up and pulls him to his feet. "We'll take it slow. For now, I just want to feel your arms around me."

He holds out his arms. She walks into them, and they nuzzle in front of the fire for a long time. When he finally kisses her, something stirs inside of her, a sense of longing and belonging like she never felt with Buford.

June wakes before Phillip the following morning. She sinks deeper beneath the covers, relishing the afterglow of a long night of lovemaking. She watches him sleeping, so peacefully, with his mouth slightly open. He's an amazing man, so caring and gentle. She won't think about the years she wasted when she chose to be with Buford instead of him.

When Phillip finally opens his eyes, a slow smile spreads across his lips. "I could get used to seeing you in my bed every morning. When are your children arriving?"

"Wednesday afternoon, in time to go to Mary Beth's for dinner. I'm sorry I have to kick you out, but I have limited bed space. Even though we're all adults, I don't approve of us or them flaunting their sexual relationships."

"I totally agree. There's nothing wrong with exercising propriety, especially when all our relationships are so new." He reaches for her, pulling her close. "But what those kids don't know won't hurt them."

They make love again, and by the time they finally venture downstairs for breakfast, it's nearly ten o'clock. Phillip makes coffee while June scrambles eggs and microwaves several slices of bacon. After they eat, she calls the party rental company and orders tables, chairs, and linens for Thursday. They spend the rest of the morning and the first part of the afternoon scrubbing the porch. A few minutes before three, they leave to meet Anne, her Realtor, out at Magnolia Estates.

"The name is a good omen," Phillip says as they drive down the magnolia-lined driveway. His breath hitches when the house comes into view. "It's stunning."

June's pulse quickens. "Wait until you see the inside. The current owner has already moved out, so the rooms are bare."

Anne unlocks the door for them but remains outside to make a phone call while they look around. Phillip falls in love with the house's worn random-width floors, oversized windows, and heavy moldings. They tour the kitchen with its marble countertops and stainless appliances before going outside.

"I'm going to raise chickens and buy two female golden retriever puppies from the same litter." June shows him the barn and shares her ideas for utilizing the space for Southern Essence.

"Well? What do you think?"

He smiles at her. "Everything about this place suits you. Make an offer before someone else snatches it up."

June sucks in a deep breath. "All right, then. Let me find Anne."

Phillip pokes around outside, inspecting the exterior of both buildings, while June discusses the terms of her contract, closing dates, and putting her house in town on the market.

"I'll submit the contract to the sellers' Realtor this afternoon. Hopefully, we'll have an answer this evening," Anne says when she walks them to the car.

June holds up her hands to show Anne her crossed fingers.

As they retreat down the driveway, Phillip says, "I hope I didn't coerce you into making an offer. This is a big deal. If you're not ready, you should take a few more days to think about it."

June glances over at him. "Are you kidding me? I love the property. It already feels like home. I've come close to making the offer a dozen times since it came on the market last week. But I wanted your approval, since you'll be spending a lot of time here."

"You have it. What say we go out to dinner to celebrate? My treat."

"We'll jinx my offer if we celebrate before the owner accepts. But since I'll be cooking all day tomorrow, I won't turn down your offer for dinner out tonight."

They leave her car at home and walk back to town, strolling up and down Meeting Avenue until they agree on Mexican. Their order has just arrived when June receives a text from Anne. She reads it out loud to Phillip. "The owners accepted your offer. Congratulations."

June sets down her phone. "They didn't even counter. I should've offered less."

"Don't go there, June. You can't put a price on your dream farm."

"You're right." A sense of calm settles over her. Everything in her life is falling into place. "My business and my new home and you, so many dreams are coming true at once."

Phillip leans across the table and whispers, "I suddenly have the urge to see your beautiful naked body."

June blushes. "And I've suddenly lost my appetite. Let's get our dinner to go?"

They ask the waiter for carryout containers and race-walk home, holding hands and laughing like children. They strip their clothes off inside the front door and make love on the Oriental rug in the hallway. It's nearly midnight before they finally get around to eating.

June lets Phillip sleep in on Wednesday morning and sets out early for the market to beat the holiday rush. Her grocery list is long, and she's gone for nearly two hours. When she returns, Phillip's rental car is missing from the driveway. She finds a note from him on the kitchen counter, saying he went to drop his stuff at Kate's and will be back soon.

But he's gone for hours. She's in the kitchen mashing potatoes when she hears his car pull in around two o'clock. He enters the kitchen from the mudroom wearing a goofy grin.

June sets down her potato masher and crosses the kitchen to greet him. "There you are. I was getting worried about you."

He takes her in his arms. "Sorry I didn't call. I ran into Lance, and he wanted to talk."

Chapter 42

Kate

During the predawn hour of Thanksgiving morning, Kate is waiting at the end of the sidewalk when Lance's Tahoe pulls to the curb. She slides in beside him and slams the door. "This is ridiculous. The sun isn't even up yet. Why can't you tell me where we're going?"

"Because it'll spoil the surprise."

"Then give me a hint."

"Hmm. Let's see." Lance drums his fingers on the steering wheel. "This is one of my family's Thanksgiving traditions." He hands her a coffee from the cupholder. "Here. You'll need this. It's going to be a long day."

She softens, thinking about the fun day ahead.

"I missed having you in my bed last night. We're adults, Kate. I'm sure your dad knows we're sleeping together."

"I'm sure he does too. But I don't feel right leaving him alone." She sips her coffee. "What do you think of Ford's girlfriend? Did you have time to talk to Charlie last night?"

"I spoke with her for a long time about which dogs make the best pets. She knows her stuff." As he drives through town,

Lance discusses the pros and cons of different breeds. "But I still think I want a lab."

Kate laughs. He's always going on about getting a dog. Little does he know, she's giving him a yellow lab puppy for Christmas. "Charlie is the girl-next-door type I would've picked for Ford. Do you think they're serious?"

Lance lifts a shoulder. "I guess. Why else would he bring her all the way here from Alaska to meet his family?"

Kate eyes him suspiciously when he turns down the road leading to the artist colony. "What are we doing here? If this is your family's tradition, why are we at my mother's house?"

"Stop asking so many questions. We need to hurry, or we'll miss the sunrise." He parks at the edge of the main field in front of the farmhouse and comes around to her side to help her out. As the first pink rays of sun brighten the sky, he drags her through the knee-high grass across the field.

"So this is why you wanted me to wear boots," she says, tripping along beside him. "I'm not into hunting, Lance. Please tell me we're not going to kill a wild turkey."

"It's nothing like that." They arrive at the sprawling live oak tree. "Here we are."

Kate raises an eyebrow. "You brought me out here at the crack of dawn to stand under a tree I've seen dozens of times?"

He presses his finger to his lips. "Stop talking and listen."

Seconds later, she hears a low-flying plane approaching. The plane comes into view, and it's towing a banner with the message *Will you marry me, Kate?*

Kate blinks her eyes and reads the banner again.

Dropping to one knee, Lance takes her left hand and slides a sparkling solitaire diamond onto her ring finger. "I'm crazy in love with you, Kate. Please, say you'll be my wife."

Kate doesn't hesitate. "And I'm head over heels in love with you. Yes! I will be your wife." She pulls him to his feet and plants a kiss on him that makes him groan.

"I don't believe this. I wasn't expecting a proposal. But what about your family's tradition?"

He shrugs and gives her a goofy expression. "I had to say something to get you out here."

She looks down at her hand. "This ring is gorgeous."

"I'm glad you approve. The diamond belonged to my grandmother. I had it reset for you." His smile fades. "I hope you don't think it's too soon. We've only been together a few weeks, but you've been living in my heart for years."

Her lips part in a broad smile. "I feel the same way. We're not getting any younger. What's the point in waiting when we know we're meant to be together?"

He places an arm around her and walks her back across the field. "I hope you don't mind. I invited our parents here to join the celebration. They are waiting for us in the farmhouse kitchen."

She nudges his ribs with her elbow. "You're awfully sure of yourself. What if I had said no?"

"Then I would need our parents to console me."

Cheers and applause greet them in Honey's kitchen. Lance's parents are here, along with Phillip, June, and Honey. Everyone takes turns congratulating the newly bethrothed, and when Honey pops the cork on a bottle of champagne, the two fathers offer heartfelt toasts.

"You'll be a gorgeous bride," June says. "I hope you'll let me help plan the wedding."

"I would love that." Kate admires her ring again. "You've worked so hard to prepare for Thanksgiving. I hate to steal your thunder today, but I don't think I can keep this a secret from Scout and Mary Beth."

June laughs. "Today is about all of us. Our families are

finally reunited again. I can't think of better news to share. Everyone will be thrilled."

~

June's Thanksgiving table is set on the porch with her Woodland China, sterling flatware, and sparkling crystal and decorated with mums and gourds in autumn colors. After serving their plates from the buffet in the kitchen, family and friends find their seats and bow their heads while Phillip offers the blessing.

His gaze travels the table. "For as many years as I can remember, Kate and I have celebrated Thanksgiving with the same group of friends in New York. My favorite part is when we share something or someone we're particularly thankful for this year. I'd like to continue that tradition by saying I'm ever so grateful we've reunited our extended family. I'm glad to finally have Ford back with his family where he belongs. We are all experiencing changes in our personal lives, but I hope we will grow together as a family unit."

June smiles at him. "I won't even try to top that lovely sentiment. But I would like to say how overjoyed I am to have all my children together again." She looks from Ford to Scout to Mary Beth to Kate. "Genetics aren't important to me. In my heart, all four of you are my children."

Kate risks a glance at Honey sitting next to her. Her expression is solemn, and Kate worries she was wrong about inviting her to join them for Thanksgiving. She recalls Honey's comment about June in the chapel. *I could never live up to her. No one can live up to perfection.* June's lovely home and exquisite dinner are a reminder of Honey's failures as a wife. Not everyone is cut out for homemaking. But Kate has learned so much about Honey's other talents during the last few weeks.

Not only is her mother an accomplished artist, she's a patient and gifted teacher.

Mary Beth is next to speak up. "I'd like to take a minute to remember Alice. She was a good person who led a troubled life. She's in a better place now. But I feel blessed, because her death brought us all together again."

"Correction," Scout says. "You, Mary Beth, are the one who brought us together, and I will always be indebted to you for that."

"As will I," Kate adds. "And I will always be indebted to Mary Beth for bringing Lance and me back together." She holds up her left hand, showing off her engagement ring. "He proposed at sunrise this morning. We're getting married." She leans toward him and plants a kiss on his cheek. "If not for Mary Beth, we would never have found each other again."

The table erupts in cheers and congratulations.

"That's awesome news, Kate. I'm thrilled for you both." Scout rests her head on Barrett's shoulder. "Barrett and I aren't ready for such a big commitment. We're still enjoying the newness of our relationship. But when our leases run out at the beginning of the year, we'll be looking for an apartment together."

"I'm so happy for you," June says. "You make a wonderful couple."

Ford clears his throat. "Since we're telling all . . ." He rests an arm on the back of Charlie's chair. "Charlie and I are having a baby."

Jaws slacken as silence settles over the table. Scout is the first to speak. "Whoa, bro! That was fast."

Ford and Charlie both laugh. "You're right, Scout. It happened very fast. The night I arrived home from Alabama, I went straight to Charlie's house and confessed everything about my past. We declared our feelings for each other, and we made a baby. Accidentally, of course, but we couldn't be happier about it."

"I'm gonna be a grandmother!" June cries, getting up from the table to give Charlie and Ford a hug. "I'm thrilled beyond words."

Ford smiles up at her. "Thanks, Mom. We will eventually tie the knot, but for now, like Scout and Barrett, we're simply enjoying being together."

Mary Beth waits for June to return to her seat. "It's my turn for a news flash. Come next July, Billy will have a baby brother or sister."

More cheers and whistles erupt from the table.

Mary Beth's eyes bounce from Scout to Ford to Kate. "Even though we're not biological siblings, I would love for the four of us to raise our children as cousins."

Scout and Ford eagerly nod their heads, and Kate says, "I love that idea."

They have much to talk about during the rest of dinner, babies and weddings and new relationships. Honey is noticeably quiet, and when they take a break from eating to clean up before dessert, Honey thanks her hostess, and Kate walks her out.

"Thank you for coming," Kate says, giving her a hug. "Having you here meant a lot to me. I hope it wasn't too much."

"Not at all. I had a nice time. But I promised my sisters I'd have dessert with them." Honey opens her car door. "If you're thinking of having a casual wedding, our field is lovely in the spring when the world comes alive. You could be married under the tree where you got engaged. It's just a thought."

"Lance and I haven't talked about what style wedding we want, but I'll keep that in mind."

Kate closes her mother's car door and watches her drive away before removing a large gold box with a robin's egg blue satin ribbon from the back seat of Lance's Tahoe. Returning to the kitchen, she hands the box to June.

June looks down at the box and up at Kate. "What's this?"

"Open it!"

Setting the box on the counter, June unties the ribbon, lifts the lid, and removes a powder blue cashmere coat.

"I wanted you to have the prototype. I designed it as more of a swing coat than a wrap coat. It has pizazz like you. Preorders for The June are already sold out on our website."

June slips on the coat and spins around. "It's fabulous, Kate. You outdid yourself. I'm honored. And flattered. This gesture means more to me than you know."

Kate smiles. "*You* mean more to me than you know. Growing up, you were the closest thing to a mother I had. Now that you and Dad are seeing each other, maybe you'll get married and make it official. I would love to have you as a stepmom."

"Let's not get ahead of ourselves," June says with a laugh. "But your father is a special man, and I will cherish our time together. And you're a very special young lady. I look forward to spending many Thanksgivings with you and Lance in the future."

Chapter 43

Scout

While the others are finishing dessert, June pulls Scout and Ford aside in the family room. She appears nervous, wringing her hands with eyes darting about the room. "This may come as a shock to you. It certainly did for me. You know how hard I've fought to keep this house. I never imagined moving." She takes a deep breath. "I've made an offer on a small farm outside of town. The size of the house is more manageable, and there's a small barn I plan to convert into a workshop and offices for my business. The current owners have accepted my offer, and I will put this house on the market in the coming weeks."

Scout's face brightens. "That's wonderful news, Mom. A fresh start is just what you need, and this house has some seriously bad juju."

"No kidding!" Ford drags the back of his hand across his forehead, as though wiping off sweat. "I'll be honest, Mom. I don't enjoy being here. There are too many ghosts."

June sighs in relief. "I was worried you'd be upset. This is your childhood home."

"The good memories are safe here"—Scout plants her hand

in the center of her chest—"in my heart. The important thing is for you to be happy."

"I agree," Ford says, giving June a half hug.

"When everyone leaves, if you're interested, I'll drive you out to the farm to see it."

"Cool!" Scout says, and Ford adds, "I get first dibs on bedrooms."

"No way! You got the best room in this house. I get first pick."

June laughs. "It does my heart good to hear you two arguing like siblings again. Unfortunately, we won't be able to see the inside today, but I can show you around outside."

When their guests leave, Scout, Ford, and their significant others pile into the car with their mom.

"You might get a new car too, Mom," Ford says about her ancient Volvo station wagon. "I was a little boy when you bought this thing."

June glances over at him. "Why do you think I kept it all these years?" She strokes the dashboard. "I drove you kids to school and birthday parties and dances in this car. I couldn't stand to get rid of those memories."

"You're going to be a grandmama," Scout says. "Time for you to buy a new car and make some new memories."

"I guess you're right. Maintaining this old heap costs me an arm and a leg," June says as she backs out of the driveway.

She drives five miles in the direction opposite town and makes a right turn at a sign that marks the place as Magnolia Estates.

The magnolia trees lining the driveway take Scout's breath. "This is stunning."

When he sees the house, Ford says, "Seriously cool, Mom. It fits you."

They take their time strolling about the property, peeking in windows and choosing a spot for June's new rose garden. When Barrett's parents call to wish him a happy Thanksgiving, he steps away to talk to them. While Charlie gives June a lecture on raising chickens, Ford and Scout venture over to an old swing, dangling from a large maple tree.

Scout play-punches her brother in the arm. "Charlie is amazing. I really like her."

"Thanks. I think so too." Ford, casting his eyes on Charlie, says, "She reminds me of you, you know. I realized it when I came back to Alabama in October, when I saw you again after so many years. Like you, she's feisty on the outside but a total pushover on the inside. Not only does she love animals, she's an advocate for the underdog, always willing to help others. Also like you."

Scout's throat thickens. "Gee, Ford. I might cry. That's the nicest thing you've ever said to me."

He hangs his head. "I'm sorry I was so mean to you when we were in high school."

"You weren't mean. You were dismissive of me. I grated on your nerves, and you didn't want me around."

"You put me on a pedestal, and I couldn't live up to your high expectations."

Scout spins the swing around. "I'm sorry if you felt that way. I loved having a football star for a brother. What high school girl wouldn't? Truth is, the real Ford was always good enough for me. I'm proud of you for remaining true to yourself. That's not easy to do in today's complicated world."

"Why do you think I live in the Alaskan wilderness?" He gives the swing a push. "You seem so put together. Are you sorry you skipped out on veterinary school?"

"Not really. I doubt I would've had the grades to get in anyway. I'm doing something meaningful with my life. Like you said, instead of helping runaway animals, I'm helping runaway kids."

Ford pulls the swing high and lets it drop. Squealing like a little girl, Scout closes her eyes and tilts her head back as she flies through the air.

"You know I wrote a song about you," he calls out to her as he gives the swing another shove.

Scout opens her eyes. "You mean 'Sunshine'? Isn't that song about Kate?"

He grabs the swing to stop it. "Why would you think that? Did you listen to the lyrics?"

Scout slips off the swing to her feet. "The song is about a brother who loves his little sister. You were closer to Kate than you were with me."

"The little sister who was the light of her brother's childhood. That was you, Scout. Not Kate. As kids, my sun rose and set on you."

Scout throws her arms around his neck. "I've waited a long time to hear you say that." A dam bursts inside of her, and the tears gush out. "Don't you ever disappear on me again."

"You have nothing to worry about," he says, holding her tight. "My problems were never about you, Scout."

"I could've helped you, if only you'd confided in me." She sobs into his chest.

He holds her at arm's length. "You were my little sister. I had to protect you."

"Well, I'm a big girl now. I can protect myself."

"We'll look out for each other," he says, pulling her close again.

"Amen to that." Scout presses her face to his chest. Listening to his heartbeat and inhaling his familiar woodsy scent triggers a memory she's thought of often during the years Ford was missing.

On a blustery early November afternoon, Ford and Scout were lying in a pile of yellow gingko leaves in their backyard. "What do you wanna be when you grow up?" he asked.

"I wanna be like Mama," Scout said without hesitation. "I wanna live in a big house and have three kids, five dogs, four cats, two bunnies, and a bird that talks." She rolled over to face him. "What do you wanna be?"

"I refuse to work in a boring office like Dad. I wanna live far away, in the wide open, where I can be outside every day. Maybe I'll be a farmer or a builder or work on a shrimp boat."

Tears stung Scout's eyes. "I'll miss you if you move far away."

"You'll visit me. And I'll come home to visit you." He took her tiny hand and placed it on his chest. "No matter where I am, or how far away I live, you'll always be here, close to my heart."

Also by Ashley Farley

Virginia Vineyards

Love Child

Blind Love

Forbidden Love

Palmetto Island Series

Muddy Bottom

Change of Tides

Lowcountry on My Mind

Sail Away

Hope Springs Series

Dream Big, Stella!

Show Me the Way

Mistletoe and Wedding Bells

Matters of the Heart

Road to New Beginnings

Stand Alone

On My Terms

Tangled in Ivy

Lies that Bind

Life on Loan

Only One Life

Home for Wounded Hearts

Nell and Lady

Sweet Tea Tuesdays

Saving Ben

Sweeney Sisters Series

Saturdays at Sweeney's

Tangle of Strings

Boots and Bedlam

Lowcountry Stranger

Her Sister's Shoes

Magnolia Series

Beyond the Garden

Magnolia Nights

Scottie's Adventures

Breaking the Story

Merry Mary

A Note from the Author

Scent of Magnolia is technically my first novel. I learned the craft of writing while working on the originally titled *Legend of a Rock Star*. (The rock star being the brother who vanishes into the night on Christmas Eve.) I wrote this novel from every point of view and verb tense imaginable. At the time, I lacked the experience to make the many moving plot components work. So I abandoned the project and moved on to write *Saving Ben*. When these beloved characters recently resurfaced in my imagination, I revisited the project. I searched all my hard drives for the original files but came up empty. Starting over allowed me the fresh perspective the project needed to come to fruition.

Because I already knew these characters so well from previous time spent with them, I was able to dive deeper into their motivations. They led me down different paths, which resulted in plot changes that make the story much stronger. I have poured my heart into the Montgomery family drama. Fasten your seatbelts. You're in for a wild ride.

I'm forgiver indebted to the many people who help bring a project to fruition. My editor, Pat Peters. My cover designer, the hardworking folks at Damonaz.com. My beta readers: Alison Fauls, Anne Wolters, Laura Glenn, Jan Klein, Lisa Hudson, Lori Walton, Kathy Sinclair, Jenelle Rodenbaugh, Rachel Story, Jennie Trovinger, and Amy Connolley. Last, but certainly not list, are my select group of advanced readers who are diligent about sharing their advanced reviews prior to releases.

I'm blessed to have many supportive people in my life who

offer the encouragement I need to continue my pursuit of writing. Love and thanks to my family—my mother, Joanne; my husband, Ted; and my amazing children, Cameron and Ned.

Most of all, I'm grateful to my wonderful readers for their love of women's fiction. I love hearing from you. Feel free to shoot me an email at ashleyhfarley@gmail.com or stop by my website at ashleyfarley.com for more information about my characters and upcoming releases. Don't forget to sign up for my newsletter. Your subscription will grant you exclusive content, sneak previews, and special giveaways.

About the Author

Ashley Farley writes books about women for women. Her characters are mothers, daughters, sisters, and wives facing real-life issues. Her bestselling Sweeney Sisters series has touched the lives of many.

Ashley is a wife and mother of two young adult children. While she's lived in Richmond, Virginia, for the past twenty-one years, a piece of her heart remains in the salty marshes of the South Carolina Lowcountry, where she still calls home. Through the eyes of her characters, she captures the moss-draped trees, delectable cuisine, and kindhearted folk with lazy drawls that make the area so unique.

Ashley loves to hear from her readers. Visit Ashley's website @ ashleyfarley.com

Get free exclusive content by signing up for her newsletter @ ashleyfarley.com/newsletter-signup/